CHARLES SHEFFIELD

CONVERGENCE

BAEN BOOKS by CHARLES SHEFFIELD

CHARLES SHEFFIELD

CONVERGENCE

The Return of the Builders

BAEN

CONVERGENCE

This is a work of fiction. All the characters and events portrayed in this book are fictional, and any resemblance to real people or incidents is purely coincidental.

A Baen Books Original

Baen Publishing Enterprises
P.O. Box 1403
Riverdale, NY 10471

ISBN: 0-671-87774-7

Cover art by Gary Freeman

Printed in the United States of America

To Ann, Kit, Rose, and Toria;
and to Mary Q. and the San Diego crowd,
who made me change it

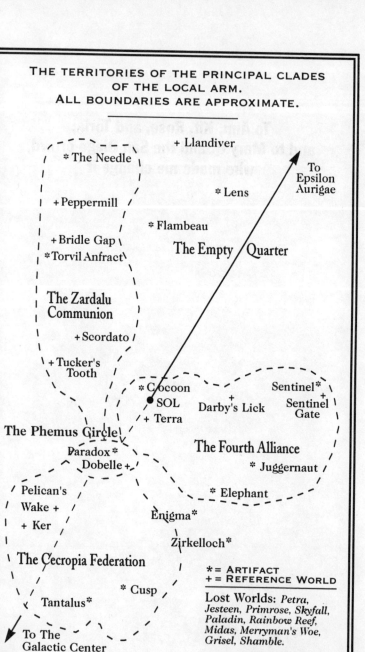

THE TERRITORIES OF THE PRINCIPAL CLADES
OF THE LOCAL ARM.
ALL BOUNDARIES ARE APPROXIMATE.

+ Llandiver

* The Needle

To
Epsilon
Aurigae

* Lens

+ Peppermill

* Flambeau

+ Bridle Gap
* Torvil Anfract

The Empty / Quarter

The Zardalu
Communion

+ Scordato

\+ Tucker's
Tooth

* Cocoon   Sentinel *
• SOL   +   Sentinel *
+ Terra   Darby's Lick   Gate

The Phemus Circle

Paradox *
Dobelle +

The Fourth Alliance

* Juggernaut

Pelican's
Wake +
+ Ker

* Elephant

Enigma *

Zirkelloch *

The Cecropia Federation

* = ARTIFACT
+ = REFERENCE WORLD

* Cusp

Tantalus *

Lost Worlds: *Petra,
Jesteen, Primrose, Skyfall,
Paladin, Rainbow Reef,
Midas, Merryman's Woe,
Grisel, Shamble.*

To The
Galactic Center

*(Taken from the private note-
books of Captain Alonzo
Wilberforce Sloane (Retired).*

✦ Introduction: The Expanding Heritage Universe

When Einstein in 1915 published the field equations of general relativity in their final form, he applied them to the study of the whole universe. Soon he discovered something surprising and disconcerting: any universe with matter in it will not stand still. According to his equations, it must either expand or contract.

To get around that problem, Einstein introduced a term into his equations that he called the "cosmological constant." A decade later, it was found that the universe does not stand still. Distant galaxies are receding. The universe is expanding. Einstein at that point described his use of the cosmological constant as the worse blunder of his life. He had been in a position to *predict* the expansion of the universe, long before it was measured, and he had blown the chance. The cosmological constant, brought in to stop the universe expanding, became a monster that was hard to kill—it survives in theories to this day.

Einstein's reputation is in no danger. He will be famous as long as humans are doing physics. However, any writer who has ever built a universe runs into a similar problem: the universe of the imagination wants to expand, and it does so in several different directions.

It is as much as an author can do to keep track of it, never mind control it.

The Heritage Universe began with one simple observation: there is nothing in physics that says an object cannot disappear from spacetime at one point, and instantly appear in another. In fact, quantum theory rather encourages that point of view. Sub-atomic particles constantly vanish and show up somewhere else, without anyone being able to explain how the transition took place. Relativity theory forbids the *acceleration* of an object up to or past the speed of light; nor can we send signals through ordinary space at speeds faster than light. But instant disappearance and reappearance elsewhere is not prohibited.

So let us suppose that the structure of spacetime is more complicated than it seems on the surface. Suppose certain places can be reached from certain other points without the usual process of traveling. You might call these special locations wormholes, or spacetime singularities. I call them nodes of the Bose Network.

This idea has one obvious consequence: interstellar travel becomes a lot easier. The universe, or at least the easily accessible universe, expands enormously.

There are two other consequences, not quite so obvious. First, if only certain places can be nodes of the Bose Network transforms, the usual science fiction ideas about interstellar travel must change.

To see why, suppose we have three stars that sit at the vertices of a triangle, each one five hundred light-years from the other two. Let two of the stars lie within a few billion kilometers (which is just a few light-hours) of a couple of nodes of the Bose Network. Let the other star be a full lightyear away from its nearest Bose node. Then, once travel through the Bose Network has been established, the first two stars become close neighbors. There can be frequent commerce and regular travel between them.

The third star, however, will seem to the others to be way off in the distance. A traveler who goes to its nearest Bose node still faces a multi-year journey, at a fraction of light-speed, to reach the star. The separation between points in the Galaxy is no longer given in terms of *actual* positions. The distance *from a node* is all that matters.

So far, so good. We have a rather simple fact, one that allows rapid interstellar travel. What is the other major implication? Well, before the discovery of the Bose Network, humans had been moving steadily out to the stars using hibernation and robot spacecraft. The process was necessarily slow. The nearest stars are lightyears away, and travel speeds must be slower than the speed of light. Trip times of hundreds of years were the norm.

But now, at a stride, comes the power to make a transition from one Bose node to another, spanning many lightyears in no time at all. The slow ships, crawling through space, will find other humans *waiting for them* when they reach their destinations.

That would be shock enough. But it gets worse. Humanity, racing out through the galaxy, will not find it devoid of intelligence. Once outside "crawlspace," the few hundred lightyears of the spiral arm explored by sub-lightspeed ships, we encounter aliens as smart as we are—and with the same high opinion of themselves.

Those aliens have their own spheres of influence. The Cecropia Federation lies roughly in the direction of the galactic center (see the map), and it contains half a dozen intelligent species. The Fourth Alliance, another independent region, is the main domain of humans. It centers on Sol, has an overlap region with the Federation that is known as the Phemus Circle, and bulges away into the area of Earth's night sky spanned by Aldebaran, Betelgeuse, and Epsilon Aurigae. A handful of near-intelligent aliens can be found in the

Fourth Alliance, but nothing as formidable—or dangerous—as the Cecropians.

The Zardalu Communion lies along a different heading, in the direction of Arcturus, though it begins far beyond that star. The original developers of the Communion territory, the Zardalu, are now (thank Heaven) extinct, but in their time they were the terror of the Spiral Arm. A narrow corridor of the Zardalu Communion also approaches the Phemus Circle. The latter group of worlds is well situated to be fought over by the major clades—if anyone were fool enough to want such an impoverished and dismal backwater.

Scattered throughout these diverse regions are the ancient and enigmatic structures of an ancient and vanished race, known only as the Builders. The uses of some of the relict Artifacts can be guessed at—more or less—but most remain totally baffling. Naturally, both humans and aliens are eager to understand the ancient Builder constructs, and to know where the Builders themselves have gone. In an attempt to reach that understanding, many of them converge on a single system, Dobelle, to witness an event known as *Summertide*.

They meet, they interact, and at that point they run out of control. Humans, Cecropians, Zardalu, Hymenopts, Lo'tfians, Varnians, Ditrons, Decantil Myrmecons, Bercians, and Chism Polyphemes bubble and boil and fume and fight all over the Spiral Arm. They explore dozens of Builder Artifacts: Sentinel, Lens, the Torvil Anfract, Serenity, Cocoon, Umbilical, Elephant, Paradox, the Eye of Gargantua, Flambeau, Cusp, Dendrite, Glister, Labyrinth, and a wide variety of Phages. Driven by fear, greed, or curiosity, they show up on dozens of planets: Teufel, Styx, Quake, Darby's Lick, Opal, Miranda, Sentinel Gate, Ker, Bridle Gap, Polytope, Rumbleside, Genizee, Scaldworld, Jerome's World, Terminus, Pelican's Wake, Merryman's Woe, Shasta and Grisel and Peppermill.

What began as a single book, *Summertide*, expands to a second, *Divergence*; then it extends into a third, *Transcendence*. And finally there is a fourth, *Convergence*.

Note that I said *finally*. With that fourth book, the tetralogy is over. The Heritage Universe has—at last—stopped its expansion.

I think.

I assume.

I hope.

Would someone kindly pass me the cosmological constant?

✦ Chapter One

It was a sobering thought: to contemplate a whole world, with all its diverse environments and its swarming life-forms. And then to reflect that you were apparently the only one of those myriad forms who *sweated*—or needed to.

Louis Nenda wiped his forehead with a fuzzy piece of cloth, and as a second thought mopped his bare chest and his dripping armpits. Although it wasn't yet noon in Genizee's forty-two-hour day, the temperature had to be around a hundred. Humid, hot, and horrible, like the inside of a steam boiler. Nenda looked up, seeking the disk of Genizee's orange-yellow sun. He couldn't see it. The annular singularities that shielded the planet were strong today. Louis saw nothing more than a swirl of colors, shifting in patterns that defeated the eye's attempt to track them.

A whistling grunt brought his attention back to more mundane concerns. Half a dozen Zardalu were dragging a ten-meter cylinder along the flat sandy shore for his inspection. No sign of discomfort in *them*. The midnight-blue bodies of the land-cephalopods, protected by their waxy outer leather, seemed impervious to either heat or cold.

The Zardalu paused respectfully, half a dozen paces from Louis Nenda, and bent to touch their broad heads to the beach.

"The Great Silent One found this in one of the interior tunnels."

Nenda stared down at the prone figures stretching their tentacles six meters and more along the beach. The leading Zardalu was using the clicks and whistles of the old language, the ancient Zardalu Communion slave talk. It lacked a decent technical vocabulary, but Louis was willing to put up with that. The master-slave relationship was all that mattered.

"She told you to bring it here?"

"The Great Silent One *indicated* that to us. I am sorry, Master, but we are still unable to understand the Great Silent One's speech."

"Atvar H'sial's not easy to understand. Maybe you'll catch on one day, when you get a bit smarter."

Louis prayed, not for the first time, that this particular day would be a long time coming. If the Zardalu ever really caught on . . .

"Do you think, Master, that this might be the missing component?"

"Could be. Have to study it before I can be sure. Leave it here. Now get back inside, and help the Great Silent One."

"Yes, Master. Let us pray that this is indeed the necessary component. For all our sakes."

Nenda watched them as they retreated toward one of the holes that led to the interior. They weren't groveling as much as usual. And that last crack hadn't sounded quite as subservient as it should. "For all our sakes." Maybe it was his imagination, but it sounded more like a threat than a prayer.

Even so, he was glad to see them go. Those huge beaks were big enough to bite him in half. The great tentacles could tear a human limb from limb. Louis had seen it done.

And some day soon, he might see it done again. Or *feel* it.

How long had it been? He squinted up again toward the invisible sun. Nearly two months. He and Atvar H'sial had stalled the Zardalu for all that time, pretending that they had the know-how to take the *Indulgence* out to space and away from Genizee. When the Zardalu found out that Nenda and Atvar H'sial were as trapped on the planet as they were, it would all be over.

It wasn't the ship; he was sure of that. The *Indulgence* was perfectly spaceworthy. It was those damned annular singularities, the eye-twisting glow that he was peering at now, and the Builder Constructs that controlled them. They made space off-limits to anything that started up from the surface of Genizee. How long before the Zardalu latched on to the fact that Louis was as helpless as they were?

Louis went across to the cylinder that they had dumped on the beach, and sat down on one end of it. He inspected it, bending over with his head tucked down between his knees to examine its hollow inside. An old piece of air circulation ducting, by the look of it. About as able to fly into space as Louis himself.

The sweat was trickling down his inverted face and into his eyes. Louis straightened up and mopped again with the sodden cloth. The sea, a hundred yards away across the beach, was cool and tempting. Louis would have been in for a dip hours ago, if he hadn't long since learned of the fanged horrors that swam beneath the calm surface. They made the Zardalu seem tame.

He might as well head for the tunnel system and see how Atvar H'sial was doing. It would be dark there, and clammy, but it would be cooler.

Louis eased his way off the air duct and stood for a moment in thought. Something felt a little bit different. What was it? Maybe sitting with his head down had made him dizzy. It sure wasn't any improvement in the weather. It was hotter than ever. Even the top of his skull felt as though it was burning up.

He put up a hand to rub at his dark matted hair.
He *was* burning up. His hair felt *hot*. Maybe he was
getting sick. That would be just what he needed, to
catch some alien planet's bug, out in the ass-end of
nowhere, where the native drugs and painkillers didn't
work unless you happened to have a beak and blue
tentacles.

Louis removed his hand from his head. As he did
so he caught a flicker of movement on the ground in
front of him. He stared, blinked, and stared again. He
was seeing something there: something that could not
be. He was seeing a *shadow*.

His own shadow. Louis spun around and stared up.
The unshielded sun was visible, bright and glaring. For
the first time since he and Atvar H'sial set foot on
Genizee, the swirling light of the annular singularities
had vanished.

Louis gazed directly at the marigold sun for at least
two seconds—long enough so that when he stopped
he saw nothing but dark, pulsing circles. Even before
they faded, he was running.

He had to get to the interior tunnels. He had to
find Atvar H'sial, and bring her to the surface before
any of the Zardalu saw what had happened and realized its possible significance.

The sun's after-images blinded him to what lay ahead.
Close to the entrance of the tunnel he ran full tilt into
a springy surface that bounced him away onto the sand.
Nenda heard a deep grunt. Three jointed limbs reached
down and raised him effortlessly to his feet.

"Louis Nenda, save your energy for the future." The
pheromonal message diffused across to him from Atvar
H'sial, with a subtext of concern and warning. "I fear
we have troubles ahead."

The giant Cecropian set him gently onto the sand.
The creature towering over Nenda inclined her white,
eyeless head, with its pair of yellow open horns below

two six-foot fan-like antennas. Beneath the head was a short neck banded in scarlet-and-white ruffles, leading to the dark-red segments of the underbody. The whole effect, propped up on six jointed bristly limbs, was the stuff of nightmares.

But not to Louis Nenda. He did not give the Cecropian's anatomy a second thought. He had seen too many aliens to go by appearances. "Trouble? What kind?" Nenda's pheromonal augment went into action, even though he was too winded to speak.

"The interior of Genizee is changing, in ways that I cannot explain." The pheromonal language of the Cecropian, unlike the slave talk of the Zardalu Communion, possessed degrees of subtlety and shading denied to even the richest of human tongues. Atvar H'sial's speech included images of collapsing walls, closing tunnels, and vanishing chambers, deep within the planet. "If this continues, our pretence of the need for interior exploration will be destroyed. The Zardalu will demand that we demonstrate to them the powers that we have so long claimed, and take them to space."

"It's not just the inside that's changing." Nenda pointed upward, knowing that the pleated resonator on Atvar H'sial's chin was bathing him with ultrasonic pulses, and the yellow horns were using the return signal to provide a detailed image. The Cecropian could "see" Louis's gesture perfectly well—but what she could not see was the vanishing of the annular singularities, and the emergence of the naked sun. No Cecropian could sense light, or other electromagnetic radiation shorter than thermal wavelengths.

"Up there, At," Nenda continued. "The singularities have gone. They just vanished, a couple of minutes ago."

"Why?"

"Damned if I know. Or care. But we've got to get over to the *Indulgence*, and take her up."

"And if we are returned once more to the surface, as we were before?"

"Then we're in deep stuff. But we're in that anyway if the interior tunnels are closing."

"Everywhere. As far as my signals could penetrate, the interior constructions of Genizee are vanishing. It is as though the work of the Builders there never existed."

While Atvar H'sial was still speaking, she acted. Without asking for approval from Louis Nenda, she picked him up and curled him tightly in a pair of forelimbs. She went springing away across the surface in long graceful bounds, her vestigial wing cases wide open behind her. Louis had his breath knocked out of him at every leap, but he did not complain. A Cecropian in full flight was much faster than any human.

The *Indulgence* lay midway between a twisted thicket of gigantic moss plants and five jutting towers of sandstone that formed homes for the senior Zardalu. Nenda rubbed his aching ribs as Atvar H'sial placed him on the ground—Didn't she realize her own strength?—and glanced across at the towers. At this time of day most of the Zardalu should be working in the ocean or the interior tunnels. Just his luck, if today they had decided to take a vacation.

At least the *Indulgence* was intact. But the ship was useless, as it had been for the past two months. Nenda had checked the engines every day. They were in perfect condition, with ample power. There was just one problem: they refused to carry the ship up from the surface of the planet. Something—the annular singularities themselves, or more likely the Builder Constructs who controlled them—had inhibited every attempt at takeoff.

"Quickly, Louis Nenda. This is no time for introspection."

It hadn't been more than two seconds since Atvar H'sial dropped him on the ground with his chest half crushed.

"Get off my back, At. Gimme time to breathe." Nenda swung the hatch open. "If the engines don't work this time, it'll be the last shot of introspection we'll ever get."

The lift-off sequence had been waiting in the computer for two months. The navigation system was primed and ready. Louis was in the pilot's seat two seconds after the hatch opened. Unfortunately, the power build-up of the *Indulgence*'s engines took a minimum of three minutes, and it was far from silent.

Three minutes. Three minutes of sitting, staring at the screens, wondering when the first head of midnight blue would peer curiously out of one of the towers, or lift from the calm sea.

"What do we do if the engines don't work this time, At?" Was that the curling end of a long tentacle, or just a ripple on the blue water?

"We will chastise the Zardalu, blaming them for the inadequacy of their assistance to us in refurbishing the ship."

"Right. Lots of luck." It *was* a tentacle. And now a head had broken the surface. The Zardalu were swimming rapidly for shore, four of them, and now half a dozen more. They must have felt the vibrations, and known that they came from the engines of the *Indulgence*.

Still over a minute to go. Was it time to send Atvar H'sial to man the ship's weapons system? Maybe they could swing it one more time; persuade the Zardalu that another day or two was all it would need to give them access to space. But that persuasion would have to be done *outside* the ship, without weapons. . . .

"Has it occurred to you, Louis Nenda, that if we do achieve orbit, and depart Genizee, we will once again be leaving empty-handed?" Atvar H'sial was crouched by his side, her echo-location vision useless to see what was happening outside the ship. "We did not have the foresight to stock the *Indulgence* with samples of Builder technology. We do not even have Zardalu trophies. I blame myself for a major lack of foresight."

Thirty seconds to go. The ship was vibrating all over as power build-up hit sixty percent. Zardalu were boiling up out of the water and whipping themselves along the shore toward the ship. The nearest was less than forty yards away. Others were appearing from the sandstone towers. And Atvar H'sial was bemoaning the lack of mementoes!

Nenda gripped the controls, a lot harder than necessary. "At, you can have my share of trophies, every one of 'em. I'll be glad to get out of here with my ass and hat. Hold on tight. I'm going for a premature lift."

The nearest Zardalu was reaching out long tentacles toward the ship. Power was less than seventy-five percent, below the nominal minimum. The *Indulgence* shuddered at Nenda's lift-off command and rose three feet off the ground. It hovered for a moment before sliding lazily sideways and down to the soft earth.

Too soon!

Forty seconds were recommended between engine power pulses. Nenda managed to wait for a quarter of that, until he heard something slap at the hatch and begin to turn the handle. He gritted his teeth and hit the lift-off sequence again.

The *Indulgence* shivered and began a wobbling, drunken ascent. Nenda watched the ground as it drifted past on the viewscreens. They were at six feet—ten feet—still within reach of questing tentacles. The shoreline was approaching. The ship was crabbing sideways, slowly lifting. Engine power was nearing eighty percent.

"We're going to make it, At. We're lifting, and nothing aloft is stopping us." Nenda glanced at a viewing screen. "Hold on, though. We got a problem. There's a whole line of Zardalu, right at the edge of the beach. We might be low enough for them to grab us."

"What are they doing?"

Nenda stared hard. He didn't speak the Zardalu slave tongue all that well, and the body language was even harder to read. But the splayed lower tentacles and the upper two raised high above every Zardalu head, together with the wide-open gaping beaks, were an easy signal.

"You won't believe this, At. But they're cheering."

"As they should be. For are we not demonstrating to them that, as promised, we are able to leave the surface of Genizee and go to space?"

"Yeah. But they won't cheer so loud when they find out we're not coming back. They were relying on us to get them off the planet and back into the Spiral Arm. They're going to be mad as hell."

"Perhaps so." The ship was rising steadily, and the waving Zardalu were no more than blue dots on the grey-brown beach. Atvar H'sial settled into a more comfortable position at Nenda's side. "But they ought to be most grateful."

"Huh?" The *Indulgence* was moving faster, above the thick haze of Genizee's lower atmosphere. Louis gave the Cecropian beside him only a fraction of his attention. Already he was beginning to worry about the next step. They might be off the planet, but they were still deep within the convoluted spacetime of the Torvil Anfract.

"I assert, they should be grateful." The pheromonal message carried with it an overtone of sleepy satisfaction. There was no hint that half a minute earlier Atvar H'sial had been facing possible death. "Think about it, Louis. We have been very good to them. We did not exterminate them, although the very name of

Zardalu strikes terror through the whole Spiral Arm. We did not kill or mutilate them, although that is their own habit with slaves. We have not taken their most prized possessions—a short-sighted omission on my part, I admit, and one for which I take full responsibility. And we have even left them their planet."

"You're all heart, At."

"In Zardalu terms, we have been Masters both kind and generous." Atvar H'sial settled lower on the cabin floor. "However, we have done one other thing for the Zardalu, which pleases me less. We have demonstrated that the road to space from Genizee is now open."

"No thanks to us that the singularities went away. That just happened. Maybe they'll come back." Nenda caught another drift of pheromones, with an unmistakable molecular message. "Hey, you better not be falling asleep back there. This isn't the time for it. We're still in the middle of the Anfract. Suppose it's changing, too? The flight plan we made before may not take us out."

"We escaped from Genizee." The Cecropian was closing the twin yellow horns, turning off her echo-location receivers. The six-foot antennas on top of her head were furling their delicate fan-like receptors. "I have no doubt that you will find a way to take us out of the Torvil Anfract. Wake me when we are clear. Then I will compute a trajectory to take us to the *Have-It-All*."

"Don't try to get off the hook by talking about my ship." Nenda turned to glare at Atvar H'sial's body, with the six jointed legs housed comfortably along its sides. "You need to stay awake and alert. If I don't handle the exit from the Anfract just right, it could kill you."

"But not without also killing you." The Cecropian's thin proboscis curled down, to tuck away into the pouch at the bottom of her pleated chin. "You should be gratified, Louis," she said sleepily, "pleased that I have such confidence in you. And confidence, of course, in your finely-developed sense of *self*-preservation."

✦ Chapter Two

The Torvil Anfract has a bad reputation, but the reality is worse. Phrases like "multiply-connected spacetime" and "macroscopic quantum phenomena" don't tell the half of it. *Anfract* is the noun formed from the adjective *anfractuous*, which means full of twists, turns, and windings; but that gives no more than a flavor of the real thing. Even the knowledge that the whole Anfract is a Builder Artifact, of unimaginably vast proportions, fails to deliver the right message.

Of more significance is the fact that less than a quarter of the ships that have entered the Anfract have ever come back to report what they found there. If getting *in* is difficult, it is nothing compared to the problem of getting out.

Louis knew all that. For seven full days, the *Indulgence* had crawled alongside granular sheets of quantum anomalies, seeking an opening, or eeled its way through knotted spacetime dislocations. For all that time, Louis had watched Atvar H'sial snoozing, and had thought dark thoughts.

Cecropians were accustomed to having sighted slaves who did all their dog work. Atvar H'sial, deprived of her Lo'tfian slave, J'merlia, seemed to be taking Louis Nenda for granted as an acceptable substitute. She never gave a thought to the fact that Louis might miss his own Hymenopt slave, Kallik, at least as much as she missed J'merlia. And she blithely assumed that he would bring them out of the Anfract, with not one ounce of help from her.

For seven days Louis had got by with catnaps in the uncomfortable pilot's chair. He had made bathroom runs—literally—and wolfed down his meals in spare seconds. Atvar H'sial, for the few hours a day that she had been awake, had spent her time in the galley, making evil-smelling liquid refreshments to suit her exact tastes.

The worst of it was that Atvar H'sial was right. The *Indulgence* had been designed for piloting by a five-armed Chism Polypheme, with all the arms on one side of his body. Louis Nenda found the pilot's seat inconvenient, to put it mildly, but at least he and the Polypheme both possessed *eyes*. If blind Atvar H'sial had tried to take the *Indulgence* out of the Torvil Anfract, she and Louis Nenda would have died in the first hour of flight.

That was logic, and undeniable. But Louis was not interested in logic. Whenever there was a free moment he turned to glare at the sleeping hulk of his business partner; he thought about reprisals.

Not physical ones. That wouldn't work with someone twice his size and four times his strength. The most effective revenge on Atvar H'sial was to *cheat* her. But how was he going to do that, when neither of them owned anything? Even their slaves were gone. If he managed to find his way back to Glister and his beloved *Have-it-all*, that ship was *Nenda's*. It was hard to see any way to use the *Have-it-all* to cheat Atvar H'sial.

Revenge is a dish best eaten cold. Louis kept that in mind, while he brooded over Atvar H'sial. What sort of stupid creature was it anyway, who saw using sound, and talked using smell? And in spite of this, his partner thought herself *superior* to humans and everyone else in the Spiral Arm.

As he schemed and fumed, the *Indulgence* under his careful guidance crept clear of the Anfract. His annoyance was so absorbing, it was almost an anticlimax when the panorama of star-dogs and the pinwheel fireworks of rotating micro-galaxies suddenly ended, and he saw ahead a clean, undistorted starfield.

It brought him fully awake for the first time in days. He realized then how exhausted he had become. He was so tired, so gritty-eyed bone-weary worn out, it was amazing that he had remained awake for so long. It would have been so easy to have killed them both by falling asleep in the middle of the Anfract. Maybe he should have done that. It would have served Atvar H'sial right. The trouble was, she would never have known it. And of course he would be dead, too.

He *was* tired, when that passed for thinking.

Nenda went over to the sleeping Atvar H'sial and nudged her with his boot.

"Your turn. I've done my bit."

The Cecropian awoke like the unfolding of a gigantic and hideous flower. Six jointed limbs stretched luxuriantly away from the dark-red body, while the yellow horns opened and the long antennas unfurled like delicate ferns.

"No problems?" The pheromones generated by Atvar H'sial were a statement more than a question. The Cecropian lifted her white, eyeless head and scanned around her.

"Nothing you want to hear about. We're out of the Anfract." Nenda sniffed noisily and headed at once for the sleeping quarters. They were designed for a Chism Polypheme, a nine-foot tall corkscrew with helical symmetry; even so, they should be a lot better than the pilot's chair. "Don't bother waking me for the Bose jumps," he said over his shoulder. "Just let me know when we get to the Mandel system."

That might take a day, or it might take a month.

Louis felt ready for something nicely in between—say, four or five days of sleep— when he collapsed onto the bunk. He tried to shape his body to the awkward spiral padding.

Everything depended on how tricky Atvar H'sial could get. The Torvil Anfract lay in remote Zardalu Communion territory, hundreds of lightyears away from the Phemus Circle. Mandel's stellar system was located within the Circle. The *Have-it-all* had been left near a gasgiant planet, Gargantua, that orbited Mandel. But linear distance was quite irrelevant. The *Indulgence* would negotiate a series of superluminal transitions, jumps through the nodes of the Bose Network. Travel time was a function of operator cunning, node loading, and energy budget.

Atvar H'sial could see nothing at all in human terms, but she had a remarkable power to visualize. Louis knew that when it came to manipulating the nonlinear connectors of the Bose geometry, she left him standing.

So he felt a strange mixture of pleasure and annoyance when, twelve hours later, she came to where he was still trying to fit his body—unsuccessfully—to a corkscrew shape, and announced: "I have a problem, Louis. I would welcome your counsel."

"What's up?" Nenda abandoned any attempt to sleep and swung his legs over the edge of the bunk.

"I am wondering. When you were navigating our way clear of the Torvil Anfract, did you notice anything unusual about it?"

"You gotta be kidding!" Nenda stood up and massaged his thighs, trying to get the stiffness out of them. "The whole Anfract is unusual. You find anything normal in there, it don't belong. Why'd you ask?"

"Like any serious student of the Bose Network, I have learned certain preferred node combinations— shortcuts, in effect, both for energy and total transition time. Those preferred modes of transport, naturally, depend critically on the spacetime structure of the Network itself."

"Is that right?" Nenda's pheromonal message carried an expression of total disinterest, one that Atvar H'sial could not miss.

The blind head nodded. "Hear me out, Louis Nenda, before you scoff. Except over very long time-scales, of centuries or more, the preferred node combinations ought to be invariant."

"Sure."

"But they apparently are not. For the past twelve hours I have been examining alternative routes to Mandel. Not one of the fastest and cheapest employs my standard node combinations. Instead I am coming up with an alternative to take us from here to Mandel with incredibly low cost and high speed."

"So you missed a good one." It was hard to keep the pleasure out of the pheromones. "Hey, At, anyone can goof up now and again."

"To err is human? Just so. It is not, however, Cecropian. Accept my assurances, Louis Nenda, that I did not overlook a cheap path for transition. That path was not present when we entered the Anfract, just a couple of your months ago."

"But you just said—"

"I know what I said. The travel times associated with particular node combinations should be stable for very long periods. They must be so—provided that the overall structure of spacetime in the spiral arm is not subjected to major perturbations. Now do you see the reason for my question concerning the structure of the Anfract? Had it substantially changed since we entered?"

"If it did, I have no way of knowing. You see, I didn't plan our way out, At, I felt the way out. Seat of my pants. I'm a pretty good pilot, even if I'm not up to Dulcimer's level."

"I agree; and if we are in confessional mode, let me also make an admission. I lack the experience to make a full evaluation of the new route to Mandel that I have discovered. It should prove considerably shorter than anything I have met before. On the other hand, since it is new there is a possible risk factor. A Node used for our transition could lie too near to a star or a chasm singularity."

"Lovely thought. You know me, At. I'm a natural coward. I say, go slow, but go safe."

"And again I agree. Or I would, if these were normal times. But since the moment of our first meeting, Louis, has it not been clear that something exceptional has been happening within the Spiral Arm? The changes to Quake at the time of the Grand Conjunction, the rogue Phages around Glister, our encounters with the Builder Constructs, the passage through the Builder transportation system, the re-awakening of the Zardalu—"

"Hey! Don't let me spoil your fun, but I don't wanna hear any of that. So we've been through some strange stuff together. Are you suggesting that we go lookin' for more of the same, with your special fast trip to Mandel?"

"Worse than that, Louis. I am asking the question, what next? Suppose that great changes continue to occur in the Spiral Arm. Suppose that those changes were eventually to include a failure of the Bose Network. Suppose our progress from this point on were to be restricted to subluminal speeds—"

"Don't *say* that. We'd be stuck in crawlspace for the rest of our lives, just the two of us with each other for company, out at the ass-end of the known universe."

"A dismal prospect indeed—though worse for me, I suggest, than for you. But that is why I awakened you—to ask, should we risk the fast transit to Mandel?"

"You call that a risk? Go do it—get that new flight plan into the computer."

Atvar H'sial inclined her head, in a gesture common to humans and Cecropians. "It is already there, Louis, ready for execution. I did not doubt that, faced with the alternative, you and I would once more find ourselves in full agreement."

✦ Chapter Three

Four days and six Bose Transitions later, Louis Nenda was beginning to have second thoughts. The *Indulgence* was on its final, slow, subluminal leg of the journey from the Torvil Anfract, heading out from the star Mandel toward its gasgiant planet, Gargantua. Nenda's own ship, the *Have-It-All*, should be where they had left it months earlier, on Glister, the little artificial planetoid that orbited Gargantua.

The journey from the edge of the Anfract had gone without a hitch. They had found no sign of the changes to the Spiral Arm that had worried Atvar H'sial. And that, when you got right down to it, was the source of Nenda's own uneasiness.

He was a squat, muscular human, born (though he could certainly never go back there) on the minor planet of Karelia, in a remote part of Zardalu Communion territory. Atvar H'sial was a towering Cecropian, from one of the leading worlds of the Cecropia Federation.

He preferred brutal directness; she was all slippery tangents. He might kill in moments of anger. She never seemed to feel anger, but she would destroy through calm calculation. They happened to be able to speak to each other, because Nenda had long ago obtained an augment for just such a purpose, but their overlap ended there. He and Atvar H'sial seemed to have nothing in common.

And yet . . .

They had first met on the doublet planet of Quake and Opal, in the Mandel stellar system where they now moved. Somehow, like had called instantly to like. When it came to business practices, Nenda knew that he did not need to ask Atvar H'sial's opinion. It was enough to sound out his own. In Louis Nenda's view, all sensible beings had the same business principles.

And what were they?

Sensible beings did not discuss such matters.

Which meant that if Atvar H'sial ever had an opportunity to cheat Louis Nenda, without risk to herself, she would surely do it.

Mutual need had held them together on Genizee, but that was over now. He could not see *how* she might be setting him up, but a good scam was never discernible in advance. And of course, there was another reason why he was not a good target: the only things he owned in the whole world, now that his slave was gone, were the clothes he stood up in; plus his ship, the *Have-It-All*—if they ever got that far.

Louis Nenda sank back into uneasy sleep.

He had spent most of the journey to Mandel napping, or trying to, as much as the corkscrew template of the Chism Polypheme bunk permitted. When discomfort and boredom finally drove him once more to the control room, he found that Atvar H'sial had been busy. She had rigged the electronics so that the visual signals of Nenda's display screens were converted to multi-source ultrasonics. She now "saw" just what he saw, although so far as he could tell it was not in color.

And what she claimed now, as the result of that "seeing," roused Nenda's worst suspicions.

"As I anticipated, Louis," she said. "There have been changes in the Mandel system, and profound ones. See."

Nenda found himself staring at the display, wondering

and waiting. The screen contained an image of the gasgiant planet, Gargantua. The atmosphere, with its smog of photo-dissociated organic compounds, showed as swirling bands of orange and umber. They glowed like high-quality zircon and hessonite, separated by thinner streaks and dots of blue-white ammonia clouds.

"I have arranged this as a time-lapse sequence of images, in order that you will see at once what took me many hours of observation to discern." Atvar H'sial reached out a clawed forelimb, and the display began to move. Gargantua was rotating on its axis, the image speeded up so that the planet's stately ten hours of revolution took less than a minute.

Louis watched, but found nothing to see. Just a stupid planet, turning on its axis as it had done for the past few hundred million years, and as it no doubt would for the next.

"Do you see it?" Atvar H'sial was hovering beside him.

"Of course I see it. D'you think I've gone blind?"

"I mean—do you see the *change*?"

It took another whole revolution before Louis felt his breath catch in his throat. He had it at last. "The Eye!"

The Eye of Gargantua. The orange-red, atmospheric vortex that peered balefully out of the planet's equatorial latitudes. A permanent circulation pattern, a giant whirlpool of frozen gases, a hurricane forty thousand kilometers across—sustained not by nature, but by the presence at its center of the vortex of a Builder transportation system.

"The Eye has gone!"

"It has indeed." Atvar H'sial's eyeless white head nodded her assent. "Vanished without a trace, even though it has been there for as long as humans have been in the Mandel system to observe it. And that inevitably sets up a train of thought. If the Builder transportation system on Gargantua has gone, then there seems a good chance that the entry point to that system, on the planetoid Glister, has likewise vanished. And indeed I can detect no trace of Glister at all, even with the ship's most powerful detection devices. Now, since Glister has vanished—"

Nenda roared with rage. He was way ahead of her. Glister had gone. And his ship—the *Have-It-All*, the only thing that he owned—had been left on Glister.

The whole thing must be part of some scam that Atvar H'sial was trying to pull on him.

He dived at the Cecropian, and went in swinging.

Louis had been wrong about Atvar H'sial's physical power. She was not four times as strong as he was. Ten times was more like it.

She held him effortlessly upside-down in her two front limbs, and hissed reprovingly—her echo-location equivalent of a rude gesture.

"To what end, Louis Nenda? And *how*? Like you, I have been on this ship continuously since we rose from the surface of Genizee. Modesty is not a quality usually ascribed to me, but in this case I confess that cheating you in the way that you are thinking is beyond my powers—whether or not it might be beyond my desires. I say again, how could I make Glister and the *Have-It-All* disappear, while traveling from the Torvil Anfract?"

Louis had stopped struggling, except for breath. A Cecropian's restraining hold was almost enough to crack a man's ribs. It was just as well that pheromonal speech did not need the use of lungs.

"Okay, Okay. You can put me down now. Easy!" Too rapidly inverted, he staggered as his feet met the deck. "Look. Try to see it from my point of view. If the *Have-It-All* was your ship, and I came along and told you it had vanished away—wouldn't you get angry, and do just what I did?"

"Anger, if it implies loss of control, is alien to a Cecropian. And given the disproportion of our sizes and strengths, it is well for you that I not respond as you did."

"Sure. But you get my point."

"As surely as you have missed mine. The loss of the *Have-It-All* is unfortunate, but the vanishing of the Builder transportation system is incomparably more significant. No longer can we hope to visit the artifact of Serenity, with the Builder riches that it contains. Even beyond that, my conviction that important changes continue to occur throughout the Spiral Arm remains unshaken. The events on and around Gargantua point more clearly than ever to the Builders as the agent of that change."

"Don't kid yourself, At. They've been gone at least three million years."

"What goes, can return. Builder Artifacts still dominate the Spiral Arm. We need the use of an expert on the Builders. I almost wish I could—"

"Could what?" Nenda had caught a hint of something hidden in the pheromones, a person's name about to be revealed, and then just as hastily disguised.

"Nothing. But with the Eye of Gargantua gone, and Glister vanished, there seems little point in approaching closer to Gargantua itself. I wonder . . ."

The pheromones carried no word pattern. Louis Nenda saw instead the doublet worlds of Quake and Opal, spinning about each other.

"Want to go back there, At, take another look at Quake? Summertide's a long time past; it's probably real quiet now."

"A landing, no. But a close approach might be . . . interesting."

Atvar H'sial refused to say more as the *Indulgence* approached the doublet planet. Which left it to Louis

Nenda to peer at the displays, and puzzle over what "interesting" might mean.

Quake and Opal were sister worlds, Quake just a fraction the smaller, spinning madly about each other. The closest points of their surfaces were only twelve thousand kilometers apart, their "day" was only eight hours long. But in everything except size, the two worlds were a study in contrasts: Opal, the water-world, had no land other than the floating soil-and-vegetation masses of the Slings; Quake, the desert world, was inimical to human life, shaken by great land tides at the doublet's closest approach to the parent star, Mandel.

Stretching between the two, like a slender tower with bases on both worlds, was the Umbilical.

Nenda stared at the screen, and waited for the Umbilical to become visible. Its thread of silvery alloy was bright, but it was no more than forty meters across. The first part to come into view would surely be the Winch, located roughly midway.

Except that it wasn't happening. Nenda had made the approach to Quake and Opal before. Last time, he had seen the Umbilical from much farther away.

Where was it?

He glanced at Atvar H'sial. She, intent on her own ultrasonic displays, was frozen at his side.

"I can't see it, At. Can you?"

He thought at first that his message had gone unreceived. The reply, when it came, was diffuse and hesitant. "We do not see it, because it is not there. The Umbilical was also a Builder Artifact. And it too has vanished. Quake and Opal are no longer connected."

"What's going on, At?"

"I do not know."

"But, hell, you *predicted* this."

"I expected a possible anomaly. But as to *why* . . ."

Nenda waited in vain for a continued message. As

he did so, he caught the faintest hint of a name in the pheromonal emissions—the same name that had occurred before in Atvar H'sial's thoughts, and had as rapidly been suppressed.

"Darya Lang!" Nenda shouted the words aloud, as well as sending them in a pheromonal flood. "I know where we can find her."

Atvar H'sial froze rigid. "Why do you say that name?"

"Because you've been thinking it, and trying to keep it from me. Darya's the Arm's top expert on the Builders. You know it. You think she'll understand what's going on."

"I doubt that Darya Lang's comprehension is better than my own." But Atvar H'sial's pheromonal words were soft-edged and unconvincing.

"Another half-lie. It doesn't have to be better for the two of you to make progress. Two heads are better than one—even if one of them is a Cecropian."

It was a deadly insult, and a deliberate one. Nenda was making his own test. And Atvar H'sial's response, when it came, was revealingly mild.

"I do not question Professor Lang's competence—in her specialized field. I do, however, question the wisdom of meeting with her. Even if, as you say, you can predict her location."

"She's back home on Sentinel Gate, sure as shooting. But if you're afraid of coming off second-best with her . . ."

"That is not my concern, and you well know it." The Cecropian's message was tinged with acid. "I worry about meeting with her not for my sake, but for yours."

"Hey, *I* don't claim to be the Builder expert."

"Enough deliberate innocence. You know why I worry about your meeting. Deny it as you choose, Louis Nenda, but you have a powerful emotional attachment to that human female. In previous encounters Darya Lang has diverted your attention, blunted your limited powers of ratiocination, and made your every decision suspect."

"You're full of it. Didn't I leave her behind, to fly with you on the *Indulgence* when we thought there was profit to be had? Anyway, you don't know humans. Darya Lang already picked her man. She chose Hans Rebka, that trouble-shooter from the Phemus Circle."

"A choice which you, at least, have not accepted. Human females are not like Cecropian males, mating until death."

"Don't you trust her?"

"Neither her, nor you. Although I admit that it might be useful to confer with Darya Lang, in order to learn more of the Artifact changes."

"Listen to me." Nenda advanced to stand directly below the thorax of Atvar H'sial, where the pheromonal messages were most distinct. "Here's the deal. We go to Sentinel Gate, and we see what we can learn from Darya Lang. Straight facts, pure business, nothing personal. Stay there no more than one day. Soon as we have all we can get from her, we leave. Just you and me. And we find a way to make some money out of what we learned. End of story."

"You pledge this?" Atvar H'sial was on the point of believing him—or pretending to, for her own reasons.

"Cross my heart." Nenda made the sign on his chest.

"An activity which, as you well know, has no meaning to a Cecropian." There was a cinnamon whiff of regret, together with a scent of acceptance. "Very well. I agree. We go to Sentinel Gate—and there will be no emotional coupling with Darya Lang."

"Trust me. That's not the sort I had in mind, anyway."

But Louis did not offer his last sentence in pheromonal form.

✦ Chapter Four

Life on Sentinel Gate was worse for Atvar H'sial than for Louis Nenda. Any rational being would agree with that statement. The permanent sentient population was exclusively human, the gravity and atmosphere and food perfect for humans. Humans felt *right* there. But to a Cecropian, designed by nature for a small, cloudy world lit by a faint, red dwarf star, Sentinel Gate was hot, dry, massive, and blindingly bright. Appropriate liquid nourishment was hard to find. Cecropians felt *strange* there.

All the same, any rational being would be wrong. Life on Sentinel Gate was worse for Louis Nenda.

Sure, Atvar H'sial on Sentinel Gate was a freak, no doubt about that. There was no way she could *not* be a freak, with her alien appearance, size, and metabolism. Everyone would recognize that, and accept it.

But Louis Nenda was a freak on Sentinel Gate, too, and one without Atvar H'sial's excuses. The average inhabitant—women included—loomed half a head or more above him. They were fair of complexion. He was dark and swarthy. Their eyes were wide-open and innocent. His were deep-set and bloodshot. The men favored shorts and an open, sleeveless vest that left the chest and arms bare.

Bare arms and legs were all right, even if Nenda's rated as too short and hairy. But his chest was the site of his augment, an array of grey mole-like nodules and deep pock marks that emitted and received the pheromone molecules. No way was he going to show *that* off in public, even if it did not excite comment. It was one of his secret weapons, something that gave him an edge in reading *human* emotions as well as Cecropian conversation.

Louis did it the hard way. He emerged from Immigration with arms, legs, chest, and throat clothed in close-fitting black. His hair was tucked away inside a tight and uncomfortable cap. If he had to be a freak, he'd be a *complete* freak.

He emerged to a world where even the building interiors were filled with birds and light and flowers, where every structure seemed to reach effortlessly for the sky. It was hard to believe, standing here, that down-scale worlds like Karelia and Peppermill and Opal and Quake even existed. Hard to accept that every day, throughout much of the Spiral Arm, life was a struggle for simple existence—hardest of all to believe what Atvar H'sial was at pains to assert, that there were events taking place in the Spiral Arm, right now, that might change everything for everybody, including the favored few of this lucky planet.

Louis was not sure that he believed it himself.

Darya Lang worked at the Artifact Research Institute of Sentinel Gate, a fact which Louis had long ago committed to memory. The problem was, no one at the spaceport seemed to have heard of such an institute. He went from one information desk to another, conspicuous in his odd clothing, and even more conspicuous because of the huge and colorful Cecropian at his side. Atvar H'sial was, relatively speaking, on her best behavior, but she received inquiring glances—and gave as good as she got.

Nenda's sixth inquiry won a condescending nod, and a terse set of travel instructions. By the sound of it,

Darya's research institute was down near noise level on the list of Sentinel Gate's significant activities. Louis Nenda was apparently judged to be of the same level of importance. He was an oddity, but not a *rewarding* oddity.

The institute was located in a foothill town called Bower. Louis made more inquiries, and came back to Atvar H'sial shaking his head.

"They stared at me like I was nuts. All I did was ask how much it would cost for the two of us to get there."

The answer was the most mind-boggling thing of all—more than the riotous flowers and the soft breezes and the sweet-smelling air. Travel on Sentinel Gate was *free*, a basic right so taken for granted that no one ever thought about it.

No one except Louis. On Karelia or Scaldworld, a trip halfway around the planet would be filled with risks and cost a good part of a life's savings. On Sentinel Gate, people seemed amazed at the very idea of *buying* a ticket.

They reached Bower using a combination of ground car, hypersonic aircraft, rail car, and hovercraft. Almost broke, Louis had wondered how they would pay for food. By now he ought to have learned. Like travel, simple meals on Sentinel Gate came free. The seats on every vehicle were broad and comfortable, perfect for sightseeing or sleeping. It was life as it ought to be lived, but never was.

A pilotless hovercraft finally dropped them off at the top of a gentle incline. "The Artifact Research Institute is straight ahead, at the foot of the hill. Beyond this point, vehicles are not permitted." The onboard computer even managed to sound slightly apologetic. "It will be necessary to walk, or to call for other assistance. Do you wish to remain here, or continue to some other destination?"

"Leave us here. We'll walk." Louis Nenda waited until the hovercraft floated away across the hillside, then turned to his companion. "You know, At, I'm not sure what sort of reception we're likely to get. Last time we saw Darya Lang, we sneaked away without tellin' anyone where we were going."

"As it turned out, Louis Nenda, we did not *know* where we were going. Are you suggesting that we will be greeted with some degree of animosity by Professor Lang?"

"I'm saying I don't know how we'll be greeted. Why don't you sit right here for a while, and let me go down there and try to make contact? You know, just check things out."

"Contact, you mean, with Darya Lang?" The Cecropian crouched down so that her head was level with Nenda's. "That human female. Did you not pledge— have we not already agreed—"

"*Business*, At. Nothing personal. Straight business, just like I promised. If I'm not back in half an hour you can come and get me."

Atvar H'sial rose to her full height, then slowly subsided to a crouched position. "Half an hour. No more. Enough time for you to locate Professor Lang, and explain that I wish to consult with her. But I do not want you to offer any explanation of my concerns, until I am present. I wish to make my own assessment of her response."

"Don't you trust her?"

"Not her. And not you." The Cecropian's yellow horns began to close. "Half an hour, Louis Nenda. I will be timing you."

The research institute was a five-minute walk down the hill, long enough for Louis Nenda to survey the place and wonder how he was going to greet Darya Lang. The last time he had seen her, months before,

they had just escaped death at the hands of the Zardalu.
He had looked like a hero. Now the conversation was
to continue on her home ground, where he looked like
a buffoon.

The institute was laid out on an open plan; graceful
white buildings, all clear windows and vine-covered
balconies, connected by trellised walkways. Nenda
searched in vain for signs on the buildings. All the
structures were of roughly equal size. He slid open
the door of one wooden building and peered inside.
It was clearly the main dining-room, and just as clearly
deserted. A squat serving-robot came trundling along
bearing an empty porcelain tureen. It ignored his
questioning. He went to stand in front of it and asked
again, "Darya Lang? Do you know where she is?" It
halted and waited, until at last he gave up and went
back outside.

A woman, poised and elegant, was strolling toward
one of the flowered arbors.

"Hey! You there." Nenda saw her languid turn, and
watched the expression of disbelief as it spread across
her face. As he strode toward her, he confirmed his
first impression. She was tall, she was slim, she was
blond, she was beautiful, she was perfumed; she was
a good foot taller than Louis; and she was *staring*.

A freak by any other name. Louis abandoned any
pretence of politeness. He took off his uncomfortable
cap and threw it on the ground, allowing his sweaty
and uncombed hair to blow in the breeze.

"My name is Louis Nenda. I'm looking for a professor called Darya Lang. She works at the institute.
Do you know where her office is?"

The woman didn't answer at once. Instead she lifted
her hand to her forehead, in a gesture that Louis saw
as wholly theatrical. "Nenda. Louis Nenda. Most interesting. Now where have I heard that name before?"
She tilted her head down to inspect him, from his

clumsy footwear to his dark, greasy hair. "You are Louis Nenda? I am Glenna Omar. I work at the institute."

"Yeah?" Louis was quite sure that he had never met the woman before, and he had no interest in playing the name game, especially with somebody who inspected him like he was an escapee from a carnival sideshow. "If you work here, you must know Darya Lang. Where's her office?"

She pouted, her glistening and bright-red lower lip pushing out at him. Whatever she might think of Louis, she obviously didn't have much time for anyone who wanted to talk about Darya Lang instead of Glenna Omar. One arm, slender and white and bare, waved at a building in a dismissive gesture.

"Second floor. Will you be staying here?"

"Don't know. Could be." As Louis turned and hurried away along the flower-lined path, he knew that the woman was still poised there staring after him. He wished he hadn't thrown down his cap, but there was no way he was going back to retrieve it while she was around.

The building had a list of names and office numbers posted inside the entrance. DARYA LANG, SENIOR RESEARCH SCIENTIST. ROOM 211.

So. Now came the awkward part. Louis stood thinking for a few seconds. He had read about situations like this, but he had never experienced one. He went back outside. Glenna Omar, thank goodness, had vanished. He stared up the hill, making sure that the hilltop and Atvar H'sial were not visible from his location. Finally he walked across to the path and picked from the flower border a single blossom, of apricot color and delicate perfume.

The second-floor corridor, like the stairway, was clean, carpeted, functional, and indefinably *pleasant*. What must life be like, day after day of peaceful research in such surroundings? Louis walked, not quite tiptoeing, past the closed doors until he came at last to Room 211. Its door too was closed.

To knock, or not to knock? Louis gently tried the door. It was not locked. He eased the door open and stepped softly inside.

The office was dominated by rows of wall screens and a long desk by the window. In front of the desk sat a single chair, broad, high-backed and with plush black armrests.

The office was occupied. Louis could see the chair moving, rocking a little on its base as though its occupant was relaxing or thinking hard.

Holding the flower out in front of him, Louis moved to stand beside the chair. "Surprise. Here I am again."

The chair swiveled. Louis found himself looking down at a slightly-built, large-headed man whose hands and feet seemed a bit too big for his body.

He dropped the flower to the carpeted floor. "You!" he said. "What the hell are you doing here?"

Even before his question was answered, Louis could see some irony in the situation. Back in the Mandel system, he had carefully explained to Atvar H'sial that he was not interested in Darya Lang, or she in him. She already had a man, Hans Rebka, the trouble-shooting specialist from the Phemus Circle. He had been with Darya, the last time that Louis had seen her. It ought to be no surprise that he was with her now.

But it was. The only good news was that Atvar H'sial would be pleased when she found out.

"What are you doing here?" Louis repeated. "And where is she?"

Rebka, after the initial moment of shock, was scowling. "I hoped I'd seen the last of you."

"Mutual. Where is she, Rebka? What you doing in her office?"

The scowl was replaced by a different expression. Guilt, if Louis was any judge.

"She's not here." Hans Rebka stood up. "But thanks for the flower. It's nice to know you care."

"She's not at the Institute?"

"Not here, not on Sentinel Gate."

"Then where is she?"

Again, that shifty look on Rebka's face. Louis wished that Atvar H'sial was present. This was a case for some high-class reading of pheromonal messages.

"I don't know where she is."

"You think I'll swallow that? Come off it, Rebka, you went muff-sniffing after her the minute you first met her. You chased her all over Opal and Serenity and Genizee. Damn it, you were sitting in her own chair when I came in." Nenda pointed at the name plate on the desk, and had a sudden suspicion. The window overlooked the path. Darya Lang might have seen him. She could have watched his approach to the building, even his picking of the flower. "Did *she* tell you to get rid of me?"

"She hasn't mentioned your name once since you and your bug friend left us." That at least sounded true—Hans Rebka acted too pleased for it to be a lie.

Louis took a step closer. "Well, I'm not leaving this place until I find out where she went. What have you done with her? This is important."

Rebka took his own step forward. The scowl came back. All the signs for a fight were there, and in spite of Rebka's tough-guy reputation Louis was looking forward to it.

But then, unpredictably, Hans Rebka's mood shifted. Instead of raising the testosterone level further, he shook his head and sighed.

"You want to know what's happening with Darya? All right, I'll tell you. But let's go to the dining-room."

"Why not do it here?"

"Because we'll need a drink and somewhere comfortable to sit. This is going to take a while."

Nenda's own sense of time suddenly cut in. "How long?"

"Depends how many stupid questions you keep interrupting me with. What's it matter how long it takes?"

"Give me two minutes, and it won't matter." Louis Nenda headed for the door. "I'll be right back. There's someone else has to hear this."

The introduction of an adult Cecropian into the small faculty dining-room at the Artifact Research Institute had one desirable effect. A little group of loungers, seated snacking at a couple of tables and chatting about their work, took one look at Atvar H'sial and hurried out.

Score one for Karelia, Louis Nenda thought with some satisfaction, as he arranged chairs to make room for the Cecropian. You'd never have separated inhabitants of his home world from their food that easily. They'd have stayed, and fought Atvar H'sial or a dozen other monsters for their meal if they had to.

Hans Rebka hadn't been overjoyed at the sight of her, either, although he knew her well.

"I didn't say anything about including your partner-in-crime in this conversation," he had said, when Louis appeared with Atvar H'sial in tow.

"She's no more a criminal than I am." Louis saw Rebka's reaction to that, and hurried on before it could start another argument. "Soon as we get settled in, I'll summarize At's thinking for you. Then you'll know just why we're here on Sentinel Gate."

But that explanation, when Nenda hung his muscular arms over the back of a dining-room chair and talked to Hans Rebka, sounded thin and feeble. Builder constructions inside Genizee fading and vanishing before your eyes. Builder Artifacts, stable for millions of years, suddenly gone. Massive and inexplicable changes to the geometry of the Spiral Arm. Suspicions that the Bose Network itself, the keystone of galactic travel and commerce, might be affected. It was none too persuasive, not when all around Nenda the serene world of the Artifact Research Institute—the very place where such changes ought to have drawn most attention— went quietly about its usual business.

"Pretty far-out, eh?" Nenda said defensively, as he came to his final comment, of the need to consult with Darya Lang. Then he saw Hans Rebka's face. The other man was not looking skeptical, far from it. He was watching and listening open-mouthed.

Had Louis said something he shouldn't have? If so, he couldn't think what. He straightened up, gripping the back of the chair in his muscular hands. "Anyway, that's why we're here. So now, tell us what's goin' on at your end."

Rebka shook his head. "I told you it would take a while to explain. But after what you've said . . ."

"It gets shorter? You've been hearing the same things?"

"No. It gets *longer*. Make yourselves comfortable, and sit tight. I'm going to have to start in on this from the very beginning."

✦ Chapter Five

The high that Darya experienced on her return to Sentinel Gate had to end. She knew that. She just hadn't expected to come down so far and so fast.

It was not that she was hoping for a big parade, or cheering crowds at the spaceport. What she had accomplished was hot stuff, but only to the scattered specialists for whom the *Lang Universal Artifact Catalog* (Fourth Edition) had become a kind of bible.

What *had* she done? Well, she had confirmed all new Catalog references, and verified their sources. With the Fifth Edition ready to go to press, Professor Merada should be ecstatic.

Her group had also returned from Genizee with an infant Zardalu in their possession, proving to the whole Spiral Arm that the old menace was back and breeding. That *was* important, but she claimed little credit for it—less than she gave to Hans Rebka and Louis Nenda. They had done all the work. And the little Zardalu would never come to Sentinel Gate. It had been taken to Miranda, for careful inspection.

Her personal ego-boost would come at the Institute, and only at the Institute. But there, at least, she was bursting to tell her story; and they should be bursting to hear it.

"Calm down, Darya." That was Hans, sitting by her

side on the final leg of the journey. "Relax, or you'll blow a circuit."

Sound words. It wouldn't be good to let Professor Merada or Carmina Gold or any of the other Institute heavies know how excited she felt. They prized calm, cool logic—or claimed to. You would never know it by listening to the screaming arguments at faculty meetings.

Darya did her best to follow Hans Rebka's advice. E. Crimson Tally, the embodied computer sitting in front of her, had turned questioningly at Rebka's final words. She smiled at him reassuringly. "'Blow a circuit' is just a figure of speech, E.C. I don't have circuits to blow—a blood vessel, maybe. But really, I'm fine."

And she was—or would be, as soon as she was inside and had Merada's ear. Darya jumped out of the hovercraft before it stopped moving. She hurried into the building, up a flight of stairs, and along the corridor to the Administrator's office.

Something odd about the corridor itself? She was too full of ideas and suppressed excitement to pay attention.

Professor Merada was not in his office. Nor was Carmina Gold, two doors farther down, in hers. Nor—now Darya knew what was wrong with the corridor—was *anyone*, although at this time of the morning the whole faculty would normally be present.

Darya ran the length of the corridor, and back downstairs. No one on the first floor, either. The building was deserted. She hurried outside, in time to catch sight of Hans Rebka vanishing around the corner of another building. A tall blond woman in a white silk dress swayed at his side.

"Hans!" But he was gone. Darya turned to E. Crimson Tally, still standing patiently by the side of the hovercraft. "E.C., the place is empty. Where is everybody?"

"They are presumably in the main lecture hall." Tally pointed to the notice board at the entrance to the building. "As you will see, it is described as a two-day event."

Darya stared at the board. The announcement was certainly big enough. You could only miss it if you were obsessed by something else.

SPECIAL TWO-DAY SEMINAR: QUINTUS BLOOM WILL PRESENT FULL DETAILS
OF HIS NEW AND REVOLUTIONARY THEORY:
THE NATURE AND ORIGIN OF THE BUILDERS.

"'The nature and origin of the Builders.' E.C., I've devoted my whole damned life to that subject. But I've never heard of Quintus Bloom. Who is he? And where did Hans go?"

"I do not know. But if you are aware of the location of the main institute lecture hall, it should be easy to find an answer to your first question."

Tally pointed again at the board. Darya read the rest of the announcement. In the main lecture hall—the way Hans Rebka had been heading. And it had started yesterday.

Darya ran, without another word to E.C. Tally. She had missed day one. Unless she moved fast she would miss most of day two.

Darya knew every research member of the Institute. Quintus Bloom was not one of them. So who the devil was he?

Her first impression of the man was indirect—the lecture hall was packed as she had never seen it, to the doors and beyond. As she tried to eel her way inside she heard a roar of audience laughter.

She grasped the loose vest of a man who was leaving. "Jaime, what's going on in there?"

He paused, and frowned in recognition. "Darya? I didn't know you were back."

"Just got here. What's happening?"

"More of the same." And, at her blank expression, "Yesterday, he went over the physical properties of all the Builder Artifacts. Today he's supposed to present his general theory of the Builders. But yesterday he didn't quite get through, so he's wrapping up the rest of the Artifacts this morning. I've got something back at my office that just has to go out today—wish it didn't—but I'll be around for the main event. *If* I can just get out of here."

He was pulling Darya, impatient to be on his way. She held on.

"But who *is* he?"

"He's Quintus Bloom. Came here from the Marglom Center on Jerome's World, to present his new theory."

"What's the theory about?"

"I don't know. No one knows. The only one who has heard it so far is Professor Merada." Jaime pulled again, freeing his vest from Darya's grip. "Word is out, though, that it's something special."

He pushed away her reaching hand, slipped past a couple standing in the entrance, and was gone.

It was no time for hesitation. Darya ducked her head and pushed her way forward, ignoring the grunts of protest and outrage. She kept her head low. It was like swimming underwater, through a sea of grey and black jackets.

Darya kept going until she saw light in front of her. She surfaced and found she had reached the front row of standing-room-only. The stage was below her and directly ahead. Professor Merada sat in an upright chair on the left side of a big holograph screen. He was looking straight at Darya, probably wondering about the disturbance created by her shoving to the front. He did not respond to her nod and little wave. By Merada's side, spurning the use of the lectern to the right of the stage, stood a tall and skinny man dressed in a white robe.

It had to be Bloom. His forehead was flat and sloped slightly backwards, his nose was beaky, and his teeth were prominent and unnaturally white. He seemed to smile all the time, even when he was speaking. Darya studied him, and was sure that she had never seen him before. She had never heard of the Marglom Center on Jerome's World. Yet she believed she knew every significant human worker in the field of Builder research, and every center where Artifact analysis was being conducted.

"Which disposes of one more Artifact," Bloom was saying. "*Elephant* bites the dust. There are two hundred and seventeen more to go. You will be pleased to know, however, that we will not have to work through them, one by one, as we did yesterday. We got all the detail work out of the way then. With the taxonomy that I established, we will find that we can put all the Artifacts very rapidly into one of my six overall categories. So. Let's do it."

The display behind him began to show Artifacts, rapidly, one after another. Bloom, without seeming to look at them, offered one-sentence summaries of their salient features, and assigned each to some previously-defined group.

Darya, in spite of herself, was impressed. She knew every Artifact by heart. So, apparently, did Bloom. He spoke easily, fluently, without notes. His summaries were spare and exact. The audience laughter—and there was much of it—came from wry, humorous comments that illuminated what he was saying. Darya had heard many speakers use humor as a distraction, to cover ignorance or some weak point in their argument. Not so Quintus Bloom. His wit arose naturally, spontaneously, from the text of his speech.

"Which brings us," he said at last, "to the relief I am sure of everyone, to the end of Part One. We have finished the Artifacts."

Darya realized that she had been in the lecture hall for more than an hour. No one had moved. She glanced quickly around, and saw Hans Rebka, far off to her right. He was standing next to Glenna Omar, who wore a dazzling flaunt-it-all dress. So that's who it had been, walking beside Hans as he vanished from sight. It certainly hadn't taken them long to make contact. Glenna seemed able to *smell* any man who came from off-planet. Couldn't Hans see her for what she was— Miss Flavor-of-the-Month?

Quintus Bloom was continuing, pulling Darya's attention back to the stage.

"We have completed the data reduction phase. Now comes, if you will, an *analysis* phase. Finally we will perform the *synthesis* phase."

The hologram display blinked off, and Bloom moved a little closer to the center of the stage.

"Twelve hundred and seventy-eight Builder Artifacts, scattered around the Spiral Arm. Every one mysterious, every one ancient, and every one different.

"Let me begin by asking a question that I suspect has been asked many times before: Can we discover, in all the great variety of Artifacts, any properties that seem common to all? What features do they share? They are of wildly different sizes. Their functions range from the totally comprehensible, like the Umbilical transit system between Opal and Quake in the Mandel system, to the wholly baffling and almost *intangible*, like the free-space entity known as Lens. They appear to be totally different. But are they?

"I suggest that their striking common property is *spacetime manipulation*. The Builder Artifacts came into existence millions of years ago, but the Builders themselves must possess an ability to work with the structure of spacetime—or of space and time—as easily and flexibly as we mould clay or plastics. With that ability comes something else, something that I will discuss in a little while."

Something else. It was a deliberate tease, inviting the audience to work out for themselves what Bloom was going to say. Darya herself had wondered many times at the apparent ease with which the Builders fabricated spacetime anomalies, from the simple Winch of the Umbilical to the monstrous puzzle of the Torvil Anfract. Did Quintus Bloom believe that he had something new to say, when so many others had thought about the problem for so long? Did he even realize that the Anfract *was* a Builder construct? Behind the casual marshalling of facts and the easy audience command, Darya sensed a massive arrogance.

"Now I want to ask a rather different question. Within the past year, we have seen what appears to be an unprecedented number of *changes* to the Artifacts. It is fair to ask, is this real, or is it merely something of our own imagining? Are we perhaps guilty of *temporal chauvinism*, believing that our own time is uniquely important, as all generations tend to think that their time is of unique importance?

"We can answer that question, thanks to the work of one of your own researchers, here at the Institute. Professor Darya Lang did the statistical analysis that shows the recent Artifact changes to be unlike any recorded earlier."

Darya felt the shock, and a rush of blood to her face at hearing her own name when she least expected it. Professor Merada was leaning forward and saying something to Quintus Bloom. White teeth flashed, and the beaky nose turned to point in Darya's direction.

"Professor Merada informs me that Darya Lang is herself in the audience today, after being away from the Institute for a long period. I feel honored, and I hope that we will have a chance to meet after this seminar ends.

"But let me continue. We have available the statistical evidence that recent events involving the Artifacts are in fact unique. But it is well known that statistics are not an *explanation* of anything. We have to ask and answer the question—*why*? Why has there been a spate of changes in the Artifacts, unique in our history of them? Professor Lang's important work, with all due respect, does not answer that question."

The knife, sliding in hidden behind the compliment. "With all due respect" meant "with no respect at all." Darya held her face expressionless, while people in the audience turned to look at her. Bloom went on, ignoring the reaction.

"What is unique about our own time, sufficient to cause a basic change in Builder Artifacts—in *all* Builder Artifacts? Why did the new Artifact, which I described yesterday and called Labyrinth, come into existence?"

A *new* Artifact? But every one was at least three million years old! Bloom must mean there was a *newly-discovered* Artifact. Even that was hard to believe. Darya had scoured every record in the Spiral Arm. She wanted to interrupt, to make Bloom stop and repeat whatever it was he had said the previous day. But she could not do it, and he was sweeping on:

"I want to suggest an answer, and also to make a prediction. The changes are occurring *because the Artifacts have at last achieved their intended purpose*.

"And what is that intended purpose? It is to shape the development of the Spiral Arm, so that it follows a certain path into the future. Now we can ask, how is it possible that the Builders *knew* what shape the future might take?

"To answer that question, I return to my earlier point. The Builders, we know, had a mastery over space and time that is far beyond us. It is far beyond us, *literally*, because the Builders are not from the distant past, an ancient race who built their Artifacts and then somehow vanished. They are from the *future*, the far future, where they built the Artifacts and *returned them to the past*. The Builders are beings from the future, who have mastered time travel. Let me say that again, in other words, because it is so important. The Builders did *not* vanish from the Spiral Arm at some time in the past. They were never in the Arm in the past— that is why we find no trace of them there. They are in the future.

"And which beings are they? Given their interest in human affairs, and the way that they have shaped human affairs, there is only one plausible answer: the Builders are *us*—our own distant descendants. *We* are, or will be, the Builders.

"And so, my overall prediction: the Builder Artifacts have achieved their main purpose, steering us along the desired path of Spiral Arm development. Since that primary purpose is fulfilled, the Builder Artifacts will continue to change, and even to disappear from existence. They will return whence they came—to the future."

The lecture hall was in an uproar. Only Merada, who had known what was coming, remained calm. Quintus Bloom was standing at the front of the stage, gesturing at Darya.

"I wonder, Professor Lang." His voice carried over the hubbub. "I wonder if you have any comments. I would appreciate your opinion."

But Darya's mind was spinning. She could not give her opinion. Not because Bloom's suggestion that the Builders were time travelers from humanity's own future was unthinkable.

No. Because Darya had considered that possibility *herself*, long ago—and rejected it, for reasons too subtle to present off the cuff, and in public. She shook her head at Quintus Bloom, turned and began to push her way back toward the entrance. She had to think. If there really was a new Artifact, as he had suggested, she had to find out all there was to know about it; then she had to re-evaluate everything she had ever thought and done in her whole blessed career.

"So that was it. The talk by Quintus Bloom left Darya fit to burst. Anyone could tell that by looking at her. After she'd had a session or two with Bloom she took off. Left Sentinel Gate."

Hans Rebka stopped speaking. He showed no signs of starting again.

Louis Nenda, who had been offering pheromonal simultaneous translation for the benefit of Atvar H'sial, glared at him. The transition had been abrupt, from detailed description to a sudden two sentence cut-off. It was certainly not a logical end point.

"Are you saying that's *it*? That's all you're going to say about what happened, and where and why she went?"

Rebka shrugged. "I've told you all I know."

"And you *let* her go, just like that. Didn't try to talk her out of it, or stop her, or go with her?"

"I didn't."

"He is lying, Louis." The pheromonal message from Atvar H'sial came quickly. It was not necessary.

"Damn right he's lying. But why?" Out loud he said, "Were you in on the sessions she had with Quintus Bloom?"

Rebka shrugged. "I sat in on the seminar, until it was clear to me that I wasn't going to understand more than three words." He looked Nenda straight in the eye. "I don't know what they said to each other."

Nenda stared right back. "I believe you." He added to Atvar H'sial, "In a pig's eye. I can lie with a straight face as well as anybody. What now, At?"

"We have something of a problem, Louis. I do not wish to reveal to him that Bloom's prediction, of changing and vanishing Artifacts, appears to be coming true."

Hans Rebka snapped his fingers. "Oh, there was one other thing that will interest you, Nenda. Soon after we arrived at Sentinel Gate, J'merlia and Kallik rolled up at the institute."

As a distraction, it was first-rate. Nenda went popeyed. "Kallik is here now? And J'merlia? Why didn't you tell us that before?"

"Because they aren't here now. Darya took them with her."

"She can't do that! They don't belong to her. They belong to me and Atvar H'sial."

"Not any more. They have the rights of free beings."

"Nuts. I have their slave cubes, right here." Nenda began to fumble at his tight head-to-toe clothing, which proved almost as hard to get into as it was uncomfortable.

"Louis, what is going on?" The exchange between Nenda and Rebka had been too fast for Atvar H'sial to receive a pheromonal translation.

"J'merlia and Kallik. Been here—and gone. With Darya Lang."

"My J'merlia!"

"And my Kallik. I know what I said, At, but we better be ready for more than a day's stay. You and me got lots of work to do before we can leave Sentinel Gate."

✦ Chapter Six

Hans Rebka had told the truth about Darya's first encounter with Quintus Bloom, and what happened afterwards (even if it was not, for reasons that Hans preferred to keep to himself, the whole truth).

She had run from the lecture hall, so swamped with emotions that her mind refused to function. But ten minutes later she was pushing her way back in, barging past the same angry people as on her first entrance. Wrong or right, Quintus Bloom had not finished, and she had to hear the rest of it.

She knew there had to be more, if Quintus Bloom was to retain his plausibility with Professor Merada and the Institute. Merada, whatever his faults, was scrupulously honest and painstakingly thorough.

Darya herself had long ago noted—and remarked on—the mastery of time and space exhibited in the Builder Artifacts. It was easy to form a theory around the idea that the Builders had time travel. But theories were a dime a dozen. The partition that separated science and wishful thinking was *evidence:* observations and firm facts.

The odd thing was that Quintus Bloom *had* facts, more than Darya would have believed. As he spoke she became convinced. The Artifact near Jerome's World, whether it was new or not, certainly existed. Bloom had visited Labyrinth, and found a way to penetrate its coiled and re-entrant geometry. He had taken recording equipment with him. At the key moment of his presentation, the darkened stage of the Research Institute filled with scenes of Labyrinth: the scan from all angles, and the bizarre interior where nothing remained still and nothing followed straight lines.

Quintus Bloom kept his comments to a minimum. He allowed the images to speak for themselves, until at last he said, "This is the innermost chamber of Labyrinth. The scenes that follow are taken directly from polyglyphs contained within that chamber. I have performed no editing, no adding to or subtracting from. I merely display what I found revealed on the chamber walls."

The scene at first was static, a fixed panorama of points forming a rough crescent. Every audience member knew it well. It was the local part of the Spiral Arm, complete with bright stars and diffuse clouds of dark or glowing gas. Builder Artifacts were shown as minute flecks of vivid magenta. Nothing moved on the image, and the tension in the lecture hall grew steadily. When a green point flared suddenly into existence, there was a sigh from the whole audience.

"I suggest that you ignore that for the moment, and concentrate your attention *here*." Bloom indicated a region of the Spiral Arm far from the green point, which had now spread to become a close-set pattern. Soon an orange speck of light flickered into existence, to spread in its turn and swallow up the green.

"Now, if you please, watch closely where the cursor is set. A new point—now! And its location: *Earth*, the original home of the human clade." But Quintus Bloom had little need to speak. That source location was familiar to all.

So was the sequence that followed. One by one, other points brightened, moving out from Earth and

Sol in a roughly spherical pattern. "Centauri, Barnard, Sirius, Epsilon Eridani, 61 Cygni, Procyon, Tau Ceti, Kapteyn, 70 Ophiuchi . . . "The names were spoken, not by Quintus Bloom but by the audience. It was little more than a whisper in the darkened hall, the ritual recital of the nearest stars that humans had explored at crawlspeed, before the discovery of the Bose Network.

The display continued: millennia of human exploration, shown in a couple of minutes. Bright sparks of a new color appeared, far off in the Spiral Arm. They too grew in numbers, until suddenly a thousand stars burst into light simultaneously,

"The discovery of the Bose Network, and the Bose Drive." Again, Bloom's comment was unnecessary. Everyone recognized the moment when humanity had exploded into the Spiral Arm at a rate limited only by the available ships and explorers, and human space had become linked with the sprawling worlds of the Cecropia Federation.

The dance of the lights continued. The orange points, which had winked out one by one, reappeared. But now the appearance of the Spiral Arm was no longer familiar. Myriads of stars glowed, in many colors. They extended across thousand of lightyears, far beyond the boundaries of the Fourth Alliance, beyond the Cecropia Federation, past the farthest reaches of the Zardalu Communion. Suddenly everything was new, the familiar star maps swallowed up within a larger panorama.

"No longer our past. Our *future*, and the future of the other clades of the Arm." Bloom allowed the display to go on, spreading through the Arm and beyond, until at a gesture from him it suddenly vanished. He was left alone at the front of the stage.

"I know some of you had trouble with the idea, when I proposed a few minutes ago that the Builders are our own distant descendants." His voice was conversational, even casual. "That's all right. I had trouble myself, when it first occurred to me. But rather than trying to persuade you that I am right, I want to point something out to you, and let you make your own decision."

Darya had the feeling that he was speaking directly to her. Certainly he was looking her way.

"The scenes you have just seen showed the Spiral Arm as it was long ago," he went on, "and as it appears to be far in the future. Those images were taken from within Labyrinth itself. Now, is Labyrinth truly a *new* Artifact, as I have suggested? Or is it merely one that we have managed to overlook for all these years? That is not beyond possibility, since it is small, and a free-space structure. Jerome's World is the closest inhabited planet, but we are still over half a lightyear away.

"We then have two possibilities: Labyrinth is new, and recently appeared; or Labyrinth has, like the rest of the Builder Artifacts, been present for millions of years.

"Which one is the more likely? I began equally happy with either. But then I asked a question. Was it plausible that, three million years or more in the past, the Builders had been able to make a prediction—a *precise* prediction—of the way in which the clades would move out into the Spiral Arm? I do not think so. Ask yourselves the same question, and see what conclusion you reach."

Behind Quintus Bloom, the moving tableau began again from the beginning. Earth was illuminated, then the neighboring stars. The Zardalu came and went; the Cecropians appeared. The audience could again follow that precise historical pattern of interstellar travel and development. The familiar expansion through space had a soothing, almost a hypnotic effect.

"If you believe that the Builders were, millions of

years ago, able to make such devilishly accurate predictions, that's fine." Bloom was an invisible voice, lost within a sea of stars. "If not, take your thinking a little farther. Suppose that Labyrinth appeared recently— as recently as yesterday. Now, do you believe the development patterns we saw for the future? If you do, then we again face the same question: How can the Builders, *today*, know the precise pattern of expansion through the Spiral Arm as it will be hundreds and thousands and tens of thousands of years in the future? It is the same problem, merely displaced through time."

The whole Spiral Arm was aflame with stars again. Earth had vanished, the Fourth Alliance was lost in an overwhelming sea of light.

"If you answer that the Builders had that magical power to predict the far future, then you assign to them talents that strain my belief past bearing. But if your answer is, the Builders are able to show such a pattern *because it forms a part of their own past*, then your thoughts agree with mine. The Builders are not three million years in the *past*; they are who-knows-how-many years in the *future*."

Darya listened to the applause that filled the lecture hall at the end of Quintus Bloom's seminar. She said not a word, in spite of the many heads turned in her direction. She knew what they wanted. Either a fight between her and Bloom, or agreement that his ideas explained what hers could not. She would not humor them. Science wasn't a show-business talent search, conducted in large halls and decided by audience applause. Her time would come later, when she had the opportunity to probe Bloom for details and ask the subtle questions denied in the thirty-second sound bite of a public forum.

That chance would not be long in coming. Professor

Merada always hosted a private dinner for visiting scholars after a seminar. Darya would be invited, even though she had just arrived at the Institute. Her mouth watered at the prospect—and not because of the food.

Darya arrived a few minutes early. Professor Merada was already there, sitting as usual at the head of the table with Quintus Bloom on his right. Normally Carmina Gold would sit on Merada's immediate left. Tonight that had been changed. Darya circled the long table, seeking her own name card, and was surprised to find it right next to Merada, directly across from Quintus Bloom.

Bloom nodded to Darya, smiled at her reaction to the seating plan, and said, "At my request." He went on talking to Merada.

Darya sat down uncertainly. Already, in some vague way, she was on the defensive. She studied the man across the table.

Seen close up, Bloom was not the attractive figure he had seemed on the stage. His face and neck were marred by some kind of skin disease, with coin-sized red sores only partly concealed by ointment and powder. His tongue seemed far too long. Darya watched with a revolted fascination as the pink tip flicked out far past his white teeth at every pause for breath.

"Well, Professor Lang?" Merada was addressing her. "What do you think?"

I think I'm an idiot. But Darya did not say it. She, who had mixed with Zardalu and a dozen other alien forms, had been so put off by minor human variations that she had not even been listening! For all she knew, everyone on Jerome's World looked like Quintus Bloom.

"I'm sorry. What was that again?"

Professor Merada, heavy and humorless, nodded as though confirming some private suspicion. "Our guest was suggesting that perhaps it is a mistake to issue the

Fifth Edition of the Artifact Catalog. It might be out of date, even before it appears."

That was enough to grab Darya's attention—*all* her attention. The Lang Catalog—*her* catalog!—was the Institute's most respected publication. If Merada was considering withdrawing it, the influence of Quintus Bloom went far deeper than Darya had realized.

"It's certainly not out of date! The new theory is *wrong*." Darya noticed the change in the room as she spoke. Others had arrived while she was preoccupied with Quintus Bloom. She glanced along the table. Every face was familiar to her; even E. Crimson Tally's, although it was anyone's guess as to how the embodied robot had found his way in to what was supposed to be an invited dinner. And all those faces were turned in her direction, with every other conversation at the table abandoned.

Darya had had four hours between the end of the seminar and the start of the dinner. Not long, but enough to go back to her notes and review her own analyses.

"I say that the Builders are from the past, and existed millions of years ago. Whether they ceased to exist, or whether they now exist on some other plane that is beyond our senses, is not important. They were *here*, in the Spiral Arm. They made the Artifacts. The Builders were certainly far different from us, in ways that we may never understand. They were masters of both space and time, and perhaps they could predict future events as we cannot. Furthermore, their Artifacts call for a technology beyond our own, and possible changes to our understanding of the laws of physics. But that is all."

Darya glanced again along the table. She had everyone's attention. Quintus Bloom was smiling slightly, and Carmina Gold was nodding. E. Crimson Tally seemed slightly puzzled, as though what Darya had said was self-evident.

"Now compare that with what *you* are suggesting." Darya glared at Bloom. "The Builders, you say, are from the future. But that is not an *explanation* of the Builders, it is merely a source of paradox. Let me make my point simply, by asking: Which future? If you say that they are from, say, Future A, then by coming back and planting the Artifacts they will have created a different future for the Spiral Arm, say, Future B. If you reply that they did *not* create a different future, then Future A must be unaffected by the appearance of the Artifacts; if it is unaffected, then there was no *point* to introducing the Artifacts. Time travel as an explanation always has this fatal flaw: it contains the seeds of its own logical destruction. My ideas may require changes to the laws of physics. Yours are inconsistent with the laws of *logic*, and that is a far more serious problem."

It was not coming out quite right. Somehow her clear thoughts were being twisted on the way from brain to lips.

Quintus Bloom was still smiling, and now he was shaking his head.

"But my dear Professor Lang, why are you so convinced that our present understanding of logic is any better than our understanding of physics? You asked us all a question. Let me now ask you a couple. First, does anything in your ideas explain the appearance of the new Artifact, Labyrinth?"

"I don't know that it's new. I have had no chance to inspect it." That was a weak answer, and Darya knew it.

"But *I* have done so, in detail. However, since you have not seen Labyrinth, let us omit it from consideration. Will you admit that there are changes in other Artifacts, profound changes, more than there have ever been before?"

"I agree that there have been some changes. I'm not sure how great they are."

"And do your theories explain *why* there have been changes?"

"Not yet. I came back to the Institute to start a new investigation, precisely to explore those anomalies."

"Ah. A worthy objective. But I can explain them *now*, without that research program. You say there have been 'some' changes. Professor Lang, when did you last visit an Artifact?"

"I came here directly from the Torvil Anfract. It is an Artifact."

"Indeed?" Bloom's eyebrows raised, and he glanced along the table. "But it is not listed in the famous Lang Catalog, the volume which we all take as our final authority." He turned to Merada. "Unless someone with greater knowledge can correct my memory . . ."

"It's not in the Catalog," snapped Darya.

"Not even in the upcoming Fifth Edition? The *new* Edition?"

"It is not in the Catalog," Merada said. "Distinguished guest—"

"Please. Call me Quintus."

"If you prefer it. Quintus, the Torvil Anfract had never been proposed as an Artifact, until Professor Lang did so a moment ago. And it will never be listed as an Artifact, without my personal review of the evidence." Merada glanced reproachfully at Darya.

Bloom was still smiling benignly. "Very well, let us leave the Anfract for the moment. I want to ask Professor Lang: When did you last visit any Builder Artifact *other* than the Torvil Anfract? One that *is* in the famous Lang Catalog."

Darya thought back. Genizee, not in the Catalog. Serenity, not in the Catalog. The Eye of Gargantua, not in the Catalog. Glister, not in the Catalog.

"About half a year ago. The Umbilical, between Quake and Opal."

"But the greatest changes to the Artifacts have taken

place within that time! Half a year, in which you have not seen a single Artifact. Half a year, in which—"

Bloom paused. He lost his smile, turned, and stared to his right along the table. The voice of a puzzled embodied computer was steadily becoming louder.

"If the Builders are not in the future, then they can't come back and change the present so that the Builders *are* in the future, because they are not there to do it." E. Crimson Tally was staring down at the table top. "But if they *are* in the future, then the present didn't need the Artifacts to become that future, so then the future they make if they send the Artifacts back is a different future—"

He paused and froze, his eyes blank and his mouth hanging open far enough to reveal his bottom teeth.

"There!" Darya pointed accusingly at Quintus Bloom. "Now you've done it. You've put E.C. into a loop. That'll be hell to fix. I told you it was a logical contradiction, the idea that the Builders might have come from the future."

She seemed to be the only one who cared. Half a dozen conversations were starting up along the table.

Professor Merada leaned over and patted her hand. "We are all good scientists here, Professor Lang, and it is as good scientists that we must behave. We all have our cherished theories, on which we have worked for many days and months and years. Although it is hard to abandon beloved ideas, if a new and better theory comes along it is our duty as good scientists to accept it. Even to *embrace* it."

Darya bristled. The man was trying to *soothe* her. And Carmina Gold was nodding agreement. So were half a dozen others at the table. Darya couldn't believe it. They had been here for less than a quarter of an hour. The first course of the meal was still to arrive, and she had said only a tenth of what she had to say— and badly, at that. But minds along the table were already closing. Darya had lost the argument. Quintus Bloom had won it.

Darya stood up and blundered towards the door. She was quite sure that she was right, but without evidence she would never convince anyone. Quintus Bloom was too confident, too smooth and charismatic, too well-armed with recent facts.

Well, there was only one way to deal with that. She had to find more facts of her own. And she would not do it sitting in an office on Sentinel Gate.

✦ Chapter Seven

Darya would need facts, but at the moment she wanted something a good deal more personal.

She had not seen Hans Rebka since the beginning of the seminar. For all she knew he had left after the first few minutes, because she had been too preoccupied to notice. However, it was easy enough to find out which guest accommodation in the Institute was assigned to any visitor. Darya checked the central listing. Hans had a single-story building to himself, a bungalow that lay in a wooded area behind the main complex of the Institute.

Although it was raining outside and already dark, Darya didn't want to waste time going back for more clothing. The night was chilly, but she welcomed the brisk breeze as a force to blow away her worries. She walked slowly, face tilted up to catch the raindrops. It would be hard to know what to say to Hans without sounding like a whiner and a loser. Had he been there himself, to see and hear exactly what had happened? She didn't know.

Darya felt a touch of guilt. Chasing down her old notes after the seminar, then losing her temper at Merada's crazy dinner before the food even appeared— she had been too busy to give any thought to what Hans was doing. Maybe she could make up for that now.

When she was fifty yards from the bungalow, the shower quickened to a downpour. Darya sprinted for the porch and stood panting beneath it for a few moments, listening to the hiss of rain and the gurgle of runoff through gutters and downspouts.

The door was not locked, and it was—unusual for Hans—slightly ajar. The inside of the house was dark, but guest quarters were on a standard plan and Darya knew the layout well. Her eyes had adjusted to the dark. She did not turn on any light as she went quietly through the open living-room and on into the bedroom. She could make out the bed and a white sheet covering it, with a bare foot sticking out past the end.

She gripped the big toe and tugged it gently, then ran her fingers along to the ankle. "Hans? I need to talk to you. I think I just made an ass of myself."

There was a gasp from the other end of the bed, at the same moment as Darya realized that something was wrong. Hans Rebka had hard, bony feet. The foot and ankle she was holding were smooth and soft.

"Who's that?" said a woman's voice. The foot jerked free of Darya's grasp. The pale blur of a face appeared at the other end of the bed, as the woman sat upright. "What the devil are you doing?"

A light snapped on. Darya found herself face to face with Glenna Omar. "I'm sorry. I thought these were Hans Rebka's quarters."

"They are." Glenna pulled up the sheet, to cover her naked breasts and shoulders. "Didn't you ever hear of *privacy*?"

"What are you doing here?" It seemed to Darya that the other woman looked more pleased than annoyed. "And where's Hans?"

She knew the answer to the first question, even before Glenna jerked her tousled blond head to the right and said, "In there. In the bathroom."

Darya heard the sound of running water. She had taken it for the sound of rain outside. She walked across to the bathroom door and went in.

Hans stood at the sink in profile to Darya, drying his hands on a towel. He was naked and he did not look around, but he must have heard her come in because he said, "Ten more seconds, and I'll be there. Don't worry, I haven't run away."

He turned around, with a grin that changed at once to a grimace. "Oh, no."

"Oh yes. You bastard." She glared at him, from his scarred, concerned face to his bony knees and over-sized feet. All signs of sexual excitement faded as she watched. "I should have known. What they say about men from the Phemus Circle is true. Callous, faithless, sex-mad— I thought you and I *meant* something to each other."

"We do. Darya"— she had turned, to walk back through the bedroom, and he was ignoring Glenna to hurry after her —"where are you going?"

"Leaving. Leaving you, and this lousy institute, and this rotten planet. Don't try to follow me. Go back to your—your *strumpet* in there."

"But *where* are you going?" They were outside in the teeming rain. The night was turning colder, and Hans stumbled bare-footed on slippery turf and fell flat in the mud. He couldn't see a thing. "Wait a minute, and I'll come with you."

"You will not. I don't want you anywhere near me. I don't want to be on the same *world* as you."

"Who'll look after you—who'll keep you out of trouble?"

"I'm perfectly able to look after myself. Bug off, and leave me *alone!*"

Darya began to run. Hans took a couple of steps after her. This time he tripped over a bush and fell again to the ground. When he got up he couldn't see her or even the path.

He limped back to the bungalow. The door was wide open. Had it been open when Darya came? He felt sure that he had closed and locked it. He headed through into the bedroom, rubbing a bruise on his thigh. Glenna was still snuggled down comfortably in bed, the sheet pulled up to her eyes. She giggled.

"You ought to just *see* yourself. Your hair is soaked, and you have mud all over your chest and arms. You look like a Phemus Circle wild man."

"Yeah. I'm a real comedy act." Hans sat down on the end of the bed. "Hell and damnation."

"What was all *that* about?"

"You know quite well what it was about."

"I can guess. And it's all naughty little Glenna's fault, isn't it? I bet you told Professor Lang that you had nothing to do with it." A foot eased clear of the sheet, and bare toes wriggled along Hans's leg.

"I didn't tell her anything. She wouldn't listen. Right now she hates my guts." Hans frowned at Glenna as the toes crept higher on his thigh. "Quit that. What are you, some kind of animal?"

"Maybe. Try me and find out. But at least I understand men. And *I'm* not angry with you, not in the slightest. Come to bed."

Hans stood up. Glenna's expression changed from intimate to anxious. She pushed back the sheet as Hans headed for the living-room. "Where are you going?"

"I have to make a call. Just a quick one."

"To Darya Lang?"

"No. Not to Darya Lang. She wouldn't talk to me if I did. Relax. This will only take a minute."

"All right. One minute, and no more." Glenna's voice changed to a complacent purr, and she snuggled back down in the bed. "I do not know how such things are handled in the worlds of the Phemus Circle, but in our society it is not considered polite to leave a lady alone with her motor running."

✧   ✧   ✧

Hans had not lied about the need to make a call, but what he needed more than that was time to think—think without Glenna coiling herself around him and scrambling his brains.

How had he put himself into this situation? It wasn't enough to say that Glenna was as sexy, luscious, and willing a woman as you could hope to meet. Before he left the Phemus Circle that would have been quite sufficient, but not any more.

Why hadn't he waited around the Institute, then, until Darya's work with Quintus Bloom and Professor Merada was finished?

He had one explanation, but it wasn't anything to make him happy. He had been feeling horny even before he met Glenna, undeniably. But that wasn't the reason they had finished up in his bedroom. It was because he had also been *peeved*—at Darya.

He had been quite good enough for her while they were chasing around the wilds of the Phemus Circle or Serenity, or trying to escape from the Zardalu or the Torvil Anfract; but as soon as she got back to her homeworld of Sentinel Gate it was a different story. He had been pushed out of the way and ignored. She preferred her snobbish and intellectual friends—people he was apparently not civilized enough to be introduced to, still less to converse with.

During the seminar he had decided, even if unconsciously, that he would get his own back. He would show her. There were other women, sophisticated and attractive ones, who found him acceptable even by the upscale standards of a world like Sentinel Gate. He had known, from the first moment that he met Glenna Omar, that she found him intriguing. It was time that Darya learned it, too.

Unfortunately, she had done exactly that, but not at all in the circumstances of his choosing.

Had Glenna left the door open *on purpose*? Was she someone who was excited by the chance of discovery, just as danger always excited him?

Hans stared out through the still-open door at the teeming rain. He wanted to tell Darya what a fool he had been and how sorry he was, but in that dark cloudburst he had no idea how to find her. At least, though, he had to look. He would dress, and tell Glenna that she must leave.

He turned toward the bedroom, and found her standing silent in the doorway. She had taken a sheet from his bed and draped it modestly around her.

He sighed. He was angry, but it ought to be with himself and not with Glenna Omar. "How long have you been there?"

"Just a minute or two." She glided forward to his side. "I didn't want to disturb you. You looked so upset."

"I am. I think you'd better put your clothes on and get out of here."

"I know." She held out her dress and shoes. "If you don't mind, I'll borrow the sheet and just carry these with me. They'll get soaked anyway, even if I'm wearing them."

Her voice was as dreary as the driving rain outside. A cold draft blew in through the open door, and she shivered. She stepped forward to the threshold and hesitated there.

"Are you all right?" Hans moved to her side. "That sheet won't be enough. I think we ought to find you something waterproof. And I'll look for an umbrella, too."

"It's not that. Not the cold, I mean, or the rain."

"Then what's wrong?"

"It's me. Hans, I'm really sorry. This is all my fault. When we met today I was feeling lonely and awful down, and you were kind to me. You're a very attractive and sexy man, but what I wanted more than anything was company. I needed someone to talk to, someone to hold me and tell me that I haven't made a total mess of my life . . ."

Hans was horrified to see tears filling Glenna's eyes. He felt better equipped to handle an attacking Zardalu than a weeping woman. He tried to put his arm around her, tentatively, but she pulled away.

"No. I'll go now. It's not your problem, it's mine."

"You'll freeze if you go out dressed like that. You're already shivering." He put his arm around her again, and tried to lead her away from the door. "At least have a hot drink, to warm you up before you go."

"I don't think I ought to. Professor Lang—"

"She won't be coming back." That was sure enough, he thought bitterly. "And even if she did, we'll be doing nothing wrong."

"We-e-ell." Glenna allowed herself to be steered through the living room. "I don't want a drink, though."

"Something to eat?" Hans's guilt toward Darya was mysteriously turning into guilt toward Glenna, too.

"No. What I'd *really* like is just to be held for a few minutes, until I don't feel so chilled. Then I'll go. Would you do that for me? I mean, you don't have to, and I really have no right to ask you."

"It's all right. Let's sit down until you feel better."

Hans had in mind that they would sit in the living-room, but Glenna walked him into the dimlit bedroom. She put her hand on his cheek, and then to his chest.

"But you're freezing! And I've been the one complaining about feeling cold. Come on." She threw back the bedclothes. "Lie down next to me. We'll both warm up, and then I'll leave."

He was bare, sore, and muddy, and his hair was still wet. He ought to go and take a hot shower, but Glenna stood waiting by the bed.

"It's quite all right," she said. "All I want is a tiny hug. You'll be quite safe."

Hans was not so sure. He climbed into bed reluctantly, and heard Glenna squeak as his chilled bare foot touched her leg. She didn't seem cold at all. He could feel the heat radiating from her body to his. She pulled the covers over them and moved closer.

"That's better, isn't it?" She sighed contentedly. "You know, I feel quite exhausted. But we'd better not nod off. Would you put your arms around me, just for a little while? Then I'll get up and go."

After another couple of minutes Hans did as she had asked. Somewhere in the process of getting into bed, the sheet had vanished from around Glenna's body. He eased away from her, about to explain why he was doing it. Then he noticed that her eyes had closed, and her lips were slightly parted. She was breathing evenly and deeply.

After a moment of hesitation he reached out and turned off the little bedside light. It didn't seem right to disturb her. A few minutes of rest, while both their chilled bodies became warmer, could do neither of them any harm. In a little while the rain would stop and Glenna could leave.

Hans sighed, and closed his own eyes.

✦ Chapter Eight

The Bose Network permits passage between its nodes, many lightyears apart, in no time at all. Its use frees the beings of the Spiral Arm from the tyranny of slow-speed travel. Few people realize that it produces a mind-set of its own, in which all "significant" travel must be over interstellar distances.

Thus, Hans Rebka, told by Darya that she was leaving Sentinel Gate, assumed that she would head far-off through interstellar space, perhaps to the remote reaches of the Zardalu Communion, or the most distant territories of the Fourth Alliance. The truth never occurred to him as he stepped, bleary-eyed, weary, and guilty, into the balmy morning air. Inside, Glenna snored her happy head off. (If she had been exhausted last night, he wouldn't like to meet her when she felt fresh and rested.)

The truth was that Darya was still practically within sight. Using the biggest telescope on Sentinel Gate and the right adaptive optics, Hans could have actually seen her ship.

Darya was heading for Sentinel, the Artifact that sat a mere couple of hundred million kilometers from Sentinel Gate. From the planet's surface it showed as a shining and striated ball, an under-sized fixed moon in the evening sky.

She needed evidence to disprove Quintus Bloom's

theories, and no one in the universe knew Sentinel better than Darya. The sight of it had first roused her interest, as a child growing up on Sentinel Gate, in the Builders and their Artifacts. Heading for it now was like a return to the simple days of childhood.

Of course, there were differences from the old days. Some of them were hard to ignore. One of them was crouched beside her, staring at the screen where Sentinel filled the field of view ahead. The Hymenopt at Darya's side was eight-legged, with a chubby barrel-shaped body covered with short black fur. Its small, smooth head bore rings of bright black eyes all around the perimeter. At the other end, the tubby Hymenopt abdomen carried a lethal yellow sting, now safely retracted and out of sight.

There had been nothing remotely like Hymenopts, or any other aliens, in Darya's childhood. But she did not give this one a second thought. She and Kallik had been through so many difficult and dangerous times together, from Quake to Genizee, that she felt closer to the Hymenopt than to most humans.

And Kallik was *smart*. She knew as much as Darya about many Artifacts in Fourth Alliance territory, and more about everything in the Zardalu Communion. It had been a big surprise to Darya to meet Kallik and the Lo'tfian, J'merlia, at the Sentinel Gate spaceport, but a welcome one. The two little aliens and former slaves were just what she needed: someone to talk to—and someone who wouldn't deceive and betray you.

Darya turned her thoughts away from that subject, back to the Hymenopt clicking and clucking at her side. Kallik had taken Darya's own file about Sentinel, along with Darya's summary of the theories of Quintus Bloom. She had read both at lightning speed, and was beginning to form her own impressions of the Artifact ahead as the ship crept closer.

"To recapitulate." Kallik still clicked a little as she

spoke, but her command of human language, to Darya who had mastered not one whistle or chirp of Hymenopt, remained mightily impressive. "The impermeable surface of Sentinel lies at a radius of half a million kilometers from the central structure. On your own most recent visit, what was the fate of any object that sought to penetrate that surface?"

"I was there with an exploring party two years ago. First we took a look from well outside, with ultraviolet lasers. We measured a change in the size of the Pyramid, at the center of Sentinel. It was smaller, eighty-eight kilometers on a side, instead of ninety. As always, the surface was completely transparent to radiation. So we tried a probe. Its radial momentum was exactly reversed in sign as it contacted the visible surface. The probe was traveling at only eight meters per second when it met the surface, but onboard instruments recorded a brief acceleration of one hundred and eighty gee. The probe was unmanned, but anyone on board would have been killed—at least, any human would."

"Or any Hymenopt." Kallik whistled to signify humor. "You think we are tough, but there are limits. One hundred and eighty gee, for eight meters a second velocity reversal. If the surface were elastic, the permitted penetration would be only to a depth of a couple of centimeters before it rebounded."

"That's correct. The same as the last time we were there." Darya had grown used to the idea that Kallik had her own built-in mental calculator. "The penetration depth is independent of speed. That's one of the things I want to try this time. I feel sure that Quintus Bloom is wrong, but if he were right we might expect to see changes to Sentinel."

"With respect, Professor Lang." The deferential voice came from the pilot's chair, to Darya's right. "If that is the case, then based on evidence to date, Quintus Bloom's theory has much to recommend it."

J'merlia had a body as slender as a drainpipe, but as many legs as Kallik. That was more than enough to handle the ship and have plenty left over to work the displays. He brought a new screen on-line in front of Darya.

"Since you mentioned the use of ultraviolet lasers, I took the liberty of employing that same class of device while you were busy in conversation. This is the image returned from the interior of Sentinel. I see several objects, spheres and cylinders and cones. But with respect"—the Lo'tfian turned lemon-colored compound eyes on their short eyestalks toward Darya—"with respect, I see nothing that could fairly be described as a pyramid."

The bulk of Sentinel lay right ahead of the ship. Darya gazed with disbelief at the screen. The Pyramid *had* to be there. It was the most interesting object in Sentinel's interior, the object that some workers had suggested might be a central library for Builder knowledge. Darya knew exactly where it would be with respect to the other objects in the interior. It should be . . .

"It's *gone*. It really has. Quintus Bloom said it might."

"More than that." J'merlia's voice was as gentle as ever, as befitted an ex-slave. "While you and Kallik were busy with your important work, I took the liberty of bringing our ship closer and closer to the surface barrier. Naturally, I did so very slowly, so that we would not be hurt or the ship damaged when the surface repulsed us."

"You didn't need to worry about that. All the ships in the Sentinel system have a built-in safeguard that stops them when they approach too close to the repulsive surface."

"Very wise." J'merlia nodded. "Except that the system did not stop us—and we are now, according to the inertial navigation system, two kilometers inside the bounding surface. We are *inside* Sentinel."

Inside Sentinel, where Darya had so often longed to be! But there was little pleasure in the knowledge. It was more evidence that Quintus Bloom was right, and she was wrong. They might be able to make it all the way to the center, and examine objects that humans had peered at, but could not touch, for every year since Sentinel had been discovered.

But after that it would be back to Sentinel Gate, with her tail between her legs, back to grovel before Quintus Bloom and admit that everything *was* changing, that his ideas had a lot more validity than hers. (Except, dammit, that she didn't *believe* it.)

"And we are fortunate to be here to witness this also." J'merlia was talking again, more to the Hymenopt than to Darya. "You were quite right, Kallik, and it is good that we did not ask questions. He knew this, when he told us to find Professor Lang and go wherever she chose to go. He knew that there would be revelations, which we would return to report."

The light came on inside Darya's head. She had been set up for this. "You mean Quintus Bloom *told you* to come to the spaceport and find me?"

"Certainly not." Kallik clucked in self-deprecating disapproval. "I did not say it clearly enough to you, but we have never met Quintus Bloom. J'merlia is referring to Captain Hans Rebka. He called and said that we were to protect you, and bring you back safely to Sentinel Gate."

"Damn that man. He said to *protect* me? Well, screw him."

"Indeed?" J'merlia inclined his head politely, and gestured a forelimb at the control board. "Do you wish to proceed farther toward the interior? Or would you rather we return to Sentinel Gate?"

"No! I'm not going back to that bloody planet. Let's get out of here."

J'merlia's eyes rolled on their eyestalks. "With respect,

but to where? I cannot navigate, unless I am given a destination."

Darya leaned back in her chair. It was obvious what she had to do. Quintus Bloom would always have his ace in the hole, his private Artifact—until Darya went there and examined it for herself.

"Find a set of Bose transitions to take us to Jerome's World." Darya silently cursed all men, but Hans Rebka and Quintus Bloom in particular. "We're going to take a look at Labyrinth."

✦ Chapter Nine

In the light of Sentinel Gate's brilliant morning sun, Louis Nenda stood chest-high amid a thicket of flowers that threw off a riot of sensuous and heady perfume. He sniffed deeply, wrinkled his nose in disgust, and spat on the ground.

He was stuck on this pansy world, and to get off it he was going to have to deal with one of his least favorite people. Nenda and Atvar H'sial had been over the situation again and again, and seen no alternative. Hans Rebka surely knew where Darya Lang had gone, although for his own reasons he was keeping it from them. So it was Nenda's job to worm it out of him.

If only he were on a decent world, like Karelia, where things were done in a decent way. Then he could have got what he wanted out of Rebka immediately, by smashing his stupid face in to make him talk.

But standing and thinking of better places would get him nowhere. Nenda plowed through the flowers until he was at the entrance of the bungalow. He tried the door that he came to, and found it unlocked. He snorted. An invitation to burglary—but not right now. He banged on the door panel.

No one came.

Nenda went in, walking through the living-room and following a smell that appealed to him a lot more than

the scent of the flowers outside. He'd had no breakfast.

The kitchen of the house was clean, compact, and
automated. Rebka wasn't there; but someone else was.

Wrong house! Louis was all ready to mutter an
apology and retreat when he recognized the occupant
of the kitchen. It was the tall, decorative woman he
had seen when he first arrived at the Institute. She
was wearing a white robe, open at the top almost to
her waist, and split at the bottom to show more leg
than Louis had ever seen before on a woman who
claimed to be dressed.

"Sorry," he said. "My mistake. I'm looking for Hans
Rebka. I thought this was where he's staying."

"It is. But he already left."

She had obviously recognized him, though he couldn't
for the life of him remember her name. He glared
around him, as though it might be written on one of
the walls. "Do you know where he is?"

"I might. And I'm Glenna Omar, since you've obviously forgotten. You look like you want to leave, too.
You're all the same. I hate men who are all kiss and
run. I hope you're not like that. Here, help yourself."

She waved to the table in front of her, which bore
a big plate of steaming rolls and a pot of what smelled
like hot tea.

It was the price of information. Louis gave up. He
sat down opposite Glenna. Atvar H'sial would never
believe this if she found out, but at least he'd get
breakfast out of it.

Glenna leaned back and sighed. "There, that's better. Now we can get to know each other. Although I
already know you, sort of. When you said you were
'Louis Nenda,' yesterday, I couldn't think where I'd
heard your name before."

Louis said nothing. For one thing, his mouth was
crammed full of hot roll. For another, in his experience

nothing good was likely to come from people who knew your name.

"And then I remembered." Glenna leaned forward to show even more cleavage. "I work here at the Institute as an information system specialist, and I'd seen your name listed as one of the people who were with Professor Lang on one of her trips. She talked about you, too. Do you find her attractive?"

"Eh?" For Louis, with half his mind on food and the other half on Glenna's chest, the sudden change of subject was too much.

"Darya Lang. I said, do you find her *attractive*?"

Atvar H'sial must have found a way to get Glenna to ask the Cecropian's own questions. It was a trap. Louis shook his head.

"Nah. Not at all."

"Good. But you know, I think she really likes men from other planets." Glenna leaned forward farther. The view was impressive, and almost unobstructed. "Of course, it's easy to see why. There's a sort of *mystery* about you off-worlders; you don't have a dull stay-at-home job like me, making you into a boring person . . . like me."

She arched her brows, inviting dissent. Louis had her pegged now, and the knowledge helped to clear his brain. She was a collector. He had met the type before. The trick was to get the information he needed, without his head (or other important parts) finishing as trophies on the wall behind her bed.

He looked with deep and bogus sincerity into her eyes. "I guess that Darya really liked Hans Rebka. He's seen a hundred different planets."

"Probably." Glenna smiled, the cat that got the cream. "But did *he* like *her*? Not all that much, if you ask me—and I have proof. It takes more than one person to make a relationship. There has to be *mutual* attraction. Wouldn't you agree?"

"Oh, absolutely. You bet. So Hans dumped her, did he? Good—I mean, good for him. I bet she was mad."

"Livid. Said she was leaving him, and leaving Sentinel Gate, and she stormed out. But she likes off-planet men, I can tell that. You know, *you're* an attractive man, too. I can't help wondering, did Darya ever make a pass at you?"

"I wouldn't put it that way. But some imagined there was something like that goin' on."

"And I'll bet they were right." Glenna turned her face away so that she could give Louis a coy sideways glance. "You're that sort of man, I just know it. You have that certain *look* in your eye."

Right. And I'm about a foot shorter than you, and a foot wider, and I'm all scarred and hairy, and I'm swaddled in clothes so tight that I can't get out of them inside half an hour even when I want to. What sort of mismatch from hell does it take to put you off your stride? Louis tried a demure smile, which looked more like a hideous strangler's grin. "You shouldn't tempt a man like that, ma'am, not in the middle of the morning. It's not fair. You know, I've got work to do."

"So do I. Call me Glenna. What are you doing this evening?"

"Nothing much. But I had the impression that you and Hans Rebka . . ."

"Please!" A slim hand waved away the possibility. "We're just *friends*."

You mean he's already hanging there in the collection. "I'm glad to hear that."

"Anyway, he's getting ready to go somewhere, out of system." Glenna pouted. She touched Louis's arm, then slid her hand down toward his. "Maybe this evening, then, you and me?"

"Maybe this evening." Nenda took her hand and swore a solemn vow to be off-planet by sunset. "But now I have to talk to Hans Rebka. Where is he?"

"He's up at the engineering lab, fooling around with some stupid computer that got itself short-circuited during a dinner with Professor Merada." Now that she had what she wanted, Glenna was perfectly willing to be gracious. "I can point out the way to you from the front door; it's just up the hill."

Louis was already moving. There wasn't all that much time left until evening. The lab couldn't be more than five minutes away—less if he ran.

At the door, just when he thought he was free, Glenna took hold of his hand again and turned him to face her. Her blue eyes were wide and the pupils were dilated. "I've just remembered one more thing about Darya Lang's report on you. She said that you've been *augmented*." Glenna shivered, and bit her lower lip. "That sounds absolutely fascinating. I've been wondering anyway what you have hidden under all those clothes. You've *got* to promise to show me."

Louis didn't recall running, but he made it to the engineering lab in two minutes. He entered, and found himself in the middle of what appeared to be a gruesome murder.

The body of E. Crimson Tally sat in a metal chair. Fiber tape around his arms and legs and torso held him tight. His skull had been cleaved horizontally just above the ears, so that the cranium was sheared off and had been turned, to dangle in front of his face by a flap of skin on the forehead.

Hans Rebka stood behind the chair. He held an object like an ice pick, but with a much thinner spike, and he was thrusting it deep into the grey ovoid of E.C. Tally's naked brain.

Nenda moved forward to stand next to Rebka. "What happened? He blow a gasket?"

Rebka went on probing, and didn't look up. "Sort of. He got into a closed loop at a dinner two days ago.

I called the people on Miranda, and there's a general logic fix on the way. Meanwhile, they told me how to do a cold start."

"Why the tape?"

"Protection. Miranda says there may be transients while he's booting. We don't want him walking through the walls."

Rebka had found the point he wanted, and gave a final poke. The body in the chair jerked. Rebka grasped the dangling top of the skull, turned it over, and fitted it into position. The bone lines clicked to form a neat seal, hidden by skin and hair.

"Going to take about thirty seconds of internal set-up before we see anything happen." Rebka straightened to his full height and stared at Nenda. "What do you want? I told you everything I know last time we met."

Nenda stretched upward too. He and Rebka were eye to eye, but still half a head shorter than anyone else on Sentinel Gate. He could feel the tension. If they had been a couple of dogs, the skin would be pulled back from their fangs and the hair along their backs would be bristling. Someday, the two of them would have a real go at each other. Rebka was as keen to try it as he was, Louis knew it. But it couldn't happen today.

Nenda took a deep breath before he spoke. "I heard you're heading out. Leaving Sentinel Gate."

"What of it? I'm a free agent."

"If you're following Darya Lang, I want to propose a deal. Let us go with you. We have information that she'd like to have, and we want to know what she's thinking."

"We?"

"Me and Atvar H'sial."

"I ought to have guessed that. Two crooks together, and both of you still trying to get Kallik and J'merlia back. Give it up, Nenda." Rebka stepped closer. "They're not your slaves any more."

The fight couldn't be today.

It was the worst possible time.

But perhaps it would be today, anyway.

"You're not a good liar, Rebka." Nenda felt his nostrils flaring. "Yesterday you said you didn't know where any of them are."

"And I don't. Can't you get that into your tiny pea-brain? *I don't know where Darya Lang is, or Kallik, or J'merlia.* Is that clear enough?" Rebka scowled, but there was more frustration than anger on his face. "Why the devil haven't they called me?"

"Darya?"

"No. She hates my guts. She wouldn't call me if I begged her to."

"Good. I mean, that's bad, 'cause I have to find her."

"I was talking about Kallik and J'merlia."

"Did you tell 'em to call you?"

"No. I told them to find Darya and go with her, but I didn't tell them to call."

"Then you're even dumber than I thought. Whether you believe it or not, they still act like *slaves.* If you don't tell 'em, they won't do it. Wait a minute." Nenda glared pop-eyed. The other part of what Rebka had said was finally sinking in. "You *told* them to go? *You* ordered my slave, and Atvar H'sial's slave and inter-preter, to go after Darya Lang?"

The fists and teeth were showing. Knees to the groin were just seconds away. Both men had moved to an open space, dropping from a taller-than-you posture into a defensive crouch. But before the first punch could be thrown, a loud sneeze came from the middle of the lab.

It was followed by a groan, a clearing of the throat, and a great belch. E.C. Tally was wriggling in his chair, tugging at the restraining tapes and peering squint-eyed around him in bafflement.

"What happened to the dinner table? And the people?"

Rebka hurried to his side. "Are you all right?"

"Of course I'm all right. But where am I?"

"In the engineering lab. I had to cold-start you. What's the last thing you remember?"

"I was sitting at the dinner table, listening to Quintus Bloom and Darya Lang. And Professor Lang began to comment on the logical implications of Bloom's assertion that the Builders are time travelers, humans from the future." Tally's eyes began to roll upward in his head. "Which implies—"

"You're going to screw him up all over again!" Nenda jumped forward and shook the embodied computer, cutting off his speech in mid-sentence.

"God, you're right." Rebka held up his hand. "E.C., stop it there. I want you to steer clear of every thought to do with time travel until we hear from Miranda about a software fix for you."

"But if the Builders are from the future—"

"Stop that! Think about something else. *Anything* else. Think about—what, for God's sake? Come on, Nenda, help me. E.C., talk about space travel. Tell Nenda what you and I said we wanted to do, after we had been to Sentinel Gate."

"You mean our plan to visit Paradox? Certainly. We will seek entry using some of my special capabilities, although as you all know, entry and successful return have never previously been accomplished. The Artifact known as Paradox implies that the Builders—"

"*Don't talk about the Builders!* Talk about Darya Lang. E.C., you were with Darya at dinner. Do you have any idea where she might have gone? Nenda thinks I know, but I don't."

"I can speculate." E.C. Tally turned to face Louis Nenda. "I have considered the question of a next logical investigation, in great detail. Darya Lang is almost certainly exploring one of the Artifacts, but which one? Before reaching Sentinel Gate I computed and stored for each Artifact the probability of a fruitful new exploration. The results can be summarized as follows, in order of decreasing probability: Paradox, 0.0061; Torvil Anfract, 0.0045; Manticore, 0.0037; Reinhardt, 0.0035; Elephant, 0.0030; Flambeau, 0.0027; Cocoon, 0.0026; Lens, 0.0024; Umbilical, 0.0023; Magyar, 0.0022; Cusp, 0.0019 . . ."

Nenda glared at Hans Rebka as E.C. Tally droned on. "Can't you stop him? He has twelve hundred to go."

"Why bother? It's keeping him out of trouble." Rebka glared right back. "Still want to start something?"

"Love to. But right now it's a luxury I can't afford." Nenda took four steps backward, out of distance for easy action. "I need to find Darya Lang, and you can't tell me where she is. So I'll have to work it out for myself. And wasting time fussin' with you won't help me. I'm going."

At the door to the lab he turned for a final scowl. "Have fun on Paradox, you and the dumb dinglebrain. Who knows, maybe I'll see you both there. But I hope not."

Rebka returned the snarl. "Go to hell."

"Fambezux, 0.0015," intoned E.C. Tally.

"And the same to you," growled Louis Nenda.

✦ Chapter Ten

Less than one year ago, Darya Lang had been a quiet and dedicated research scientist at the Artifact Institute. She had never in her life left the solar system containing Sentinel and Sentinel Gate. The production of successive editions of the Lang Catalog was the high spot of her existence.

Then came the trip to the Dobelle system. That had started her whole strange odyssey, to Quake, to Glister, to Serenity, on to the Torvil Anfract and Genizee, and at last back home.

All that, in less than one year. Now it was hard for Darya, seeing herself as a hardened and sophisticated traveler through the farthest reaches of the Spiral Arm, to believe that the quiet research worker had ever existed.

But sometimes she had direct proof that her new experience was very recent—and very limited.

Darya studied the Bose Network and plotted out a series of transitions to take their ship, the *Myosotis*, from Sentinel to Labyrinth by way of Jerome's World. It took many hours of careful work, but she was rather proud of the result. As she was transferring the file to another data base from which the sequence could be executed, Kallik happened to see what she was doing.

"With respect." The little Hymenopt bobbed her dark

head. "Is this by any chance your first experience using the Bose Network?"

"I've *used* it before, but this is my first opportunity to plan my own sequence of transitions."

Kallik was studying the file closely. Darya waited, expecting words of appreciation. Instead Kallik hissed, whistled, and said, "Excuse me. But is it permitted that I examine the energy budget associated with one or two of these nodes?"

"Of course."

Kallik made a copy of the file and retreated to her own terminal, one more suited for a being with eight polydactyl limbs. After a few minutes she transferred another file to Darya's terminal. It came without a word of comment, but Darya saw at once that it was an alternative path through the Bose Network. She listed the transit time. It was less than half of hers.

She displayed the energy budget. It was less than a quarter of hers.

"Kallik. How did you *do* that?"

The Hymenopt inclined her head. "With respect, Professor Lang, great intellectual power, even at the level that you possess it, is not always a substitute for humble practical experience. In service to Master Nenda, I employed the Bose Network many, many times."

It was as close as Louis Nenda's former slave would ever get to telling a human that she was an ignoramus and had blown the whole Network computation. Darya took Kallik's travel plan and prepared to put it into effect.

The journey would involve a peculiar mixture of subluminal and superluminal components. That, in turn, called for the Bose Drive and the standard drive to be used in sequence, sometimes with odd delays or advance power delivery.

Darya pondered the first jump, her hands poised

above the keyboard. She was wondering where to set the subluminal break-point when she became aware of J'merlia hovering at her shoulder. The Lo'tfian's eye-stalks were fully extended in different directions, so that he could monitor both keyboards and displays.

"With respect." J'merlia reached around Darya with four stick-like limbs. Hard digits rattled against the keys, far too fast to follow. When they withdrew a few seconds later, Darya saw that ship commands had been provided for every stage of the journey of the *Myosotis* from Sentinel to Labyrinth.

She didn't bother to ask how J'merlia had done it. She didn't want to hear again that the job called for no real talent, just a little experience. Instead she retreated to her cabin, aware that she had become a supernumerary on her own ship.

Where next would her skills be found deficient? Darya did not know, but a voice in her ear kept reminding her that in all previous leaps into the unknown (like the coming exploration of Labyrinth) she had benefited from the skill and long-time trouble-shooting experience of Hans Rebka—Rebka, the rotten, faithless, lecherous, Phemus Circle swine.

She went back to where J'merlia was sitting in the pilot's seat.

"Can you set up a superluminal circuit with Sentinel Gate?"

"Certainly. It will be expensive, because it must employ three Bose Nodes."

"Never mind that. I want to talk to Hans Rebka."

"Very good." Instead of beginning his task, J'merlia hesitated.

"What do you want?" Darya had dealt with him long enough to know that a pause like this usually meant a request that he was diffident in making.

"When you talk to Captain Rebka, Kallik and I would appreciate it if you would ask him a question from us."

"Of course."

"Would you please ask him, just *why* did he instruct us to seek you out at the spaceport, and accompany you on this trip? We have pondered this question, but have been unable to answer it. We are of course supposed to protect you, but from what? We are uncomfortable when we are not sure that we are correctly interpreting a command."

"I'll ask him." *Protect* her, that irritating word again! He must think she was too stupid and naive to look after herself. "You bet I'll ask him, the superior bastard. Get me that circuit!"

The connection took a while to set up. Darya sat and seethed. Finally it came, and she found herself staring at the face of a near-stranger, a communications operator at the Institute.

"I wanted to talk to Hans Rebka."

The head on the screen nodded. "I know. But we can't do it, that's why the call was passed through to me."

"Has something happened to him?" Darya's anger was suddenly touched with worry.

"Not so far as we know. He's all right. But he's gone. He left the Institute this morning."

"Damn that man. Did he say where he was going?"

"Not to me. But an embodied computer, E. Crimson Tally, left with him. And Tally told me they were going to explore an Artifact called Paradox. Are you feeling all right?" The operator had seen Darya's expression. "Can I connect you with someone else?"

In a way, the disappearance of Hans Rebka made everything simpler. Darya was on her own.

Hans had told her, more than once, "People talk about the *game* of life. But if it's a game, it's nothing like poker. In life you can't turn back cards you don't like and hope you'll be given better ones. You play the hand that's dealt, and you do your best to win with it."

Hans hadn't mentioned the stakes, but in his own case it had often been his life, and the lives of everyone with him. Darya wasn't sure what the stakes were this time. At the most trivial level, it was her own self-esteem and reputation. Beyond that, it could be anything from the future of the Artifact Institute, up to the future of the Spiral Arm.

High stakes, indeed.

There was less question about Darya's hand. It was herself, with all she knew about Builders and Artifacts, and two aliens. Smart aliens, no doubt of that, but aliens so used to being slaves that it was hard for them to take an initiative.

There was one other thing, an asset which so far Darya had found no opportunity to evaluate. She had brought with her a complete copy of a file about Labyrinth, bestowed as a gift to the Institute by Quintus Bloom. It had all his recent written work, data analysis and theory, and Darya would certainly study that; far more significant, however, were the raw data: the exact chronology of the discovery and exploration of the new Artifact, all the physical measurements, and the images taken both outside and inside Labyrinth.

Everything was stored in the computer onboard the *Myosotis*. The journey to Labyrinth, even with Kallik's superior travel strategy, would take days. And with J'merlia having quietly taken over all the piloting functions, Darya had nothing to do.

Nothing except *real* work, the work she had trained for all her adult life. The cramped cabin of the ship lacked the pleasant surroundings of an office on Sentinel Gate, but when Darya was concentrating she never noticed her surroundings. As an opportunity to study, the trip out to Labyrinth could hardly be beat.

She made herself a nook in the ship's cabin and

settled in. First came Quintus Bloom's description and discussion of the "old" Artifacts. Darya knew every one like an old friend. She expected to learn little new about them, but perhaps a good deal about the real Quintus Bloom, the man behind the affable, self-confident, seemingly omniscient authority onstage at the Institute.

Universal Artifact Catalog, Entry #1: Cocoon.

Form: Cocoon is a system of forty-eight basal stalks. They connect a free-space structure of four hundred and thirty-two thousand filaments to the surface of the planet, Savalle . . .

Bloom was following the order that Darya had established in her own catalog of the Artifacts. She read through his description of Cocoon. There was nothing new, but she formed a grudging admiration of his writing style. It was spare and exact. The only thing that brought a frown to her face was his final sentence:

Classification: Transportation system, for movement of materials to and from the surface of Savalle.

It was quite a leap from the physical fact of Cocoon's form and structure, to that unequivocal statement of its intended purpose.

Darya went to *Calliope*, the second artifact in the list. Then to the baffling singularities of *Zirkelloch*, the third, which Quintus Bloom classified as *Anomalous*—meaning that his classification system could not handle it! Then to *Numen*, the fourth, which had been worshipped by the Varnians long before humans came on the scene with their own ideas of divinity. Darya nodded. Who knows, maybe the Varnians saw something that humans didn't.

The task was absorbing, almost soothing—a carry back in time to the days when research meant the study of objects remote in time and space, the analysis of places where Darya never expected to go. And it was time-consuming. Hunger at last drove her back to the outside world, to discover that most of a day had passed. She had ground her way through about half of the Artifact descriptions. She also realized that an idea was sitting inside her head, without her being aware of how or when it had arrived.

Darya peered out from the depths of her hideaway. J'merlia was at the ship's controls, while Kallik lay in an easy sprawl of legs at his side. The Hymenopt might be asleep, but just as likely she was bored. And a second opinion would be useful.

"Kallik? Will you take a look at something?"

Darya copied the file to a workstation convenient for Kallik's use and went down to the galley to find something to eat. Maybe Kallik would read what Darya had read, and draw a different conclusion. Maybe there was no conclusion to be made. Or maybe the second half of the description of the Artifacts contradicted the impression that she had formed from the first half.

That thought made Darya grab her food as soon as it was ready and hurry back to work. *Lens, Scrimshaw, Paradox, Maelstrom, Godstooth.* . . . Whatever the Builders were, or would be, they had prized diversity. No two Artifacts had more than a superficial resemblance. But Quintus Bloom had somehow grouped them all into six basic classes. *Forced* them in. No one else had ever produced a satisfactory taxonomy of the Artifacts. Was this one satisfactory?

Darya awoke from her own spell of concentration to find Kallik standing patiently at her side.

"Finished already?" That would be amazing, even allowing for the speed and efficiency of a Hymenopt's central nervous system.

Kallik blinked both rows of eyes. "No. I apologize for my slowness, but the list is long. I interrupt your important thoughts only to point out that J'merlia needs a flight option to be defined. Should he take us direct to Labyrinth, or should we go by way of Jerome's World?"

Darya had postponed making that decision, then forgotten all about it. The question was, had Quintus Bloom told the full story about Labyrinth's difficulties and possible dangers? The direct path was more economical, but there was that small voice talking again in her ear. The voice was a nuisance, but Darya had learned not to ignore it.

"How far are you in the description of the Artifacts?"

"I am studying the hundred and thirty-third."

"Do you have any overall comment?"

It was an unfair question. Darya had not reached even a tentative conclusion until she had reviewed five times that number of Bloom's Artifact summaries.

Kallik's exoskeleton permitted no facial mobility. But she did jitter a pair of forelimbs, which showed that she was not quite at ease. "I have an impression. It is too unformed to be termed an analysis."

"Say it anyway."

"The distinguished Quintus Bloom is a most accomplished writer. His descriptions are always clear, and they contain no redundancies. The taxonomy of Artifacts that he offers is unlike anything that I have ever seen before."

Kallik paused. Darya waited. So far, the comments matched her own feelings exactly. Was there more? Kallik seemed to be paralyzed, not even her eyes moving.

"I have only one concern." This time the pause was even longer. "In assigning an Artifact to one of his defined classes, Quintus Bloom never misuses or misinterprets any part of an Artifact description. Occasionally, however, it seems to me that he does neglect to mention some relevant aspect of an Artifact. And those omitted elements tend to be ones that would argue against assignment of an Artifact to the class he chooses."

Jackpot! Darya could have hugged Kallik, only you didn't take liberties like that with a Hymenopt.

What Kallik had said agreed precisely with Darya's own growing conviction. Quintus Bloom was smart, he was creative, he was plausible. He had done an excellent job in summarizing the Artifacts, and displayed great originality in devising his system of Artifact classes. His sin was something that scientists had done for thousands of years. Scientists didn't usually *change* data, not unless they were outright charlatans. But when facts didn't agree with theory, there was an awful temptation to find reasons for rejecting the offending data and hanging on to the theory. Ptolemy had done it. Newton had done it. Darwin had done it. Einstein had done so *explicitly*. And now Quintus Bloom was at it. The big question was, had he done it just this once, or was this a pattern than ran through all his work including his description of Labyrinth? Did that Artifact have some unmentioned hidden property, one that might kill unwary explorers?

"I hope that my premature thoughts are of some use to you." Kallik was still standing in front of Darya, but not looking at her.

"They were *exactly* what I needed." Darya followed the rows of watching eyes, and saw to her surprise that half a sandwich lay soggy and forgotten on the console. Even though she was starving, she had been too absorbed to eat. She picked up her food and took a huge bite. "That makes the decision for us," she said, through a mouthful of bread and salad. "Thank you. Tell J'merlia that we have to visit Jerome's World before we go to Labyrinth. We have to find out more about Quintus Bloom. I want to know what he was doing *before* he started work on Builder Artifacts."

✦ Chapter Eleven

The sun was setting on Sentinel Gate, and Louis Nenda was watching it.

Amazing. No outpouring of poisonous gases, which you had to look forward to when the sun went down on Styx. No screaming gale, which marked sunrise and sunset on Teufel. No torrents of boiling rain, like Scaldworld, where anyone outside at the wrong time was brought back in medium-well-done. No mosquitoes the size of your hand, like those on Peppermill, dive-bombers that zoomed in and sank their three-inch probe into any square centimeter of exposed flesh.

Just people laughing in the distance, and bird song, and flowers that faded in the dusk and reserved their most delicate and subtle perfumes for the evening hours.

And, any minute now, Glenna Omar.

Atvar H'sial could think what she liked, but Louis was not looking forward to this. At least, not all that much.

He had protested, perhaps rather more than was justified, in an earlier discussion with Atvar H'sial.

"I do all the work, while you sit here loafing."

"Are you suggesting that I am a plausible substitute for you in this activity? That my body is an acceptable alternative to yours, in your bizarre human mating rituals?"

"You'd drive her screaming up the wall. But what

about *me*? Am I supposed to be offered up as a sort of human sacrifice to Glenna Omar, on the off-chance that we'll learn from her where J'merlia went? You just want your interpreter back, that's all, so you can communicate easily with humans."

"I am working on alternative communication methods. And if I locate J'merlia, you also locate Kallik, *and*"—Atvar H'sial's speech took on sly pheromonal insinuations—"you locate the human female, Darya Lang. I need to discuss with her the changes in the Builder Artifacts, but I wonder if your implied rejection of the female Glenna Omar derives from some prior commitment on your part to the Lang person. I wonder if *that* is the primary cause of your reluctance to meet with Glenna Omar."

"Did I say I wouldn't meet with Glenna? Of course I'll meet with her. Tonight. We already arranged that." *And if a few hectic hours with Glenna Omar was what it took to banish Atvar H'sial's suspicions about Louis and Darya Lang, it was a small price to pay.*

Louis was prepared to pay it now. At sunset, in the third arbor down the hill from where Hans Rebka had been staying.

It was sunset, it was the third arbor, he was here. But where was Glenna?

He heard a woman's laughter from higher on the hill. Half-blinded by the setting sun, he squinted in that direction. He heard a braying male laugh in reply.

Glenna was approaching; and she was not alone.

Relief and disappointment both seemed premature. Louis stood up and walked toward the couple. Glenna came undulating along the path, her hand laid possessively on the arm of the tall man at her side. She was wearing a long-sleeved, high-necked gown of pale green that left a minimum of exposed skin and made her appear positively virginal.

"Hello, Louis." She smiled at him warmly. "I hoped

we'd find you here. There's been a change of plans. I was in the middle of a discussion with Professor Bloom—"

"Quintus."

"Quintus." Glenna snuggled close to her companion. "And we hadn't finished talking. So he invited me to continue through dinner. And naturally . . ."

"No problem." Louis meant it. He admired real nerve, and there was no hint of apology in Glenna's manner. "Hello, professor. I'm Louis Nenda."

"Indeed?" Bloom removed his arm from Glenna's grasp and offered a limp-fingered wave of the hand. He regarded Louis with the enthusiasm of a man meeting a Karelian head louse, the sort that popped out of a hole in the rock and nipped your head off with one snip of the mandibles. "And what do you do?"

"Businessman, mostly, for exploration projects. Last trip I was out at the Torvil Anfract, came back via the Mandel system."

"Indeed?" Bloom had turned to look back up the hill even before Louis answered the question.

Glenna lingered a moment, her fingers on Louis's bare arm.

"He's an absolute *genius*," she whispered. "I do hope you understand, but given a chance like this . . ."

"I said, no problem." *I know that game, sweetheart. You take the one you want right now, but be sure to put the other one in cold storage in case you need him later*. "Go and enjoy your dinner."

"Some other time, though, you and me?"

"You bet."

Glenna squeezed his arm happily. But Quintus Bloom had turned, and was sauntering back with a frown on his face.

"I say. Something you said just now. Did you mention the Torvil Anfract?"

"Sure did. I just came back from there, way out in the Zardalu Communion."

"That's the name that the Lang woman mentioned the other evening at dinner." Bloom was explaining to Glenna, while managing to ignore Louis. "She said that it was a *Builder Artifact*, but of course as Professor Merada pointed out, there is no evidence of that. If it *were* an Artifact, however, that could be a finding of enormous significance." Bloom at last turned directly to Louis. "Do you know Darya Lang?"

"Certainly."

"Was she at the Anfract with you, by any chance?"

"At it, and in it. Right in it."

"Three days ago, after our dinner, she left the Institute." Bloom lifted his gaze above Louis's head, and stood staring at nothing. "She told no one where she was going. So almost certainly . . ."

Quintus Bloom didn't spell out his thought processes to Louis. He didn't need to. Louis had the answer to the next question ready, even before Bloom asked it.

"If I were to provide you with a ship, could you fly me to the Torvil Anfract?"

"Could, and would. I even have the ship. If the price is right, I mean."

The last sentence had come out without thinking, but Louis didn't try to kid himself. The 'right' price? Even if Bloom didn't have more than two cents, it would be enough.

Daybreak on Sentinel Gate was, if anything, more spectacular than sunset. The air was magically clear, the flowers and shrubs touched with fragrant dew. The birds, awake but not yet in motion, sang a dawn chorus from within their hidden roosts.

Glenna, strolling back to her house, noticed none of this. She was frequently heading home in the early daylight hours, and the charms of daybreak's plant and animal life left her unmoved. She was, in fact, feeling faintly disappointed. Quintus seemed to *like* her well enough, and to enjoy their long hours together. They had talked, and laughed, eaten and drunk, and talked again. They had wandered arm-in-arm around the Institute, inside and out. They had watched the romantic setting of Sentinel Gate. The touch of his hand on Glenna's shoulder had set all her juices flowing. And then, when everything seemed ready to go full speed ahead, *he* had gone back to his own quarters instead.

Glenna sighed. Maybe the demure dress had been a tactical error? Without spelling it out in detail, she had known *faster* men. In the case of Quintus Bloom, that slowness might be a deadly drawback. He was a career man, a man on the move, heading upwards and already itching to leave Sentinel Gate. In retrospect, it was a pity that she had introduced him to Louis Nenda, with his talk of the Anfract, because they would soon be on their way. Glenna might not get a second chance—at either of them.

She was close to home, near enough to see the soft light that she left burning at night by her front porch. Near enough to see that the porch door, which she was sure had been left open, was now closed. Someone had been inside her house. Perhaps they were still in her house.

Glenna frowned—in puzzlement, not in alarm. Theft and violence were almost unknown on Sentinel Gate. She lived alone. Maintenance and cleaning robots were punctiliously careful to leave a house's doors and windows exactly as they found them.

She felt the delicious tingle of a desired though unexpected treat. Quintus Bloom had disappointed. He had proved regrettably diffident. But Louis Nenda would not be like that. He was a real out-worlder, a wild man from one of the rough-and-tumble planets of the

Zardalu Communion. She had postponed his date, and all that went with it. But *he* wasn't willing to wait.

She just loved an impatient man.

Glenna slipped off her shoes, eased open the door, and drifted inside. The living-room was empty, but she could smell a faint, alien musk. Of course, he would already be in the bedroom, lying waiting for her on the soft, over-sized bed. Would he have removed those dark, tight-fitting clothes? Or would he have waited, to let Glenna do it? Waited, if he was the man she hoped he was. He must know how eager she was to explore for herself the ways in which he had been augmented.

Glenna tip-toed into the bedroom. As she approached the bed itself she paused. Louis was not lying on it. And crouched beside it—

A great nightmare shape rose up, as high as the ceiling. A pair of long, jointed limbs swept Glenna from the floor, and her scream was muffled by a soft black paw. She was drawn in toward a broad, eyeless head, and to the thin proboscis that quivered at its center. Faint, high-pitched squeaks sounded in her ears.

Glenna struggled, but not as hard as she might have. She had recognized the intruder. It was a Cecropian. She knew through the Institute's grapevine that a female of that alien species had recently arrived there. Arrived, according to Glenna's informant, with Louis Nenda.

"What do you want?"

It was wasted breath, because everyone knew that Cecropians didn't speak. But the eyeless white head nodded at the sound, and carried Glenna back to the door of her living-room. One black limb pointed silently through the doorway to Glenna's communications terminal, then to a grey box that sat next to it. Glenna found herself placed gently back on the floor at the doorway. She was at once released.

She could flee—Glenna's intruder would have a difficult time squeezing back through into the living-room, though she must have entered that way. However, it was hard to believe that anything that intended her real harm would have placed her where she was free to run away. Glenna walked unsteadily across to the communications terminal, and stood there waiting.

The Cecropian eased her way through the door and crept across to the grey box. Nimble black paws began a complex dance of movement in front of it. The terminal screen came to life, displaying words: SPEAK YOUR HUMAN SPEECH. THIS DEVICE WILL INTERPRET IT.

"Who are you? Who are you?" Glenna had to say it twice, she was so breathless. "What do you want?"

The screen flickered to a longer statement.

MY NAME IS ATVAR H'SIAL. I AM A CECROPIAN, AND A BUSINESS PARTNER OF THE HUMAN, LOUIS NENDA. IF YOU ARE THE HUMAN FEMALE GLENNA OMAR, I WISH TO TALK WITH YOU.

"That's me." Glenna stared at the grey box, then at the dark-red carapace and the open twin yellow horns on the head. As she spoke, she again could hear those faint bat-squeaks of sound. "I thought that Cecropians *saw* with sound, and spoke to each other using some sort of smells."

This time the words on the screen came painfully slowly.

THAT IS INDEED THE CASE. I HAVE BUILT A DEVICE WHICH TAKES HUMAN SPEECH, AND CONVERTS IT TO A TWO-DIMENSIONAL PATTERN OF SOUNDS BEYOND YOUR FREQUENCY RANGE. I SEE THAT PATTERN AS A PICTURE, WITHIN WHICH ARE THE FORMS OF MY OWN WRITTEN LANGUAGE. I AM THUS "READING" YOUR WORDS WITHIN THAT VISUAL SOUND PATTERN. I AM "SPEAKING" IN A SIMILAR WAY, BY THE CONVERSION OF MY OWN GESTURES TO A TWO-DIMENSIONAL

IMAGE, WHICH IN TURN MAPS TO THE ONE-DIMEN-
SIONAL SOUNDS THAT YOU CALL WORDS. IT IS A CRUDE
METHOD OF SPEECH, AND AN IMPRECISE ONE, BUT
THE BEST THAT I CAN ATTAIN. BEAR WITH ME. TO
MAKE NEW SPEECH, WORDS THAT I HAVE NOT
ALREADY RECORDED, IS MOST DIFFICULT.

"But what do you want?"

I WISH TO OFFER YOU AN UNUSUAL OPPORTUNITY.
I BELIEVE THAT YOU VERY MUCH WISH TO PERFORM
SEX ACTS WITH MY PARTNER, LOUIS NENDA, AND
WITH THE HUMAN QUINTUS BLOOM.

"Well, I wouldn't put it quite that way." Glenna did
her best to make allowances for a Cecropian's lack of
understanding of the finer points of human social habits.
"But just for the sake of discussion, what if I do?"

A screenful of words flashed into existence. Atvar
H'sial must have prepared the whole speech in advance.

IN ORDER TO DO THAT, YOU NEED TO HAVE CONTIN-
UED ACCESS TO THEM. THE MAN BLOOM, TOGETHER
WITH LOUIS NENDA AND MYSELF, WILL SHORTLY BE
LEAVING SENTINEL GATE. WE HAVE BEEN ASKED TO
GUIDE QUINTUS BLOOM TO A REGION OF THE SPIRAL
ARM KNOWN AS THE TORVIL ANFRACT, WHERE HE
BELIEVES THAT THE HUMAN FEMALE DARYA LANG IS
CURRENTLY ENGAGED IN EXPLORATION. NENDA AND
I KNOW THE ANFRACT REGION WELL, AND CAN EASILY
TAKE BLOOM THERE. BUT IF NENDA AND BLOOM
LEAVE SENTINEL GATE, YOUR DESIRE TO COUPLE WITH
THEM WILL NOT BE FULFILLED, NOR WILL YOU HAVE
FURTHER ACCESS TO THEM. HOWEVER, I CAN ARRANGE
FOR YOU TO GO WITH US ON OUR EXPEDITION, AS AN
INFORMATION SYSTEMS SPECIALIST. OFFICIALLY YOU
WILL BE HELPING ME TO ACHIEVE BETTER COMMU-
NICATION WITH HUMANS, EMPLOYING THE MEANS
THAT WE ARE USING HERE. UNOFFICIALLY, YOU WILL
HAVE FEW DUTIES, AND YOU WILL BE FREE TO PUR-
SUE YOUR OWN ENDS.

"You really think I'm that keen for it? Don't bother translating and answering that. Suppose that I say I'm interested?—and I might be. I don't understand what's in it for *you*."

Atvar H'sial was silent for a long time. Whether she was thinking, or just having trouble translating, Glenna could not be sure. The words came at last: MY SLAVE AND INTERPRETER, J'MERLIA, IS WITH DARYA LANG. TO GET HIM BACK, I AM MOST ANXIOUS THAT LOUIS NENDA AND I GO ON THIS JOURNEY. HOWEVER, I HAVE FOR A LONG TIME BEEN CONCERNED THAT NENDA MAY BE EMOTIONALLY UNBALANCED CONCERNING THE HUMAN FEMALE, DARYA LANG. YOU ARE, I GATHER, AN EXCEPTIONALLY ATTRACTIVE HUMAN FEMALE. AND HE IS, I BELIEVE, SUSCEPTIBLE TO YOUR CHARMS. IF YOU WERE TO TRAVEL TO THE TORVIL ANFRACT, AND LOUIS NENDA WAS TO BE EXPOSED TO BOTH OF YOU . . .

"No contest." Glenna had taken Hans Rebka from Darya without any trouble at all; she could do the same with Louis Nenda. She was intrigued. It was at the same time something of a challenge, and a chance to become closer to Quintus Bloom. Nenda would be interesting for a while, but Bloom was something else. It would be no bad thing to wander the Spiral Arm as the regular consort of a recognized genius. As for his apparent shyness, she knew ways to cure that.

Glenna had only one question left. "I'm sure I can make Louis forget that Darya Lang ever existed. But I wonder about you. You're not *jealous* of Lang, are you? I mean, I realize that you are a female, yourself. But I thought that there was no way that humans and Cecropians—that Louis Nenda and you—I mean, how do male Cecropians handle the females, anyway, in your mating?"

Maybe Glenna had gone too far. Certainly there was a long delay.

YOU HAVE THE WRONG IMPRESSION. IT WOULD BE MORE ACCURATE TO ASK: HOW DO WE FEMALE CECROPIANS HANDLE THE MALE DURING MATING? AND ALSO AFTER IT.

A pair of forelimbs began a rhythmic crushing movement, moving in toward the dark red underside of Atvar H'sial. After a few more seconds the long proboscis reached down, questing.

HOWEVER, THAT IS A PERSONAL QUESTION, WHICH I PREFER NOT TO ANSWER. LET ME SAY ONLY THIS: YOU WOULD PERHAPS BE LESS DISTURBED BY THE ANSWER THAN WOULD EITHER LOUIS NENDA OR QUINTUS BLOOM.

✦ Chapter Twelve

Jerome's World orbits the yellow dwarf star Tetragamma, only forty lightyears from Sentinel Gate. Almost directly between the two lies the bright blue star, Rigel. Rigel is a true supergiant, fifty times a standard stellar mass, a hundred thousand times standard luminosity, blazing forth with intense brilliance and dazzling power. Few observers of the night sky from Sentinel Gate would ever notice the wan gleam of Tetragamma, tucked away close to Rigel's line of sight. And no one on Sentinel Gate would see the mote of Jerome's World, gleaming faintly in Tetragamma's reflected light. Darya could not remember anyone mentioning the name of that world during all her years at the Institute, until the arrival of Quintus Bloom.

She glanced at the planet a couple of times as the *Myosotis* approached for landing. That Jerome's World was a thinly populated planet was obvious from the absence of city lights on its night side. It must be a poor and backward planet, too, or Darya would have heard more about it. Yet according to Quintus Bloom, this was his home world. It was also the closest inhabited planet to the Artifact he had discovered and named Labyrinth.

Darya saw nothing to change her first impressions as the *Myosotis* completed its landing and she disembarked. The Immigration staff, all one of him, greeted

Darya cheerfully enough, but he stared pop-eyed at Kallik and J'merlia. Interstellar human visitors were rarity enough. The Jerome's World entry system had no procedures at all for dealing with wildly non-human creatures from the Cecropia Federation and the Zardalu Communion.

While the officer scratched his head over old reference materials and kept one uneasy eye on the two aliens, Darya came to a decision. She had planned to spend only a day or two on Jerome's World before proceeding to Labyrinth. The red tape surrounding the entry of Kallik and J'merlia might take all of that, just to produce clearances.

"Suppose these two were to remain on the ship?"

The officer didn't voice his relief, but his face brightened. "No problem with that, if you follow the standard quarantine rules. Food and drink can go in, but no plants or animals—" he glanced uncertainly at the two aliens "—or anything else can come out."

Kallik and J'merlia raised no objection. It was Darya who felt bad, as she endured a meaningless entry rigmarole and was at last pronounced free to leave the port. Not long ago the two aliens had been slaves, and here again they were second-class citizens. It was little comfort to know that in the Cecropia Federation the situation would have been reversed, with J'merlia free to wander while Darya was impounded and regarded with suspicion.

Her guilt vanished within minutes of leaving the spaceport. Kallik and J'merlia weren't missing a thing— perhaps they were even the lucky ones. She didn't know who Jerome was, but if he were dead he was probably turning in his grave, having a backwater world like this named after him. The planet was right at the outer limit of habitable distance from Tetragamma. This was the winter season, and the days were short. The sun was a bright cherrystone two sizes too small in the sky;

the air was thin and cold and caught in your throat, and the straggling plant life was a pale, dusty grey-green. The people that Darya met seemed equally pale and dusty, as they directed her to the air service that served the Marglom Center.

That, she supposed, was the good news: Quintus Bloom's home could have been on the other side of the planet, rather than a mere couple of thousand kilometers away. The bad news was that the aircraft stopped at half a dozen places on the way.

The plane that Darya boarded was big enough to carry twelve people. The flight had exactly two passengers, Darya and an obese man who overflowed his seat. She studied his thick neck and close-shaved head from behind as the craft prepared for takeoff. He looked a good candidate for a research center. He was certainly too fat for any form of manual work.

Sitting next to him was not a possibility. After take-off Darya went forward, to the seat in front of him. She turned to peer over the seat back. Talking to strangers was something that she hated—she knew how much she resented the invasion of her own thinking space by other people—but she needed information.

"Excuse me. Do you happen to be going to the Marglom Center?"

The fat man apparently shared Darya's view of gratuitous interruptions from strangers. He glanced up and scowled at her.

"I'm going there myself," Darya went on, "and I'm hoping to visit a man named Quintus Bloom. I wondered if you know him."

The scowl was replaced by the smile of a man pleased to deliver bad news. "I know him. But you won't find him. He's away from the Center. In fact, he's off-world." He pushed the knife a little deeper. "He's in a different *stellar* system, giving some invited talks."

"That's a shame. I've seen some of his work, and I think it's brilliant."

Darya waited. The man said nothing, and turned his eyes down.

"I wonder if there's anyone else," Darya continued. "Anyone at the Center who could discuss his work with me. Is there?"

He sighed in irritation. "Quintus Bloom is the most famous person at the Center. Almost anyone there can discuss his work with you, from the Director on down. If they choose to. Which I do not."

"The Director?"

"Kleema Netch. And now, if you don't mind . . ." He turned his eyes determinedly away from her.

"Sorry that I interrupted your work."

The man grunted. Darya went back to her seat. It was progress, of a sort. Bloom was famous, and his work was well-regarded. It surely must include research performed before the discovery of Labyrinth, and before his new theory about the Builders.

The flight would take another two hours, and her companion was likely to explode if she tried more conversation. Darya's thoughts went back to her one and only discussion with Quintus Bloom. She had not liked what he had to say, but she could not dismiss it. She *did* believe, as he had asserted, that there had been recent and unprecedented changes in the Artifacts of the Spiral Arm. But nothing in her own theories could explain the appearance of the new Artifact, Labyrinth. Worst of all, Bloom's discoveries on Labyrinth seemed to demolish the idea that the Builders had left the Spiral Arm millions of years ago, and never returned. How, at a time when humans were no more than primitive hominids, could the Builders make a precise prediction of the way in which humanity would achieve space travel and move out to explore the Spiral Arm?

Very well. Suppose that the Builders had not left.

Suppose that they were still around in the Spiral Arm, in a form or a place that humans and the other clade members were unable to contact or even to perceive. Bloom had also provided, with his evidence from Labyrinth, an apparently impossible obstacle for that idea. He had shown *future development patterns* for the Spiral Arm, and asked the question: How could the Builders, *today*, know the pattern of expansion through the Spiral Arm for tens of thousands of years into the future? Unless, as Bloom insisted, the Builders were time-traveling humans *from the future*, placing the Artifacts back in their own past.

Darya rejected that explanation as contrary to logic. It was also contrary to her own instincts about the Builders. They were, in every sense that Darya could describe, too *alien* to be humans, even future humans. They were far more alien than Cecropians, or Hymenopts, or Ditrons, or Lo'tfians, or even Zardalu. They had probably developed in an environment where no human or other clade could survive. Their relationship to space, and even more to time, was mystifying.

So time-traveling humans were not the answer. But then she could not escape the challenge laid down by Quintus Bloom. She had to conceive of a race of beings who could somehow know what humans and the other clades would be doing a thousand or ten thousand years from now. It was not a matter of looking at the past, and extrapolating it. Humans could do that easily enough, but all such extrapolations failed horribly after a few hundred years. The Builders didn't just *predict* the future of the Spiral Arm, as humans might. They could somehow *see* the future, as clearly as Darya could look forward out of the aircraft window and see an approaching line of snow-capped hills. She could not make out detail there, as she would when she was closer; perhaps the Builders also could not distinguish long-term future detail, but they perceived the overall picture of the Spiral Arm's future, as Darya could see the large-scale sweep of the landscape beyond her.

The hills were approaching. Darya could indeed see detail now, including a sizeable town standing amid the snow. The aircraft was descending, heading for a clearing a mile or two to the west of the town.

Darya watched as more and more detail became visible in the scene ahead. She could see buildings, and a line of stunted trees.

To *see* in time, as she *saw* in space? Faint in the distant future, with only the largest features visible. Then the near future would be clearer, with more visible specifics.

It felt right. The persistent little voice deep inside her insisted that it *was* right. In some incomprehensible way, Darya sensed that she had penetrated one level deeper into the mystery of the Builders.

Darya didn't like to lie. Sometimes, though, it made things so much easier.

"From Sentinel Gate, yes, and doing a feature article on Quintus Bloom. Naturally, I want to meet people who know him well, and understand his work."

Darya smiled deferentially. Kleema Netch leaned back in her reinforced chair and nodded. The Director of the Marglom Center was *huge*, enough to make Darya revise her opinion of the man on the plane. Compared to Kleema, her traveling companion had been a mere shadow. Almost everyone she had met so far was fat. Maybe there was something in the diet on Jerome's World? Anyway, once it became clear to Darya that her own name meant less than nothing to Kleema Netch (so much for fame!) the lie had come easily.

"Do not quote me to the other staff members." Kleema cushioned her folded hands on her great belly. She spoke in an absolute monotone, never varying her voice in pitch or inflection. "But Quintus is by far our most brilliant star and the Marglom Center is fortunate to have him. You know him, I assume, for his work on Labyrinth. If you want to take a look at that Artifact, you can visit the Observatory while you are here."

"You mean Labyrinth is *visible*—from the surface of Jerome's World?"

"Of course I mean that. Otherwise, how could I offer to show it to you? Our telescope is not the largest on the planet, but I think it is fair to say that in terms of its daily use and its research value for unit investment . . ."

Darya blanked out. If Labyrinth were easily visible from the surface, it must be even more visible from space. Which meant that it would have been discovered long, long ago, had it always been there. So at least one of Quintus Bloom's assertions must be true.

"—in many different fields." Kleema Netch was grinding on, with what sounded like a much-rehearsed statement. Darya forced her attention back to the speaker. "I will summarize only three of them to you, then I suggest that I introduce you to some of Quintus's fellow workers. They will provide you with the details that you need for your article. First, in his early years at the center, Quintus Bloom pioneered the idea that Jerome's World had supported an indigenous population of possibly intelligent beings, who did not survive the arrival of humans on the planet. That is today a subject of great controversy, but Quintus did not remain involved. His own interests had moved on, to the mapping of all major orbiting bodies in the Tetragamma system; here, too, he offered a new and startling hypothesis, which in the long history of Jerome's World, over the many centuries of colonization . . ."

Kleema Netch was just hitting her droning stride. Darya tightened her jaw muscles and reminded her-

self that she had come here voluntarily. She had no
one but herself to blame.

By late afternoon, Darya sat alone and exhausted in
the central library of the Marglom Center. In the past
seven hours she had met with twenty-three members
of the research staff. Everyone had spoken in glowing terms of Quintus Bloom's brilliance, his erudition,
his quickness of mind; they accepted everything that
he said, wrote, or thought.

So. He was Mister Wonderful. It was time to return
to the *Myosotis*, and continue the journey to Labyrinth.

There was just one problem. Everyone that Darya
had met at the center had also been so *mediocre* (Darya
chose the most charitable word she could think of), it
would not take much to impress them. Or, if it came
to that, to snow them completely.

Faced with a maze of suspect opinion, Darya did
what came to her as second nature. She went to her
usual sources: the library banks. Words could lie, or
mislead, as easily as people. But statistical records of
background and achievement were hard to fake.

She called up Bloom's biography, along with his list
of publications. It was impressive. He had started
research work at a young age, and had produced papers
prolifically ever since. All his evaluations were in the
file, and every one of them referred to him in the most
glowing terms. He had advanced within the Marglom
Center at the maximum possible pace.

Darya went back to the very beginning of the record.
Jerome's World employed an early education system
in which human teachers formed an integral part of
the teaching process. Quintus Bloom had been born
in the small town of Fogline, lying halfway on a direct
line between the Marglom Center and the spaceport.
His parents had been killed in an industrial accident

when he was five years old, and he had been raised by his grandparents. He had attended elementary school in that same town. The name of his teacher appeared in the record, but there were no detailed reports. All his grandparents were now dead.

If the town had been in any other direction, Darya would not have bothered. Her decision to stop at Fogline on the way back to the *Myosotis* was hardly more than pure impulse.

Amazingly, Bloom's first teacher had not died, or retired, or disappeared. What he had done, as Darya learned late the next morning, was to leave Fogline and take a position in another small town, Rasmussen, about forty kilometers away.

There was no air service to Rasmussen. Now it was surely time to give up and press on to Labyrinth. Except that no aircraft flew to the spaceport from Fogline for another whole day. By mid-afternoon Darya, her impressions of Jerome's World as a primitive place confirmed, found herself on a slow shuttle creeping toward Rasmussen. She did not feel optimistic. She would arrive long after school was over, and tracking down Orval Freemont might be difficult.

She peered out of the window. Labyrinth was below the horizon at this hour, but off to the east, according to the Marglom Center library, the Artifact would appear as a seventh magnitude object in the evening sky. It would be just too faint to be seen with the naked eye. There was no way that Labyrinth could have remained undiscovered, if it had been there since Jerome's World was first colonized. Darya sank back in her seat, deep in gloomy introspection. Apparently Quintus Bloom was right again: Labyrinth was a *new* Builder Artifact. The first new Artifact in three million years.

It was dusk when Darya emerged from the bus and

stood gazing around her. Fogline had been electronics, Rasmussen was genetics. Both towns were at the minimum threshold size for automated factory production, so that although round-the-clock processing was performed, some elements of the work were still done by human effort. There were people on the streets, going to and from work.

When in doubt, ask. Rasmussen couldn't have that many teachers.

"I'm looking for Orval Freemont. He works at the school."

The third try produced results. A woman in a sable fur coat over a sheer silk lamé dress with golden thread—maybe not everyone on the street was an industrial worker—pointed to a building whose red roof was just visible along a side street.

"Better hurry," she said. "Orval lives by himself, and he's an early-to-bed type."

The woman seemed sure of herself, but the man who opened the door to Darya's knock made her wonder if she had the right house. Darya had imagined an elderly, stooped pedant. The cheerful, robust figure who stood in front of her didn't look any older than Quintus himself.

"Orval Freemont?"

The man smiled. "That's me."

Darya went into her speech—a lie came easily, the twenty-fifth time around. Five minutes later she was sitting in the most comfortable chair of the little house, drinking tea and listening to Orval Freemont's enthusiastic reminiscences of Quintus Bloom.

"My very first class, that was, when I was just a youngster in Fogline and none too sure of myself. Of course, your first class is always special, and you never forget the children in it." Freemont grinned at Darya, making her wish he had been *her* first teacher. "But even allowing for that, Quintus Bloom was something special."

"Special *how?*"

"I've probably taught other children as smart as Quintus, but never, then or since, have I had anyone who wanted so much to be Number One. He wouldn't have heard of the word *ambition*, that first day in my class. But he already had it. Did you know, that very day he changed his own name? He came to class as John Jones, but he'd already decided that was too ordinary for what he intended to be. He wanted a *special* name. He announced that from now on he was Quintus Bloom, and he refused to answer to anything else. And he tried so hard, it was frightening. He'd do anything to be top, even if it meant cheating a little and hoping I wouldn't notice." Orval Freemont noticed Darya's expression. "Don't be shocked; all children tend to do that. Of course, part of the reason in his case was that he was a bit of an outcast. You know how cruel little kids can be. Quintus had this awful skin condition, big red sores on his face and on his arms and legs, and nothing seemed to clear them up."

"He has them still."

"That's a shame. Nerves, I suspect, and I bet he still picks at them when he thinks nobody's looking. Whatever the cause, it didn't make his sores and scabs any less real. The other kids called him Scabby, behind my back. He didn't say much, poor little lad, just put his head down and worked harder than ever. If you had come to me, even then, and asked me which of my pupils over the years was most likely to succeed, I'd have said Quintus Bloom. He *needed* it, the others didn't."

"Had he any other special talents that you noticed?"

"He sure did. He was the best, clearest writer for his age that I've ever met. Even when he got something wrong, I'd sometimes give him a little extra credit just for the way he said it."

"I don't suppose you kept anything that he wrote, back from his first years in school?"

Orval Freemont shook his head. "Wish I had. It didn't occur to me that Quintus would become so famous, or maybe I would have. But you know how it is; the little kids grow older, and the next class of young ones comes in, and your mind is suddenly all on them. That's what keeps you young. I *remember* Quintus, and I always will, but I haven't spent a lot of time thinking about him."

Darya glanced at her watch and stood up. "I have to get back to Fogline, or I'll be away another whole day. I really appreciate your time. You know, I've dealt a lot with teachers, and I've learned to appreciate the good ones. If you wanted to, you could be teaching in a university instead of an elementary school."

Freemont laughed, took Darya's cup as she handed it to him, and walked with her to the door. "You mean, if I were willing to make the sacrifice, and give up the rewards." He smiled gently at her bewildered look, "By the time that you reached university age, Ms. Lang, you were already formed as a person. But come to me as a little girl of five or six, and I can have a real say in what you'll become. That's *my* reward. That's why I say I have the best job in the universe."

Darya paused on the threshold. "Do you think you did that with Quintus Bloom—shaped him?"

Orval Freemont looked thoughtful, more than he had at any point in their whole meeting. "I'd like to think so. But, you know, I suspect that Quintus was formed long before I ever had a chance to work with him. That drive, that urge to be first and to succeed— I don't know where and when it came, but by the time I met him it was already there." He took Darya's hand, and held it for a long time. "I hope you'll write something nice about Quintus. Poor little devil, he deserves his success."

Darya hurried away, through the cold night streets of Rasmussen. She had just a few minutes to make the last shuttle. As she slipped and skated on the thin coat of ice that covered the sidewalks, she tried to measure the value of her trip to Fogline and Rasmussen. She knew Quintus Bloom much better now, that was certain. Thanks to Orval Freemont she had confirmed his strengths, and learned a little of his weaknesses.

As Darya arrived at the terminal, just in time, she realized that her visit to Jerome's World had given her something else, something she might have been happier not to have. She had seen Bloom through Orval Freemont's eyes: not as the self-confident and arrogant adult, but as a driven child, a small, lonely, and sad little boy.

Maybe the visit to Orval Freemont had been a big mistake. From now on, no matter how obnoxious he was, Darya would find it harder to hate Quintus Bloom.

✦ Chapter Thirteen

Darya Lang and Quintus Bloom were not the only people speculating about changes in Builder Artifacts. Hans Rebka was full of the same thoughts, and was possibly in a better position than the other two to take the idea seriously. He was the only person who had listened to Quintus Bloom's seminar, and then heard first-hand from Louis Nenda about the changes on Genizee and the total vanishing of Glister.

But what should he do with the knowledge? He was the action type, a general purpose trouble-shooter. He was no Quintus Bloom or Darya Lang, with their encyclopedic knowledge of every Artifact in the Spiral Arm and their ability to detect even the slightest modification of form or function. A change would have to stand up and hit Hans in the face before he recognized it.

There had been one exception. And that, oddly enough, made his decision easier when he decided to leave Sentinel Gate.

In the days before he first met Darya Lang, Hans Rebka had contracted to lead a Fourth Alliance team to the Artifact known as Paradox. At the very moment he was ready to begin, he had been re-assigned to Quake and Opal—and had been furious at the switch. For weeks and weeks beforehand he had been learning everything there was to know about the spherical anomaly called Paradox. All that knowledge, so painfully acquired, then just wasted.

But maybe he could use it now, to confirm or deny the ideas of Darya Lang and Quintus Bloom. Even if he found no change to Paradox, there was still a good reason for the journey. The cold-start procedure, when Hans had been forced to open E. Crimson Tally's skull, had reminded him of another attribute of the embodied computer. This one might be the key that would unlock the mystery of Paradox.

Rebka watched the gleaming soap bubble ahead, its surface rippling in hypnotic rainbow colors. Paradox was one of the smallest of the Artifacts, only fifty kilometers across. Unlike Sentinel, or many of the others, Paradox provided no impermeable barrier to an approaching ship. Exploring vessels could simply coast right through to the interior, and emerge physically unscathed. Unfortunately, as early would-be explorers of Paradox had learned (or rather, the people who found the explorers had learned) the same was not true of a ship's crew. Paradox wiped clean all stored memories, organic or inorganic. Surviving crews emerged like new-born babies, with only the most basic instincts and reflexes left to them. Data banks and computer memory on the ships were equally affected. Their contents disappeared. Any ship function that relied on the performance of a computer—and many did—failed inside Paradox. Ships had emerged with their hatches open, their temperature down to ambient space, or their drives dead.

The effect had been named: a *Lotus field*. That did not, unfortunately, mean that anyone in the Spiral Arm had the faintest idea how or why it worked, or how to neutralize it. After the first few expeditions (the first *recorded* expeditions—no one knew how many times Paradox had been discovered, and how many times all memory of it had been erased), the Artifact was placed off-limits to all but specially trained investigators.

Investigators like Hans Rebka, with many years of experience in the fine art of avoiding disaster.

But not like E.C. Tally. The embodied computer was staring at Paradox like a child offered a new toy. "Do you think the whole inside is a Lotus field, or is it just in a surface layer?"

"Probably in the surface. We know it starts there, and we have evidence of a lot of other interior structure in Paradox from the light that passes through it." Rebka was distracted. He was happy with the overall plan of what he wanted to do, but now he was down to practical questions. What was the best way to unwind, and then to wind back, a reel holding thirty kilometers of thin neural cable? Where would the fiber best enter the spacesuit, if the suit was to be airtight? At what point must Rebka put on his own suit?

It was a nuisance to be forced to do everything in suits, but Rebka could see no alternative. Even if the interior of Paradox, by some improbable miracle, turned out to be filled with air breathable by humans, what would happen just before entry? And what was the interior temperature of Paradox? Instrument readings gave inconsistent results.

"Sit still." He was standing behind Tally, who was suited except for the helmet. "I'm going to rehearse the whole thing just one more time."

He had already passed the neural cable through a hole in the top of the helmet, made an airtight seal at the point where it entered, and attached a neural connector plug to the end of the cable inside the helmet. He let that float free and reached forward to feel the rear of Tally's head. When he pressed on three marked points and at the same time lifted, a gleam of white bone was revealed on the back of the skull. The rear pins released, so that the upper cranium could pivot forward about the hinged line in the forehead. Tally's brain was revealed as a bulging grey ovoid sitting snugly in the skull case.

Rebka carefully lifted it out. "You all right?"

"Just fine. Of course, I cannot see. The top of my head is covering my eyes."

"I'll make this as quick as I can." Rebka felt beneath the wrinkled ball of the brain, to locate a short coiled spiral that connected the embodied computer's brain to the upper end of the body's hindbrain. "Doing it— now."

He unplugged the spiral, lifted the grey ball of the brain free, and pressed the neural connector from the suit's helmet into the plug in the hindbrain. A moment later he connected the other end of the thirty-kilometer filament to E.C. Tally's disembodied brain.

"How's that?"

"Perfectly fine." E.C. Tally's hands came up, to click the top of his skull back in position. The thin fiber ran from the back of his head to the suit's helmet, and on into the disembodied brain. "I sense a slight transmission delay."

"About two hundred microseconds. It's the two-way signal travel time through thirty kilometers of cable. Can you handle it?"

"I will become accustomed to it." Tally reached up again, and closed the suit helmet. "There. I am airtight. Does that complete our rehearsal?"

"Almost. I'm happy with all the moves that involve you, but I want to check my own suit and then take us to vacuum and back. I'll do it once you're unwired. Hold still while I switch you, then in a few minutes we'll try the whole thing for real."

Rebka opened Tally's helmet and performed the operation in reverse. He hinged the skull forward and pulled the neural connector out of the body's hindbrain. He freed Tally's brain from the other end of the fiber optic cable and plugged it once more into its hindbrain socket. Finally he clicked the cranium back to its original position.

"Here we are again." E.C. Tally lifted one suited hand, then the other. "No anomalies. What next?"

"Close your helmet. I'm going to take us to vacuum."

Rebka waited until his own suit was on and they both had their helmets locked in position. He cycled the air pressure down to zero, then slid open the hatch. They could see Paradox through the opening. It sat only a few tens of meters away, a shimmering bubble seemingly close enough to touch.

"Do you mind if I examine the Artifact from outside the ship?" E.C. Tally was floating toward the hatch.

"Go ahead. Check the E/M field intensities while you're there, but make sure you don't get into trouble with the Lotus field. And remember the cable's attached to your helmet, if not to your head, so don't get tangled up."

Tally nodded. He picked up a portable field recorder and drifted out, cable unreeling behind him. Hans did not move. They were ready to start, but there was no hurry. He had survived in the past by being ultra-cautious. He wanted to review everything mentally one last time.

The steps seemed clear and simple:

- Remove Tally's brain, which would stay here with him.
- Connect brain and body through the neural cable.
- Allow Tally's body to enter and explore Paradox, remotely controlled through the cable.

They knew from a previous experience that this would work in a Lotus field, although it had been tried only over short distances. This time E.C. could in principle go all the way to the center of Paradox. Rebka wasn't sure he was that ambitious. If Tally could bring something—anything—back from the Paradox interior, they would be breaking new ground.

And if something went wrong? Rebka couldn't think what it might be. At worst, they would lose one spacesuit, plus E.C. Tally's current body. That would be unfortunate, but Tally's brain had been re-embodied once before. If necessary, it could be returned to Miranda and embodied again.

Rebka took a deep breath. *Time to begin.* Where was Tally? He had been outside for a long time.

As though he had been summoned, Tally in his spacesuit came floating in through the hatch, cable reeling in ahead of him. He watched as Rebka brought the cabin back to normal air pressure. Both of them opened their helmets and Rebka began to strip off his suit.

"Before you remove your suit completely," E.C. Tally raised a gloved hand, "I want to be sure that I understand the reason for the procedure that you propose to follow."

Hans couldn't believe his ears. They had just reviewed the whole thing. In *detail*.

Was it possible—he had a sudden awful suspicion—was it possible that E.C. Tally had done what he had just been repeatedly warned *not* to do, and entered the Lotus field?

"Did you go into Paradox while you were outside?"

"A little way, yes."

"Against my strict instructions!"

"No." Tally was unabashed.

"Yes it was. You dummy, I told you not to go into Paradox."

"No. You told me not to get into trouble with the Lotus field. And I did not." Tally came floating forward, and hovered in front of Rebka. "I want to understand the reason for the procedure that we will follow, because it may be irrelevant. Perhaps you and I have had a basic misunderstanding. Are you sure that the Artifact waiting outside the hatch is indeed the one known as Paradox?"

"Of course it's Paradox. You watched me fly us here. Have you gone crazy?"

"I am not sure." Tally put down the recorder that he was holding. "Maybe we both have. But I am quite sure of one thing. The object alongside which this ship is floating, whatever it is, does not possess a Lotus field at its surface."

They went outside in their suits. Hans Rebka was hair-trigger nervous, ready to accuse Tally of every kind of irresponsible behavior, until the embodied computer explained.

"The electromagnetic field readings of the recorder appeared too low. And they *decreased*, as I came closer to the surface of Paradox." He was holding the little recorder in one gloved hand. "I wondered if the decrease would continue, beyond the surface of Paradox. It would be easy enough to check. All I had to do was use my suit's extensor to place the recorder within the visible surface. So."

Tally attached the recorder to the extensible grip in the suit's forearm, and began to reach out toward the shimmering wall of Paradox.

"Wait!" Rebka grabbed at the extensor. "The recorder has its own computer and internal programs. The Lotus field will wipe everything—you'll ruin the recorder."

"I realized that, when the idea first came to me. However, I decided that I would easily be able to restore the recorder memory; use of the recorder as a probe could tell us exactly how far within Paradox the Lotus field began. I therefore continued with the experiment." The extensible arm carried the recorder forward, until it met the chromatic swirl of Paradox's surface. It vanished beyond. "I tried this several times, increasing the degree of extension and then bringing the recorder back to examine it, until the arm was at its maximum stretch of fifteen meters. As it is now."

Tally floated with the gloved hand of his suit just half a meter away from the rainbow wall of shifting soap-bubble colors.

"And I brought it back."

The little motor in the extensor unit hummed, and the recorder re-emerged from beyond the shining boundary. E.C. Tally turned, so that Hans Rebka could see the face of the recorder. Numbers glowed on its display.

"Ambient field values." Tally touched another key. "Exactly consistent with the values obtained before the recorder went inside Paradox. The recorder programs should have been erased beyond the Paradox surface. But it appears to be working perfectly."

"So the Lotus field does not take effect within fifteen meters of the surface. It's deeper."

That was *not* consistent with the earlier data that Hans had memorized. Also, E.C. Tally was shaking his head. "I had that thought. I therefore considered another test. The recorder results suggested that I could proceed up to fifteen meters into Paradox, without encountering a Lotus field. Even if such a field proved to be present, I could detect the onset of loss of data within myself and return safely. I therefore moved twelve meters *inside* Paradox—"

"Crazy!"

"—and found myself enveloped by rainbow colors. At that point I again used the extensor to advance the recorder another fifteen meters. And since it was not affected there by any sign of a Lotus field, I moved another dozen meters. Then another. Then another. Then another."

"Tally. Get to the point. How far did you get?"

"Not far, in terms of the whole distance to the center of Paradox. I explored only a hundred and twenty-eight meters beyond the surface. However, there was no sign of a Lotus field. Also, I was able to do what I believe no other explorer of Paradox has ever done and returned to tell of it. I went beyond the rainbow wall. I could see all the way to the center of Paradox."

The designers of E. Crimson Tally had put enormous effort into his construction. Since they were building an embodied computer, a complex inorganic brain operating within a human body, they wanted that computer to follow processes of logic that mimicked to a large extent the thought processes of a human.

Perhaps they had succeeded too well. Certainly, faced with the situation at the surface of Paradox, a totally logical entity would have had no trouble in deciding the procedure to be followed: Rebka and E.C. Tally should take their findings and return at once to Sentinel Gate. The Artifact specialists there would evaluate them. They would recommend the next step of Paradox exploration.

Curiosity is an intensely human emotion. It was a measure of the success of E.C. Tally's creators that he did not try to dissuade Hans Rebka from his actual decision. In fact, Tally egged him on. The only point of disagreement between them was on who would lead the way.

"I should certainly be the one." Tally was searching his own and the ship's data banks for a record of the tensile strength of a neural cable. It was not designed to support a large load, and its strength was not recorded as part of the standard specification. "I can readily detect the onset of a Lotus field, and return unscathed."

"You have no experience at all in getting out of tough situations."

"I fought the Zardalu."

"Sure. And they pulled you to bits. You didn't exactly *get out* of that situation—we had to carry you out in pieces, and get you a new body. So no argument. I go inside, you keep an eye on me. First sign of trouble, or if I stop talking, you haul me out."

"What trouble can there be, other than the Lotus field?—with which I am better prepared to deal than you."

"The fact that you even *ask* that means you shouldn't be going in. Trouble comes in a thousand different ways. Not usually anything you expect, either. That's why it's trouble." Rebka was looping the cable through a tether ring on his own suit, then attaching the end to his communications unit. He gave it an experimental tug. "There. That should do us nicely."

"If you are unsure, and wish me to go in your place . . ."

"I'm on my way. Listen at this end, but don't do anything unless I tell you to. However, if I stop talking, or seem unable to move—"

"I will use the cable to pull you out." E.C. Tally was superior to most humans in at least one respect. He lacked sulking algorithms. He had accepted that he was not going into Paradox, and now he was thinking ahead.

Hans Rebka headed straight for the wall of shifting colors. He felt no resistance as he entered, only the faint tug of the cable unreeling steadily behind him. "Ten meters, and all is well. Twenty meters and all is well. Thirty meters . . ." He was going to become very bored unless he found something better to say. There were twenty-five hundred ten-meter intervals between the outer surface and the center of Paradox. "The colors are disappearing now. Eighty meters. I can see ahead, all the way to the center."

He was not the first human to enter Paradox and

see clearly to its heart. He would, however, be the first person to *return* with the knowledge of what he had seen. And Paradox from the inside was different. At least, it was different from data in the old files, gleaned from radiation emanating from the interior.

"There's a small flat torus in there at the middle. Looks like a fat donut almost side-on to me. I've never heard of that in the descriptions of Paradox. My guess is that it must be a few hundred meters across. I think I see dark spots along the outer perimeter—they may be openings. I'll give more information when I get closer to the center. I don't see any other interior structures, though there should be lots of them. I also don't see evidence of color fringes, or space distortion. I must be through the boundary layer."

Rebka felt a tug at his back, halting his inward progress.

"Wait there for a little while, if you please." E.C.'s message came clearly through the fiber-optic connection.

"Problems?"

"An insignificant one. There is a snag on the reel that is winding out the cable, and for convenience I wish to free it. Do not move."

Rebka hovered in space. Twenty-three kilometers to the center. He had said that he had no intention of going that far, but now, with the exploration proceeding so smoothly, who could bear to stop?

His heart was beating faster. It was not fear, but anticipation. Hans Rebka had never thought of himself as a hero, and he would have denied any such suggestion. Some jobs carried danger with them, some did not. He just happened to be a man with a dangerous job. But it was one with its own rewards—like seeing what no human or alien had ever seen before.

"I almost have the tangle loosened." Outside Paradox, Tally sounded calm and confident. "However, it would make my task rather easier if you were to back up this way a few meters."

"Very good. Backing up."

Rebka used his suit controls to reverse the direction of his movement. He turned his head, to judge by the slackness of the cable when he had moved far enough. The fiber was still taut, a clear straight line running back to the shimmering colors of the Paradox wall.

"Are you reeling in the line back there?"

"Not yet. I am waiting for you to back up a little. Please do so."

"Wait a moment." Rebka used the suit thrusters again. The line behind him remained taut as ever. He had apparently not moved backward even a millimeter. "Is any line reeling in at your end?"

"No. Why are you not moving toward me?"

"I don't know. I think maybe I can't move that way at all. Try something for me. Move everything, reel and all, a couple of meters this way, closer to the surface of Paradox."

"That is about all I can move it, without encountering the surface. I am doing it now."

The line slackened.

"Good. Now don't move." Hans Rebka eased forward, very carefully and slowly, until the line at his back was once more taut. He watched it closely, then operated his suit thrustors to reverse the direction of his motion. The line remained bow-string taut and straight.

Rebka hung motionless, thinking. No one before, in the recorded history of Paradox, had ever had the slightest trouble in leaving the Artifact. On the other hand, no one had ever before penetrated the interior and not been affected by the Lotus field.

"E.C., I think we may have a little problem. I can move forward fine, toward the center. But I don't seem able to back up toward you."

"You have a problem with your reverse thrustors?"

"I think not. Here's what I want you to do. Wait a couple of seconds, then pull on the cable—not too hard, but hard enough for me to feel it."

Rebka turned to grip the cable close to where it met the tether ring on his suit. By taking it between gloved thumb and forefinger he could tell how much tension was in the line. It was increasing. Tally was tugging at the other end. Rebka should now be pulled toward the surface of the Paradox like a hooked fish. He was not moving.

"It's no good, E.C. I don't think I can travel outward at all. Listen to me carefully before you do anything."

"I am listening,"

"We have to face the possibility that I may be stuck inside permanently. I'm going to try something else, but if you lose contact with me, I want you to make sure that a full report on everything that has happened here goes to the Artifact Institute. Address the message to both Darya Lang and Quintus Bloom. Is that clear?"

"Completely."

"All right. Now I want you to try more force on the cable. At the same time I'm going to use my suit's thrustors, just as hard as they will push. Wait until I give the word."

"I am waiting."

Outside Paradox, E.C. Tally crouched over the reel. "Now!"

Tally moved the whole reel backward to increase the tension in the line, tentatively at first, then with steadily greater force. "Are you moving?"

"Not a micron. Pull harder, Tally. We have nothing to lose. Pull harder. Harder! Hard—"

E.C. Tally and the reel went shooting backward, turning end over end in space. Tally twisted to keep the line in sight. It was clearly free to move, whipping rapidly out of Paradox, meter after meter of it. It was also clear from its movement that there could be nothing substantial on the other end of it.

Hans Rebka was deep inside Paradox, as planned. Not as planned, he seemed to be stuck there.

The designers of E.C. Tally had done one other thing that must have seemed like a good idea at the time. It stemmed from their own conviction that an embodied computer could think better than a human.

It stood to reason. E.C. Tally had attosecond circuits, capable of a billion billion calculations a second. He could absorb information a billion times as fast as a human. He forgot nothing, once it was learned. His thinking was logical, unclouded by emotion or prejudice.

The designers had incorporated all that information into E.C.'s memory bank. It provided him with overwhelming confidence. He *knew*, with a certainty that no human could ever approach, that he was smarter than any organic mind.

And Hans Rebka had an organic brain.

Therefore . . .

The whole thought process within E.C. Tally occupied less than a microsecond. It took another microsecond for him to construct a message describing the entire sequence of events since their approach to Paradox. He went back to the ship, transferred the message at once to the main communications unit, and selected the Sentinel Gate coordinates for transmission through the Bose Network. He checked the node delays as the message went out. The signal would reach Sentinel Gate in four to five days. Darya Lang or Quintus Bloom, even if they received the message at once and set out immediately for Paradox, could not possibly arrive in fewer than ten days.

Ten days. Enough time for Hans Rebka to run low

on air in his suit, but not really a lot of thinking time for a human's slow brain.

But ten days was close to a trillion trillion attoseconds. Time enough for the powerful brain of an embodied computer to analyze any situation, and solve any conceivable problem.

E.C. Tally waited for the confirmation that his message was safely on its way to the first Bose Transition point. Then he set the ship's controls so that it would hover a fixed distance from the surface of Paradox. He turned on the ship's beacon, so that anyone approaching the Artifact would be able to home in on it.

And then he went outside and turned to face the Artifact.

E.C. Tally to the rescue!

He switched to turbo mode on his internal clock, set the suit for maximum thrust, and plunged into the iridescent mystery of Paradox.

✦ Chapter Fourteen

Why *Labyrinth*?

Why not "Spinning Top" or "Auger" or "Seashell" or "Cornucopia"? That's what the Artifact resembled, turning far-off in space. Darya's first impression had been of a tiny silver-and-black humming top, drilling its way downward. Closer inspection showed that Labyrinth stood stationary against its backdrop of stars. The effect of downward motion was created by Labyrinth's form, a tapering coiled tube that spiraled through five full turns from its blunt top to its glittering final point. Imagination transformed that shape to the polished shell of a giant space snail, many kilometers long. A row of circular openings spaced regularly around the broadest part of the shell appeared and disappeared as Labyrinth rotated.

Or, according to Quintus Bloom, *seemed* to rotate. Darya glanced from the Artifact to the notes and back again. Anyone examining Labyrinth from the outside would be sure that this was a single three-dimensional helix, narrowing steadily from top to bottom and rotating in space around a central axis. The openings appearing and disappearing around its upper rim merely confirmed what was obvious to the eye.

Obvious, and wrong, according to Bloom. Labyrinth did not rotate. Bloom reported that laser readings reflected from the edges of Labyrinth showed no sign of the Doppler shift associated with moving objects. The openings on the upper edge moved around the perimeter; yet the perimeter itself was stationary.

Darya performed the laser measurement for herself, and was impressed. Bloom was right. Would *she* have sought to confirm what appeared to be a totally obvious rotation by an independent physical measurement, as he had done? Probably not. She felt awed at his thoroughness.

Darya returned again to the study of Bloom's notes. They had occupied her since she and her companions left the surface of Jerome's World. Each of the thirty-seven dark openings in Labyrinth was an entry point. Moreover, according to Bloom, each one formed an *independent* point of entry and led to an interior unique to each. The thirty-seven separate interiors were connected, one to another, through moving "windows," rotating inside Labyrinth just as the outside openings rotated. An explorer could "cross over" from one interior to another, but there was an inexplicable asymmetry; if the explorer tried to return through the same window, the result was an interior region different from the original place of departure.

Quintus Bloom had done his best to plot the connectivity of the inside, and had produced a baffling set of drawings. Darya puzzled over them. The problem was, every connection point in Labyrinth was *moving*, so every portal from a given interior might lead to any one of the other thirty-six possible regions. And as one descended into the tighter parts of the spiral, the region-to-region connections changed.

She decided that Bloom was right again, this time in his naming of the Artifact. *Labyrinth* was better than any snail or spinning-top analogy.

Which entry point should she use from the *Myosotis*? In the long run it might not matter; every interior could lead to any other. But the "pictorial gallery" of the Spiral

Arm that Quintus Bloom had described might be present in only one of the regions. It was not at all obvious which one they wanted, or that they could reach it by at most thirty-six jumps through a moving door. The region-to-region linkages probably depended, critically, on timing.

Darya stared at a plot of scores of cross-connection notations recorded by Quintus Bloom, and struggled to visualize the whole interlocking system. Here was a mental maze, a giant gastropod merry-go-round in which different layers turned—or *seemed* to turn—at different speeds: thirty-seven co-rotating and interacting three-dimensional Archimedean spirals, sliding past each other. It was like one of those infuriating math puzzles popular at the Institute, where the trick to the solution was a translation of the whole problem to a higher number of dimensions. Twice Darya felt that she almost had it, that she was on the point of grasping the whole thing in her mind as a coherent entirety; twice it slipped away. Like so many things associated with the Builders, the interior of Labyrinth seemed to surpass all logic.

She decided there was one acceptable answer: Close your eyes. Pick an entry point. And get on with it, playing the hand you were given.

Darya emerged from her reverie over that problem, and at once faced another. She must make a decision she had been putting off since leaving Jerome's World. Someone must remain aboard the *Myosotis*. Who?

It was unfair to ask Kallik or J'merlia to enter Labyrinth. They had not chosen this mission, and any new artifact could be dangerous. That argued for Darya, and Darya alone, to make a visit to the interior. Unfortunately, Kallik had her own intense interest in Builder Artifacts, and a knowledge of them that matched Darya's. She was quite fearless, and would want to be part of any exploration party. As a final point, Kallik's years with Louis Nenda had given her more practical experience than Darya.

So that left just J'merlia. J'merlia would remain on the *Myosotis*.

If Darya was any judge, he would hate it.

She sighed, and drifted aft to find the two aliens. They had been strangely quiet for the past hour.

She found them squatting on the floor of the main control room in a tangle of sixteen legs, heads close together. They were chatting, in the clicks and whistles of Hymenopt speech that Darya had so far found quite unintelligible, but they became quiet as soon as she entered.

"I think we're ready to proceed." Darya kept her voice brisk and neutral. "It's time to explore the interior of Labyrinth. J'merlia, I want you to remain here, at the controls of the *Myosotis*."

"Of course." The Lo'tfian's eyes bobbed on their stalks, in firm agreement. "With respect for your abilities, I am the most experienced pilot."

Darya hid her relief. "You certainly are. So Kallik, you and I had better get into our suits."

The Hymenopt nodded. "And J'merlia also."

The reply was made so casually, Darya almost missed it.

"J'merlia?"

"Of course. After all, should the ship be breached in some way, so that our suits are needed, J'merlia as pilot will need suit protection no less than we." Kallik stared blandly at Darya with twin circles of unblinking black eyes. "Into which entry point of Labyrinth, Professor Lang, do you wish J'merlia to direct the *Myosotis*?"

It was so obvious—once it had been pointed out. Darya wanted to hang her head in shame. Labyrinth was forty kilometers long. The coiled spiral tubes that composed it must each be several times as long as that.

There were thirty-seven of them, making endless miles of interior tunnels. Anyone in a suit would run out of air and supplies before they had explored a hundredth part of the interior.

Every one of those dark entrances ahead was at least a couple of hundred meters across, more than big enough to admit a vessel four times the size of the *Myosotis*. In his notes, Quintus Bloom had emphasized the massive scale of the Artifact's interior. Use of a ship, with its almost unlimited supplies of air, food, and energy, was the logical way—maybe the only way— to roam the inside of Labyrinth.

Darya cleared her throat. "I'll point out the entrance we want, as soon as we all have our suits on and are a little closer."

"Very good."

Kallik's dark eyes remained inscrutable. All the same, Darya was sure that J'merlia and Kallik both *knew*. Like the conscientious former slaves that they were, they had deliberately allowed her to save face.

Not for the first time since the beginning of their journey, Darya wondered who was really in charge.

"Thirty-seven entrances. Why *thirty-seven*? Is there anything interesting about the number thirty-seven?"

Darya had not expected a reply; it was just nervous talk. But Kallik replied solemnly: "Every three digit multiple of thirty-seven remains a multiple of thirty-seven when its digits are cyclically permuted."

Which left Darya to try an example in her head (37 times 16 is 592, and 259 and 925 are both divisible by 37); and to wonder: Was Kallik's a serious answer that deserved thought, or just a Hymenopt's idea of a good joke?

In any case, the decision had to be made. Darya pointed at a circular opening, as it came into view over the right-hand horizon of Labyrinth, and said: "That one."

J'merlia nodded. "Prepare for possible sudden acceleration after entry." He matched velocity vectors with the opening, and popped the *Myosotis* inside with casual skill.

Bloom's warning that Labyrinth only appeared to rotate was valuable advice. As the ship passed through to the interior, J'merlia had to apply a hard and sudden thrust to kill their sideways movement. Darya, suited and strapped into her seat by the control board, released a breath that seemed to have been trapped inside her since she had made the choice of entry point. She tried to examine all the external displays at once.

Behind them, every sign of the entrance had vanished. The ship sat within a gigantic coiled horn, a twisted cone whose walls were visible as writhing streamers of phosphorescence. The gleaming lines converged beyond the ship, growing closer and closer until they were hidden at last by the curve of the wall itself. But the convergence below was more than an effect of perspective, for *above* the *Myosotis* the bright streamers kept the interval between them constant, any decrease due to distance cancelled by an increase in true separation.

The way to go was *down*. In that direction, if Quintus Bloom's records could be used as a guide, the seamless walls would finally give way to a series of connected chambers. If you reached the innermost chamber, there, according to Bloom, you would find the series of glyphs that recorded the past and future history of humanity in the Spiral Arm. Or rather, a series of *polyglyphs*. A *glyph* was a term she understood, it was a sign or an image marked on a wall. But Bloom had not explained what he meant by a polyglyph. Was that one of his secrets, something to protect his own priority of claim?

As Darya pondered that she considered another major problem. Quintus Bloom had found his chamber in *one* of the interiors of Labyrinth. Since Darya's choice of entry point had been quite random, there was just a one in thirty-seven chance that they would reach the chamber that Bloom had explored.

Well, that was going to be her worry, not J'merlia's. He knew which way to go and the *Myosotis* was already descending, easing its way down the center line of an apparently bottomless curved shaft. After five minutes of steady progress, Darya saw a dark oval drifting into view on one side. It was a moving doorway, a portal to one of the other interiors. Easy enough to access, according to Quintus Bloom, but there was no reason to take it until they knew what lay deeper within this one. Darya fixed the portal's direction from them in her mind and labeled it as *clockwise* from this interior. Five minutes more, and a second oval appeared on the counter-clockwise side. It might be a wasted mental effort to think in terms of direction of travel, if the successive interiors that one encountered by moves in one direction did not form a regular sequence. Could you make thirty-seven clockwise jumps, and return to the starting point? Bloom had believed that there was no way to guarantee it.

The conical nature of the tube was at last revealing itself. The cylinder they traveled was narrowing, the wall becoming noticeably closer. Darya stared at the streaming ruled lines of phosphorescence, trying to estimate how long it would be before the tube became too narrow to admit the *Myosotis*. At that point they would have to resort to suits. She was interrupted by the soft touch of one of Kallik's forelimbs. "Excuse me, but unless you have already noticed . . ."

Darya turned, and found herself looking on a screen at a swirling black vortex. It was no more than thirty meters from the ship, a roiling whirlpool of oil and ink that curved and tumbled constantly in upon itself. She knew the nature of *that* singularity very well, from her own experience. It was a Builder transportation system, able to convey people and materials from anywhere in the Spiral Arm or beyond. It was also a two-way system, sending objects with equal facility.

"Steer wide of it!" Her warning was unnecessary. J'merlia was easing them well clear. The others had their own familiarity with the ways of the Builders.

The vortex was a feature of Labyrinth unmentioned by Quintus Bloom. Had his exploration, through some other interior region, failed to discover it? Or had he, reluctant to describe what he could not explain, seen the spinning darkness but failed to record it?

The gleaming walls were nearer. If they met another vortex, the *Myosotis* would not be able to maneuver safely clear of it. The displays of the way ahead made it clear that was soon going to be irrelevant. The smooth tube was ending, narrowing to a circular opening through which no ship could ever pass.

Darya had to make another decision, but this one was easy since she had no choice. J'merlia would have to stay with the ship while she and Kallik went through the opening. He would be alone in the deep interior, facing a tricky and dangerous escape if the other two did not return. But Darya saw no alternative.

All three of them were already in their suits and equipped with maximum life-support supplies. J'merlia halted the ship about thirty meters short of the circular opening. A nod of Darya's head was all it took for Kallik to open the forward hatch, lead the way through the opening, and continue into the first chamber.

Quintus Bloom had described a series of rooms, decreasing steadily in size like matched pearls on a necklace and connected each to the next by a single narrow passageway. According to Bloom there should be six of them, including the final chamber. That one was shaped differently and ended in a narrow-angled conical wedge.

He had said little—too little—about intermediate chambers, beyond the fact that in the third one lay a moving dark aperture, which he believed led to another of the thirty-seven interiors. He had offered no recordings of any chamber except the last one. Staring about her as she entered the first room, Darya began to understand why. She and her two companions were shrouded at once by a billowing fog, a shifting grey mantle that changed constantly and held within it dozens of ghost images. Darya glimpsed another vortex ahead, pale and diminished. Beside it hovered a pair of spectral dodecahedra, like the omnivorous Phage Artifacts that she had encountered on Glister. Before she could examine them, or wonder how to avoid them, they had vanished into the mist. A drifting haze to the left drew her attention. It was no more than cloud imprinted on cloud, but she sensed a thousand-tendriled Medusa like a miniature Torvil Anfract. Next to it stood another whirling vortex, drawing all those writhing tendrils toward its dark embrace. A moment later both were fading, dissolving, merging into the restless swirl of the background.

Darya's only certainty was the walls of the chamber. She could sense their solidity, even if she could not see them through the mist. She was sure that she was still moving relative to them, and convinced that ahead of her lay the opening that would lead to the next room. The range sensors on her suit confirmed what she already knew, deep inside her.

The fog disappeared as they entered the second chamber. It was dark, but when Kallik, still leading the way, switched on her flashing suit lights the whole chamber turned into a meaningless kaleidoscope of colors. Again, Darya understood why perhaps there had been no recordings made here. The chamber walls formed perfect mirrors, light reflecting and re-reflecting a thousand times. She tried to visualize how light leaving their three suits would appear when it at last returned to them. It was impossible. A dark spot, dead ahead, pointed the way into the next chamber.

In that chamber, their experience diverged again from what had been reported by Quintus Bloom. The walls showed curving lines of light, running from where they had entered to converge and surround a dark circle at the far end. This was certainly the third chamber. There was, however, no sign of a portal leading to another of the many interiors. Labyrinth had changed, or more likely the one-in-thirty-seven long shot that they had entered Labyrinth at the same place as Quintus Bloom had not paid off.

Kallik paused at the entrance to the fourth chamber. Coming up level with her, Darya saw why. The whole inside was filled with a driving orange sleet, tiny pelting particles that blanketed the interior and ran from the entrance down toward the far end.

While Darya stood dismayed, Kallik and J'merlia backed up along the passage between the chambers. After a little more than forty meters, they halted and Kallik made small adjustments to their final positions. While J'merlia remained stationary, Kallik then drove forward and shot past Darya with her suit set to maximum thrust. At the moment of entry into the new chamber she turned off the suit's power and sailed on in free fall. Her rate of progress matched that of the storm of orange particles. J'merlia watched closely, and at last he nodded.

"Perfect." He beckoned to Darya. "Come, if you please, Professor Lang, and we will proceed together. With respect, it is better if I control the moment when we turn the suits' power on and off."

Darya was in a daze as she floated by J'merlia's side and allowed him to control her movements as well as his own. However, she did not lose her instinct as an observer. As they moved through the fourth chamber she examined the orange particles closest to her helmet, and saw that each one was like a tiny blunt dart, a miniature rocket pointed at the forward end and fluted into a four-part tail at the other. Just before they reached the tunnel at the far end of the chamber, the orange darts disappeared. They did not hit anything, but simply seemed to vanish. Darya and J'merlia went coasting on in darkness, toward the gleam of Kallik's suit lights.

Darya paused as the three met, and she took a long, deep breath. Could anything be more unpleasant than what they'd just been through?

Maybe. By the look of it, the fifth chamber was a candidate.

The space ahead was filled with transportation entry points, hundreds and hundreds of them. The ominous black vortices did not remain at rest, but skated through and past each other, rebounding from the chamber walls in a complicated and unpredictable dance. Darya did not even try to count them, but she shuddered at the prospect of weaving a way through. Hovering at the entrance, she watched in disbelief as Kallik and J'merlia set off to run the gauntlet.

Didn't *anything* scare the two aliens? Sometimes she wondered if humans were the only beings in the universe with a sense of cowardice (be charitable, and call it an instinct for self-preservation).

The swirling vortices blocked a view of the other end. It was impossible to tell if Kallik and J'merlia had made it through the chamber. It was also impossible for Darya to remain forever where she was, poised nervously at the entrance.

She took a long last breath, waited until she could see a space which for at least a moment was clear of the dark whirlpools, and plunged forward. In what felt like milliseconds the open space ahead had gone and vortices came crowding in on her. Darya envied Kallik, with her rings of eyes that could see in all directions. She jigged to the right, waited another moment, shot forward, waited again for a heartbeat, then did a quick combined up-and-left maneuver. A vortex zooming up from behind was almost on top of her before she knew it. She could feel the sideways drag of its vorticity as she spurted away, down and to the left again.

The biggest danger of all would be to be trapped close to the chamber wall, with her freedom to move automatically halved. She had been moving mostly to the left, so the wall might be near. She glanced that way, just in time to see a monster vortex bouncing straight at her. She had no choice but a maximum thrust, forward and to the right. She dived that way, then gritted her teeth when she saw yet another dark shape immediately ahead.

It was too late to change direction. The new vortex was going to get her. When it seemed just inches away she was grabbed by both her arms and a violent jerk pulled her clear. There was another dizzying moment, a spinning out of control. Then in front of her she saw a dark opening.

It was the exit to the chamber. Kallik and J'merlia floated on each side of her, holding her as she sagged against the safe and solid tunnel wall of the next chamber.

"A unique experience," said a thoughtful voice. "And an exhilarating one."

It was not clear whether Kallik was talking to her or to J'merlia, but Darya made no attempt to respond. Her own unvoiced comment, *This had better be the last damned chamber*, no longer seemed appropriate. She could already see that this *was* the last room. Instead of a sphere she was facing into a hexagonal pyramid. It narrowed at the far end to a closed wedge, and Darya saw no other exit. Looking at it positively, they had made it unharmed all the way to their destination. Their suits would support them for many days. Looked at otherwise, the only way out of this place would be to go back through the terrors they had just left. The orange hail of the fourth chamber, if nothing else, would make a return doubly difficult.

The other two were moving forward. Kallik, Darya noticed, was even cracking open her suit.

"Breathable air," she said, before Darya could protest. The Hymenopt gestured to her suit monitors.

Darya glanced at her own and saw that Kallik was correct. The final room held breathable gases, at acceptable pressure—in spite of the fact that the five previous chambers had shown on the monitor as hard vacuum, and there was no sign of any sealing barrier between them and this. Well, there had also been no sign of a barrier that could stop or absorb the sleet of orange darts, but they had vanished just the same.

Darya opened her own suit, with just two thoughts in her head. The first was that Builder technology would be forever beyond her. The second was that she was *not* cut out to be a bold and brave explorer. If she escaped from this alive, she would go back to doing what she did best: analysis and interpretation of *other people's* wild leaps into the unknown.

She wished, not for the first time, that she had not been so quick to leave Hans Rebka on Sentinel Gate. He thrived on this sort of madness. If he were beside her now, her pulse might be coming down from its two-a-second thumping.

And then all those thoughts vanished. She was able, for the first time, to take a good look at the six flat walls of the hexagonal room. She stared and stared. The walls were *wrong*. Each was covered with multicolored, milky patterns, interspersed with diffuse streaks and smears in pale pastel shades.

Not a beautiful series of time-sequenced images of the Spiral Arm, as Quintus Bloom had reported. Not a single comprehensive image of the region, as Darya had been half expecting. Not, in fact, a recognizable picture of any kind; just a hazy, confused blur, something that the eye had trouble looking at.

The walls could certainly be considered *pretty*, as an abstract design might be pretty. They were just not *meaningful*.

Darya had been hoping, though with no real basis for hope, that although the outer chambers might be different in each of the thirty-seven interiors, everything would at last converge to a single space. Now she knew her wishful thinking for what it was: desperate delusion. They had reached a sixth and final room, just as she had hoped—and it was the wrong room!

Her pulse rate started to rise again. If she wanted to learn the secrets of Labyrinth, she had no choice. She would *have* to head back, far enough to transfer to one of the other interiors—a different interior, probably with its own new and unique dangers—and explore *that* to its end.

Kallik and J'merlia might want to try. Hans Rebka and Louis Nenda would certainly have done it. But it was beyond Darya. Before another interior was reached, she suspected that her own courage and stamina would have long since given out.

✦ Chapter Fifteen

Louis Nenda had seen more than his share of horrors (he had been responsible for some of them himself). He was a hard man to shock.

But he could still be surprised.

Quintus Bloom had produced a ship, superior in performance to the *Indulgence,* to explore the Anfract.

How? Simple. Lacking funds himself, he had arranged through Professor Merada for a meeting with the Board of Governors of the Institute.

He needed, he explained, the use of a ship.

Very good. And what did he offer in return?

A whole new Artifact, one larger and more complex than anything currently known. He would prove that the whole region of space known as the Torvil Anfract, in far Communion territory, had been constructed by the Builders.

No mention, by either Bloom or Merada, of Darya Lang, although *she* had been the one who first suggested that the Anfract was a Builder Artifact. Quintus Bloom was the man of the hour, and Darya was not around to defend her claim to priority.

The Governors, with Merada's strong endorsement, had been unanimous: Quintus Bloom, representing both the Artifact Institute and the planet of Sentinel Gate, would have his ship. Like the explorers of old, he would travel with official sponsorship, and his triumphant return would bring glory on himself and on all those who had backed him.

Nenda heard of the meeting second-hand. It had not surprised him that Darya's name was never mentioned. He found it in no way odd that the Governors were supporting Bloom, in return for their share of the credit.

No. What gave Louis his surprise of the day, wandering through the interior of the *Gravitas*, was the amazing opulence of the ship's fittings. He realized a profound truth: *there is no one so generous as a bureaucrat spending other people's money.*

Sentinel Gate was one of the Arm's richest worlds. Even so, someone had given Quintus Bloom *carte blanche* on equipment and supplies.

And, presumably, on personnel. Nenda ran his forefinger along a gnarled but polished rail, hand-carved from rare Styx blackwood, and decided that he had been far too modest in his own request for pay. The *Gravitas* reeked of newness and wealth in every aspect, from the massive engines, barely broken in, at the rear of the ship, to the half-dozen passenger compartments in the bow. The passenger suite that he was now inspecting had its own bedroom, parlor, entertainment center, hydroponic garden, hot tub, kitchen, autochef, medicator, robot massager, drug chest, and wine cabinet.

Nenda paused in his exploration, reached into the temperature-stabilized wine cooler, and pulled out a bottle. He examined the label.

Trockenbeerenauslese Persephone Special Reserve.

Whatever that mouthful was supposed to mean. He opened the bottle and took a swig. Not bad. He glanced at the price on the side of the bottle and was still staring at it, pop-eyed, when Atvar H'sial wandered in to join him.

"Louis, I have disturbing news."

"So do I. We could have asked ten times what we'll make from this trip, and still been down in the petty cash. I just drank half our pay."

"Ah, yes. I see you have been examining the fixtures on the *Gravitas*." The Cecropian settled comfortably at his side. "I agree, our reimbursement will be modest. Compared with the value of the ship itself, I mean, which to any lucky owners, now or in the future . . . " Atvar H'sial allowed the rest of her comment to fade away into pheromonal ambiguity. "But that is not my news. As you know, the loss of my slave and interpreter, J'merlia, has been a great inconvenience."

"You can always talk through me, or anybody else with an augment."

"Of which there appears to be no other within a hundred lightyears. And you are not always available. I have therefore been seeking methods for more direct communication with others."

Atvar H'sial paused for thought. "An extraordinarily primitive and restrictive tool, human speech. That the same organ should have to serve a central role in eating, breathing, sex, and speaking . . . but I digress. I have employed a human assistant. As part of my interaction with that assistant, we have been receiving and examining together the news reports that arrive at the Institute from different worlds of the Fourth Alliance. One came in recently from the planet, Miranda. It was to Miranda that the infant Zardalu captured by Darya Lang"—the pheromones carried a snide hint of suspicion and disapproval along with the name—"was sent for study."

"I know. Better there than anywhere near me."

"Indeed. They were to monitor its ferocity as it grew larger, under close guard. The cunning and cruelty of the Zardalu has been a legend for eleven thousand years, since the time when they controlled most of the Spiral Arm."

"Yeah. I'm from Zardalu Communion territory, remember? I've heard that sort of talk all my life."

"Then you will be suitably surprised if someone suggests to you that it is nonsense. Yet that is what the report from Miranda indicates. The young Zardalu is powerful. It is endlessly, voraciously, hungry. But it is neither remarkably vicious nor unusually dangerous. Less so, the Miranda team suggests, than half a dozen other species in the Arm—including yours and mine."

Nenda sat down on one of the plush settees of the passenger suite and took an absent-minded gulp from the bottle. The news was another surprise, his second of the day. But was it a shock?

He sniffed. "I've wondered myself how we did it. We tangled with the Zardalu on Serenity, and then twice on Genizee. And every time they came off second best when they ought to have creamed us. You could say once was dumb luck, but three times in a row—"

"—suggests that other factors may be at work. My own conclusion exactly. Our experiences suggest that the surviving strain of Zardalu are but a feeble shadow of their ancestors, the old race who spread terror across the galaxy. The testing team on Miranda lacks our data, but they also are much perplexed. They wonder if the benign environment in which the Zardalu has been raised since infancy has had a profound effect upon its nature. To provide a possible answer to that question, they offer a reward—a most substantial reward— to anyone able to deliver, for their study, one adult Zardalu that has been reared in its natural environment. That raises a question. We are following Darya Lang to the Anfract. Suppose we find that her trail leads within the Anfract, and points directly to Genizee? What would you propose to tell Quintus Bloom, should he ask you to guide him there?"

"I'd have a sudden and terrible loss of memory. I wouldn't be able to figure out any way to get us to

Genizee—and you better not either. I don't want him grabbing a Zardalu for himself an' bagging all the money."

"Agreed. However, if you had reason to believe that at an appropriate future time, Quintus Bloom for some reason would not be present on board the *Gravitas* . . ."

"I might find I could remember again, all of a sudden. You know what a mystery the human mind can be."

Atvar H'sial nodded. The pheromones had faded to nothing, but Nenda had the feeling that she was satisfied by his answer. She lifted up onto her four hind limbs and silently left the passenger suite.

Once she had left, Louis began to have second thoughts. The idea of the Zardalu as less than ultimate monsters was one that he needed time to evaluate, but he certainly did hate the idea of Darya Lang stranded among them on Genizee. Was she there now? Should he be looking for her? If so, how was he going to make Quintus Bloom and Atvar H'sial agree to that?

Louis followed Atvar H'sial out of the passenger suite and continued his inspection of the *Gravitas*. He was a man who believed in knowing as much as possible about any ship he was asked to fly. This one was certainly worth knowing. If the news from Miranda was a surprise, the ship itself was no less of one. It was big as well as richly furnished. The only thing missing, to Nenda's knowledgeable but possibly biased eyes, was a decent weapons system.

Well, he had spotted a dozen places where that could be added, when the right time came. And for a hundredth of the value of the ship's other fixtures.

He wandered into another self-contained passenger suite, this one over-furnished in an elaborate baroque style. The autochef offered unusually exotic and spicy dishes, more likely to excite than soothe the diner. All the floors were covered with deep, soft rugs, and the bedroom, when he came to it, was dominated by a huge circular bed with mirrors set above it. He walked across the thick pile of the carpet, intending to glance at the bathroom and see if this one too was furnished with its own hot tub.

As soon as the door opened and he could see inside, he jerked backwards.

The bathroom wasn't just *furnished*. It was *occupied*. A woman was reclining in the tub, immersed so that only her head, bare shoulders, and legs from the knees down showed above the foam and the perfumed water. She turned her head at the sound of the opening door and gave Louis an unselfconscious nod of greeting.

"*Hello* there." Glenna Omar's smile was warm and welcoming. "Did Atvar H'sial tell you the news? I'm going to be her assistant! Isn't it *wonderful*? I wondered how long it would be before you and I ran into each other again. And lo and behold—here we are." She reached for the side of the tub and began to stand up. "Well, I think I've simmered enough for one day. Unless you'd like to . . . No? Well, if you would just hand me that towel . . ."

Louis had lived too long to think that closing your eyes in a crisis could help. He stared at Glenna's foam-flecked pink and white form, reached for the long towel, and swore silent revenge on Atvar H'sial.

"You, me, and Quintus," Glenna went on. She stepped forward into the held towel, and kept moving until her body was rubbing up against Nenda's. "This is going to be an *exciting* trip."

Apparently surprises, like so many other things in life, were apt to come in threes.

The *Gravitas* was one of the Fourth Alliance's most advanced ships. For all its size, it handled like a dream and could be operated by a single pilot.

That certainly suited Louis Nenda. They were going
to the Torvil Anfract, where inexperienced personnel
would be something between a hindrance and a disaster; and after the job was over, the fewer extra hands
on board, the better.

The ship had just cleared their sixth Bose Transition point, skipping in four days from the prosper-
ous and well-settled Fourth Alliance to the outer limits
of the Zardalu Communion. The travelers encountered
at the transition points had changed along the way,
from predominantly human merchants, tourists, and
government bureaucrats, to beings whose species was
sometimes almost as hard to determine as their occupation. Nenda had identified Cecropians, Hymenopts,
Lo'tfians, Varnians, Scribes, Stage Three Ditrons,
Decantil Myrmecons, what looked to Nenda like a pair
of the supposedly-extinct Bercians, and one Chism
Polypheme. That had given him a bad moment, because
he and Atvar H'sial had stolen the *Indulgence* from
a Chism Polypheme, back inside the Anfract. But this
one was not Dulcimer, seeking revenge. It merely glared
at Nenda with its great slate-grey single eye, reached
out its five little arms, growled, "Keep your distance,
sailor!" and wriggled the green corkscrew body past
him.

For Nenda, the best thing about their outward
progress was its effect on Glenna Omar. She was like
Darya Lang when Louis had first met her, straight from
the sheltered and innocent life of Sentinel Gate—
although *innocent* might be the wrong word for Glenna.
As the presence of aliens increased, together with
evidence of poverty and barbarism, she became gradually
more subdued. She would still rub her foot over Nenda's
or Bloom's at dinner, or sit nudging knee to knee. But
it was half-hearted, an automatic going-through-the-
motions with the genuine spirit lacking.

That gave Nenda time to do what had to be done,

and concentrate his mind on the Torvil Anfract. What he had told Quintus Bloom was perfectly true; he had been into the Anfract, and returned in one piece. Few beings could make that boast. What he had not told Bloom was that once he had escaped from the Anfract, he had said that he would never go back.

Sworn that he would never go back.

But here he was, piloting the *Gravitas* on its final subluminal leg. In just a few more minutes he would be taking another plunge into the depths of the Spiral Arm's most notorious chunk of twisted spacetime.

He knew what should be a safe route in, since the path they had followed on their previous entry had been recorded. It would be the identical path followed by Darya Lang, unless she had gone quite mad and added enormously to her risks (or not come to the Anfract at all).

The bad news, the thing he was afraid of, was recent *changes* to the structure of the Anfract. He and Atvar H'sial had seen signs of those, and evidence of variations in Builder Artifacts. Suppose that the entry path now led straight into a chasm singularity, or a Croquemort time-well? Even a local field of a couple of hundred gees would be quite enough to wipe out the crew, although the *Gravitas* itself would survive.

Nenda stared at the image of the Anfract, filling the sky ahead. It was reassuringly normal—which was to say, reassuringly strange. He could see and count the individual lobes, and discern the exact point where the ship would make its entry. The Anfract was huge, sprawling out over a region almost two lightyears across, but that was irrelevant. Normal measure and spacetime metrics meant nothing once you were inside. Within that perplexing interior they could follow Darya all the way to Genizee, if that was necessary, in just a few minutes.

He became aware of Quintus Bloom, peering over

his shoulder. Though he would never have expected it, during the journey Nenda had revised upward his opinion of the scientist from Jerome's World. The two men had much in common. For one thing, it seemed to suit Bloom as well as Nenda that the *Gravitas* had a minimal crew.

Nenda could follow Bloom's logic. Fewer people, fewer candidates to share the credit for discoveries. Nenda and Atvar H'sial would not count, one being considered mere crew and the other a bloated and blind horror of an alien. Glenna, the only other person aboard, was a known Quintus-worshipper whose main job would be to hang on to him and record his every sacred word for their return to glory.

Beyond that, though, Nenda sensed something else about Quintus Bloom. Bloom would do *anything*, literally anything, to get ahead in his world. That world happened to be a different one from Nenda's, with different rewards, but Louis could recognize and appreciate single-minded, ruthless drive. Bloom saw him as a nothing, a bug that you could use or step on, just as the need arose. But that worked both ways. To Nenda, Quintus Bloom was a man you had to kill with the first shot, or not fire the gun. If Louis controlled the *Gravitas* when it emerged from the Anfract, one person *not* to look for on board would be the honorable Quintus Bloom.

With Bloom's personal drive and ambition came any amount of nerve. He was leaning impatiently forward and staring at the image of the Torvil Anfract. "Can't you speed us up? Why is it taking so long to enter?"

What he meant was, "Darya Lang may be in there, making *my* discoveries. Take risks if you have to, but *get me in.*"

Nenda shrugged. He was just about ready to proceed, anyway. You could stare at the image of the Anfract until your eyes started to bleed, but once you were inside all the outside observations didn't mean a thing. The Anfract was huge and vastly complex. It could have changed in a million ways, and no external observer would ever know it.

"You might want to strap yourself in, and I'll announce it to the others. The ride last time was pretty hairy."

It was a way to stop Bloom from breathing down his neck. It was also a perfectly true statement. Nenda, whose own ambitions did not guarantee a matching supply of nerve, held his breath as the *Gravitas* started to move faster and faster toward the boundary of the Anfract. He was directing it down a dark, starless corridor of supposedly empty space. Any surprise would be a nasty one. As the ship began to vibrate, with small, choppy surges, he cut back their speed.

"Problems?" Bloom, from a seat next to Louis, was finally showing a little uneasiness.

Nenda shook his head. "It's a change in Planck scale. We may get macroscopic quantum effects. I'll keep my eyes open, but let me know if anything seems unusual."

It had happened before, and after the first time the anomalous was no longer terrifying. When it came, Nenda welcomed the quantum graininess of their environment as familiar, and therefore right. He was not upset when the *Gravitas* next appeared to be plunging straight for the photosphere of a blazing blue-white star. He explained to Bloom exactly what was going to happen. They would dive down almost to the boiling gaseous surface of the star, then jump at the last moment into a dark void.

They did.

Next they would find themselves in free fall, and lose all light and power on the ship.

They did.

And in just ten seconds or so, the power and lights and gravity would return.

They didn't.

Nenda and Bloom sat side by side in silence as the seconds wore on. And on.

Finally, Bloom's voice came in the darkness: "*How* long did you say before we have power again?"

"Just a few more seconds. What we've hit is called a *hiatus*. It won't last. Ah!" A faint glimmer of light was appearing in the control room. "Here we go."

Power was creeping back. The screens were again flickering toward normal status. An image appeared on the main display, showing space outside the *Gravitas*.

Nenda stared no less eagerly than Quintus Bloom. He put the ship into steady rotation, so that they could examine all directions in turn. He had expected them to be surrounded by the overall multi-lobed Anfract, and closer to them should be the nested annular singularities that shielded Genizee. If the earlier disappearance of those singularities was permanent, the ship would have a distant view of Genizee. They would be far enough away that the Zardalu inhabitants could do no harm.

Nenda kept his eye on the screen as the turning ship scanned the outside. There was no sign of the characteristic shimmering lobes of the Torvil Anfract—of *any* Anfract lobe. No nested annular singularities appeared anywhere on the display. Nothing remotely resembling a planet could be seen.

All the lights suddenly went out again. The murmur of the ship's engines faded to nothing.

"*Another* hiatus?" Bloom was more irritated than alarmed. This time the ship's rotation provided enough artificial gravity to prevent physical discomfort. "How many of these things are there?"

"Damned if I know." Louis was more alarmed than irritated. "I only expected one."

They waited, sitting in absolute darkness. Seconds stretched to minutes.

"Look, I'm in a big hurry. I'd have thought you would

know that by now." Bloom's face was not visible, but his voice said it all. "You'd better get us out of here, Nenda—and quickly."

Louis sighed, closed his eyes, and opened them again. Nothing had changed. For all he knew, the hiatus might last forever. Nothing he did to the ship's controls could make any difference.

"Did you hear me?" Bloom spoke again from the darkness. "I said, get us out. If not, you can forget your pay."

"I'm forgetting it already." But Nenda kept that thought to himself. He stared hard at lots of black nothing, and wished that Genizee would appear ahead and the ship would drop him back among the Zardalu. At least you knew where you were with Zardalu.

Loss of pay seemed the least of his worries.

✦ Chapter Sixteen

Darya hated the idea of slavery, but now and again she could see some advantage to being a slave. For one thing, you didn't have to make decisions.

J'merlia and Kallik had followed her—and sometimes led her—to the middle of nowhere. Now, floating in the innermost chamber of Labyrinth, they were patiently waiting until she told them what to do next.

As if she knew.

Darya stared around at the flat walls of the hexagonal chamber, seeking inspiration in their bland, marbled faces.

"We made it here safely, which is exactly what we wanted." (Think positive!) "But eventually we must find a good way to return to our ship, and then back into free space."

The two aliens indicated agreement but did not speak.

"So you, J'merlia." Darya cleared her throat to gain thinking time. "I'd like you to take another look at the way we came. See if there's some way to reach another interior, one that's easier to travel. And J'merlia!"— the Lo'tfian was already nodding and ready to go —"Don't take risks!"

J'merlia's head turned, and the lemon eyes on their short stalks stared reproachfully at Darya. "Of course not. With respect, if I became damaged I would be of no further value to you."

Except that his and Darya's ideas of risk were unlikely to coincide. He was already zooming happily off toward the entry tunnel and the chamber filled with terrifying dark vortices.

"And don't stay away too long!" Darya called after him. "No more than three or four hours."

There was no reply, just a nod of the suit's helmet.

"And I?" Kallik was staring at J'merlia's vanishing form. Darya thought she could detect a wistfulness in her voice. There was nothing the little Hymenopt would have liked better than to go racing off with J'merlia.

"You and I will examine this chamber more closely. I know it seems as though there's absolutely of interest here, though Quintus Bloom said otherwise."

Darya did not look at Kallik as she led the way to peer at the nearest wall. The multi-colored, milky surface seemed to stare back at her. Close up, the wall showed a lot more detail. The pastel shades that Darya saw from a distance were not composed of flat washes of pale color, but were created by many narrow lines of bright color set in a uniform white background. It was as though someone had begun with a wall of plain white, then drawn on that surface with a very fine pen thousands of intersecting lines of different colors. And drawn them sequentially, because wherever two lines crossed, one of them was broken by the other.

But it was still nothing like a *picture*. Darya wondered again about Bloom's term: *polyglyphs*. She glanced at Kallik. The Hymenopt was standing just a few feet from the wall. She was staring at it with bright black eyes, and swaying her head from side to side. After a few moments she began to do the same thing with her whole body, shifting first a couple of feet to the left and then moving back to the right.

"What's wrong?"

Kallik paused in her oscillation. "Nothing is wrong. But this wall shows parallax."

It was not something that Darya had thought to look for. She followed Kallik's example and moved her own head, first to the left and then to the right. As she did so, the line patterns moved slightly relative to each other. It was as though she could see down *into* the surface, and the lines were at different depths. When she changed her viewing position, the nearer lines moved more than the distant ones. Also, she noticed that no single line was at a uniform depth. One end was always deeper than the other, as though the line met the surface at a shallow angle and continued below it.

The whole wall looked like a bewildering set of lines embedded in open space above a white background. That was a three-dimensional effect, produced by the superposition of many different layers. If you imagined that the wall you saw was built up from a set of nearly transparent plates, stacked one beneath the other behind the surface, what would a *single* plate look like?

Darya went up to the wall and reached out to touch it. The surface was smooth and hard. The wall was continuous, and met seamlessly with other surfaces of the hexagonal chamber.

"With respect, I do not think that will be possible."

Kallik, at her side, had been following Darya's thoughts. Drilling, or somehow splitting the wall into layers, would not give the information they needed.

That was just as well; Darya had an instinctive reluctance to damage any element of an Artifact. "Any ideas?"

"None, I am ashamed to say. But subtle and nondestructive methods will be needed."

Darya nodded. It was infuriating, but little by little she was being forced to conclude that Quintus Bloom was her master when it came to practical research. He had examined the walls before which she and Kallik floated, and understood their three-dimensional nature. He had somehow "unpacked" that information to create a set of two-dimensional pictures, without in any way damaging the wall. But how had he done it?

The answer came to Darya as she again moved her head, first to the left and then to the right, and watched the lines move relative to each other because of parallax. She suddenly knew a method—and it was irritatingly simple. Any practical surveyor would have seen it at once. It needed an imaging system and a good deal of computer power, but their suits could provide that.

"Kallik, we have to take pictures." She paused and thought for a moment. Two images would fix position in a plane, three in space. "From at least three different positions. Let's make it more than that, and build in some redundancy. Then we'll need a rectification program."

"I can certainly construct such a program. And I will also include a parameter that allows for the refractive index of the wall's material." Kallik responded without a pause—it confirmed Darya's opinion; the Hymenopt was *quick*. She understood exactly what Darya was proposing. "The program will perform a resection and provide point positions in three-dimensional space. The primary computer output will consist of the depth below the surface of every point on every line. However, that is perhaps not what you would like to see."

"No. I'd like the output as a set of two-dimensional images. Each different image should correspond to a prescribed depth below the wall surface. Label each one of them"—recognition of Quintus Bloom's accomplishment and priority was no more than his due—"as a *glyph*."

✧   ✧   ✧

Kallik was quick and able as a programmer. In this case, though, she was not nearly quick enough to suit Darya.

Once the digital images had been recorded and registered to each other, Darya's role disappeared. She roamed the chamber impatiently, knowing that the worst thing she could do was to interrupt the Hymenopt while she was working. The temptation to kibitz was enormous.

For lack of anything better to do, Darya made stereo sets of digital images of the other five walls of the chamber, then wandered down toward the place where the hexagonal pyramid terminated. There was no sign of wear inside this Artifact, none of the pitting and crumbling and scarring that told of a three million year history. Score another one for Quintus Bloom. Labyrinth must be *new*, the only known new Artifact in the whole Spiral Arm.

At the very end, the shape of the room changed to a narrow wedge. Darya placed her gloved hand in as far as it would go. She tried to estimate the angle, and decided it was about ten degrees. That was consistent with the notion of thirty-seven interiors terminating in the sharp point of Labyrinth. If this formed, as Bloom had suggested, the very end of the Artifact, then where her hand was resting should be only inches away from the other interiors—and only a few feet away from open space. If J'merlia's search for a safe way out was unsuccessful, maybe they could smash through the wall to freedom.

Where *was* J'merlia?

He had been away nearly four hours. Another few minutes and he would be past his deadline.

"With respect." Kallik's voice came over Darya's suit communicator. "The results are now ready for final formatting. How would you like them to be presented?"

"Can you show them as a sequence on my suit display? The surface itself first, then images showing how the plane looks at different depths below the surface. Make one for every millimeter, going gradually deeper. And can you display a couple of images each second?"

"It can be done. Anything else?"

"One more thing. Reverse the polarity, so that *white* on the wall shows as *black* on the images."

Kallik said nothing, but the visor on Darya's suit darkened to become an output display device. An image formed. Darya was seeing just the top fraction of a millimeter of the wall's surface, with light and dark reversed. She caught her breath. It was a familiar sight: a blackness deeper than any night, and superimposed on it the white star pattern of the Spiral Arm.

And then it was suddenly not so familiar. "Freeze it there!"

The display sat unmoving on the visor. It was the Spiral Arm as seen from above the galactic plane, but not quite as it should have been. The familiar locator stars, the bright blue supergiants used by every species as markers, had been subtly moved in their relative positions.

"Are you sure you didn't change the look angle? The star positions are wrong."

"I did not make any change. With respect, may I offer a suggestion?"

"Sure. It looks wrong to you, too, doesn't it?"

"It does. It is not an accurate portrayal of the Spiral Arm *as it is today*. But I suggest that the scene may well be of the past or the future. Then the differences that we are seeing would be no more than the effects of stellar long-term movement. Thus."

The image held for a moment. There was a flicker, then successive image frames took their place on the display. Tiny changes became visible. The luminous locator stars of the Spiral Arm began to creep across the screen, all moving at different speeds. It seemed to Darya that the pattern became increasingly familiar, but without a reference set of current stellar positions she would not know when the display showed the Arm as it was today.

No wonder the chamber wall had been confusing, filled with sets of lines and smears. It was the image of a myriad of stars, their movements plotted over thousands or millions of years, and all added and portrayed together in one three-dimensional structure.

A bright point of green light suddenly appeared on the display, a new star where none had been before.

"What's that—"

Darya had the answer before she could complete the question, just as another glint of green appeared close to the first. Then another. The green must be showing stars where some species had reached a critical intelligence level—maybe achieved space flight. And those stars were never the blazing supergiants, which were far too young for intelligent life to have developed on the planets around them. That's why the green points seemed to spring into existence from nowhere.

They were increasing in number, spreading steadily outward from the original marker. Far off to the right, a point of orange suddenly flared into view.

"A new clade?" Kallik asked softly. "If so, then one would expect . . ."

And indeed, the first point of orange served as the nucleus for many more bright sparks, spreading out from it. The regions of orange and green spread, finally met, and began to overlap each other. The orange predominated. At the same time a third nucleus, this one showing as a single point of ruby-red, came into existence farther along the Arm.

The three colored regions grew, changed shape, and merged. The orange points spread most rapidly, consuming the green and red regions, but Darya was hardly watching. She was feeling a strong emotion—not triumph, but relief. It would have been terrible to go back home and admit that where Quintus Bloom had led, she had not even been able to follow.

She leaned her head on the soft back of the helmet and neck support, and closed her eyes.

"We did it, Kallik!"

The Hymenopt remained silent.

"We figured out the polyglyphs. Didn't we?"

"Perhaps so." Kallik did not sound satisfied. "With respect, Professor Lang, would you please look once more at your display."

Darya's helmet visor showed the Spiral Arm, positively ablaze with flecks of light. She frowned at it. All the bright sparks were orange, and the geometry of supergiant star positions looked right. The time shown had to be close to the present day.

"Is there more? Can you see what the future tableau looks like?"

"I can indeed." Kallik was polite as ever. "I chose to halt the display at this point intentionally. You will note that the stellar array appears close to what we perceive it to be today."

"Right. Why did you stop it?"

"Because the stellar colonization pattern that we see is totally at odds with what we know to be true, and with what Quintus Bloom reported that he found. This image indicates that almost every star is colonized by a *single clade*, the species represented by orange on the display."

"That's ridiculous. At the very least, there should be humans and Cecropians."

Ridiculous, but right. Darya struggled to interpret the pattern in terms of what she knew to be true. The numerically dominant species in the Spiral Arm were humans and Cecropians. Their colony worlds should appear in roughly equal numbers. But *everything* showed as gleaming orange.

Orange, orange, orange. Sometimes it seemed that the Builders were obsessed by orange, the color showed up so often in their creations. Was it a clue to the Builders themselves—eyes that saw in a different spectral region from human eyes, organs most sensitive at longer wavelengths?

If that were a clue, it was a singularly useless one. Who even knew if Builders had eyes? Perhaps they were like the Cecropians, seeing by echo-location. The one thing that humans knew for certain about the Builders was that they knew nothing for certain.

"Kallik, can you run the display *backwards*? I'd like to take a look at how each clade started out."

"I did so already, for my own information. With respect, I think that the frame most likely to interest us is this one."

An image popped into existence within Darya's helmet. It was one she had seen before, presumably representing the Arm as it had been some time in the past. Green and orange points of light were plentiful. Far off to one side glowed a single mote of baleful red.

Kallik highlighted it with a cursor on the image. "Here we have the first frame in which the third clade— the *human* clade, from the position of this point—has appeared. With respect, the green and orange lights do not, I feel sure, correspond to the clade colonization patterns."

"Then what are they?"

"That, I cannot say." Kallik did not raise her voice, but Darya heard a rare discomfort in it. "But let us go backward again, to the time when orange showed only at a single location in the Spiral Arm." The display changed, to show a scene with one solitary point of orange light. The blinking cursor moved under Kallik's control to stand beside it on the display.

"Here is the origin of our mystery clade. And here"—

the cursor hardly moved—"here is a world that we already know all too well. It is Genizee, the home world of the Zardalu. If this display represented reality, we would conclude that the Spiral Arm is now completely colonized—by *Zardalu alone*."

✦ Chapter Seventeen

Hans Rebka had spent a lot of time studying Paradox. He knew the history of the Artifact's discovery, and all about the effects of its interior on incident radiation (little) and intruding sapient species (disastrous). So far as the Spiral Arm was concerned, Rebka qualified as a Paradox expert.

Whereas . . .

He hung in space staring back toward the inaccessible outside, then ahead to the ominous-looking central region, and was filled with a sobering thought: he really knew next to nothing about the structure, nature, or origin of Paradox.

There had certainly been changes—nothing in Paradox's history spoke of irreversible movement within it, or of an isolated torus at the center. But changes how, when, and why?

Another couple of attempts showed that any attempt to move toward the outer surface was a waste of fuel and energy. He turned off his suit's thrust. That was when he realized that the situation was worse than he had thought. In principle he should be hovering at a fixed location within Paradox. In practice he was drifting, slowly but steadily, toward the center. He could move tangentially without any problem, but always there was a small radial component carrying him farther inward.

His next action was instinctive, the result of twenty

years of hard experience. He did not think about it or try to explain it, although E.C. Tally, had he been present, could have done so in his own terms. When a computing problem of exceptional size and urgency was encountered, all subsidiary computation should be halted. Peripheral activities must go into complete stand-by mode, in favor of work on the single central problem.

Of course, Tally regarded humans as very handicapped by virtue of inefficient design. A major part of human central nervous activity went into simple maintenance work, so that total power-down of peripherals or unwanted memory banks was not feasible.

But given those built-in limitations, Hans Rebka came pretty close to E.C. Tally's ideal. Rebka did not give a thought to Tally, or his own situation, or to anything that might be happening outside Paradox. He did not waste time with more experiments in tangential movement, or futile back-up attempts, or even in speculation as to the reason for his forward motion. Every scrap of his attention focused on the fat donut-disk twenty kilometers ahead of him. Unless something changed, he would be arriving there in an hour or so. Better be ready.

The outside of the donut was studded with dark markings, possible openings. They indicated that the disk was slowly rotating. At first they seemed no more than tiny pock marks, but as Hans came closer he could see a shape to each of them. They were like scores of little black diamonds, irregularly spaced around the disk, the long diagonal of each parallel to the disk's main axis. What had appeared from a distance to be a central hole right through the disk, making it into a plump torus, now was of more ambiguous nature. There was certainly a darkness at the center, but the black was touched with cloudiness and a hint of structure that did not match Rebka's concept of empty space.

He stared until his vision blurred. What could give that impression, of simultaneous presence and absence? Nothing in his experience.

No matter. Unless something changed, he would soon be able to find out by direct experience. His inward progress had not slowed. If anything, he was moving faster. Maybe ten more minutes to the center.

Now his ability to move tangentially *was* important—because he suddenly had a choice. Not much of one, in normal terms, but he could aim for one of the diamond-shaped openings on the side of the disk, or else head for the black swirl at the center.

Which?

Assume that his inability to move farther from the center continued. Then he could enter one of the diamonds, and if that proved useless he might still be able to go on and see what lay in the darkness at the disk's center. Explore the black region first, and there would be no later chance to visit the diamonds. *Maximize your number of options.* Decision made.

The disk was rotating, but very slowly. Rendezvous should present no problem. He could count half a dozen different diamonds along the edge, each looking as good as any other. Rebka picked one at random and used his suit thrustor to match angular velocity with it. Then it was only a matter of watching and waiting, making sure that no anomalous increase in his own radial speed threw him off target.

The opening was bigger than it had seemed from a distance, maybe twenty meters on the diamond's long axis and fifteen on the short. Rebka aimed right for the middle, wondering in the final seconds if he was about to be dissociated to individual atoms, squeezed to a pinpoint of nuclear density matter, or spun a hundred thousand lightyears out of the Spiral Arm to intergalactic space.

He felt a slight resistance as he entered the opening,

as though he was passing through a thin film of sticky material. Then he was inside, tensed and quiveringly ready for whatever life-preserving action might be necessary. A sharp note within his helmet told him to glance at the monitors. He observed that the temperature outside his suit had gone instantly from the bleak frigidity of interstellar space to that of a pleasant spring morning on Sentinel Gate.

What else had changed?

Speculation ahead of time would have been a waste of effort, so before entering the diamond he had not allowed himself the indulgence of wondering what he might find inside. In spite of that, he must have carried somewhere in the back of his head a list of things he definitely did *not* expect to encounter when he went through the opening. Otherwise, there would have been no reason for his astonishment at what he saw when he emerged into the interior.

He was in a room like a misshapen cube. One dimension was the full width of the disk, with curved ceiling and floor that followed the shape of the torus. On either side the plane walls stretched away, to make a chamber at least forty meters across. Every square inch of those walls was occupied by cabinets, nozzles, troughs, gas supply lines, faucets, and hoses. Thousand after thousand of them, in all shapes and sizes.

Rebka moved to the far wall of the chamber, closest to the center of Paradox. It was rock-solid, seamless, and resonated a deep boom under a blow from his fist. No way out through that.

He went to inspect the wall on his right. The first units he came to were apparently a line of gas dispensers. There were no dials, indicators or instructions, but it was hard to mistake the turncocks for anything else. Rebka cautiously cracked one open. He waited for his suit's sensors to sample what came out, then turned the gas stream off at once. Fluorine! Poisonous, highly reactive, and no knowing how much of it the unit would supply. Maybe enough to fill the whole chamber, assuming the membrane at the entrance was able to hold an atmosphere.

Hans moved along the line, trying each dispenser. Chlorine, helium, nitrogen, neon, hydrogen, methane, carbon dioxide, ammonia. Oxygen. He might starve here or die of thirst, but he was not going to asphyxiate. He could recharge the air supply of his suit, matching it to any preferred proportion of gases. In fact— he eyed the line of units, stretching away in both directions—it would not be surprising if some dispensers offered mixtures of gases. Certainly he saw far more dispensers than were needed to offer the gaseous elements and their simplest compounds.

It was tempting to test that idea. Instead, he turned his attention to smaller units farther along the wall. These provided liquids instead of gases. His suit was able to identify only the simplest as he permitted small samples of each to touch the sensors. Methyl alcohol, acetone, ethyl alcohol, benzene, ether, toluene, carbon tetrachloride.

Water.

He paused for a long time when that sample was identified. *Drink me*. Except that in this case he almost certainly could, and with no ill-effects. His suit pronounced the water pure and potable.

Far more purposefully, he headed for the cabinets and nozzles. It was no particular surprise to find that he could travel freely in that direction, even though it took him away from the center of Paradox. Something had restricted his movement before, but apparently it now had him where it wanted him. It was also no surprise to find that the things that looked like supply cabinets and feeding nozzles were exactly that. The variety of foods dispensed was bewildering, and most of it was certainly not to human tastes. But that was natural. Somewhere along these walls he could probably find a food supply suitable for any species in the Spiral Arm. It was just a matter of seeking out the ones designed for humans.

Rebka didn't bother. He had suit supplies for several days. He hovered in position close to the wall and banged on it with a gloved fist. Solid, although without the resonant feeling of the inner wall.

Time to start thinking again, and of more than mere survival. The "old" Paradox had permitted explorers to enter or leave, but wiped their minds clear of all memories before they left. The "new" Paradox did not affect the mind, since Rebka certainly felt normal, but it steered anyone entering to the central region. Where, unless something changed, they would stay.

And do what?

The ways of the Builders were a mystery, even to specialists like Darya Lang and Quintus Bloom. But who could accept the idea of carefully herding a man to the middle of an Artifact, providing all the physical necessities of life, and then leaving him alone until he died? That was not merely not logical, it was *anti*-logical.

Assume that the Builders, even if they recognized a different set of physical laws, followed the same laws of logic. Assume that the events within Paradox had been designed using those laws of logic. Then what was happening now? More important, what would happen next?

Curiously enough, Hans could think of one possibility.

Paradox was millions of years old, but it had not always been like this. A year ago, or half a year ago, or sometime recently, it had changed dramatically. Now it captured anyone who entered, and brought them to the central region. But not to die. The chamber walls showed that any creature of even modest intelligence could survive here for a very long time.

And then?

One of two things. The prisoner would remain here, until something else happened. A disquieting thought, given the huge time scales over which the Builders had operated. Or the prisoner, suit recharged, would be free to leave this chamber, and perhaps fulfill some other function within Paradox.

The second possibility meant that Hans might be able to exit the room that he was in. He wandered slowly along the supply lines, dumping used air and wastes from his suit into disposal hoses, and taking on air, food, reaction mass, and water. When his suit was charged to its maximum level, he headed for the diamond of the entrance. He could see, far off, the shimmering outer barrier of Paradox. A tiny step, in terms of normal space distances. A long, long way, if the restraining field still operated outside this room.

No point in waiting. Hans launched himself toward the opening. He went sailing outward, feeling for a second the tug of the membrane at the entrance. Then he was through, outside and floating free.

Except that he wasn't. He felt no force on him, but after a few seconds he glanced back to the surface of the torus and knew that he was not moving outward. Instead, he was slowly, very slowly, beginning the slide back in toward the waiting diamond.

Cross that one off. Rebka took a last yearning look at the outside before he dropped back into the interior. He saw the glowing surface of Paradox—the shimmering rainbow background—the stars beyond; and outlined there, like a black silhouette, a suited figure.

A suit designed for occupancy by humans. A suit that was diving at enormous speed in toward the center.

A suit that surely didn't—did it?—hold a half-witted, numbskull, embodied computer known as E.C. Tally.

"Hey!" Rebka was shouting and waving, as he slid slowly back down into the depths of the torus. "Tally, is that you? This way. Slow down! I said, *this way*, you idiot!"

The suit communicator was not working—could not be working. Certainly the approaching figure showed no sign of seeing or hearing anything. It went zooming in, on maximum thrust, toward an opening farther around the disk. While Rebka was still screaming and waving and sinking slowly into the diamond entrance, the newcomer vanished from view.

Ten seconds later, Rebka was back inside. E.C. Tally, in terms of physical distance, might be no more than a hundred meters away. In terms of meeting, or even communicating, he could as well have been in another galaxy. And Hans Rebka was face to face with his first alternative: he himself would remain, stuck in this one chamber, until something else happened.

Or?

Or he must somehow find his own way out.

Rebka had been in difficult situations before. To get out of them, you had to think at the extreme limit of your abilities. To make such thinking possible, you began with a few simple rules.

He ate some of the new food. Tolerable. Drank a little water. Perfectly acceptable.

And now the hard part. Relax. Impossible! No. Hard, but you can do it.

Rebka dimmed his suit visor. He turned his mind inward, and listened to the beat of his own pulse. Three minutes later he was asleep.

E.C. Tally had strangely mixed feelings about his body. On the one hand, he absolutely needed it, otherwise his embodied brain could neither communicate nor move. On the other hand, he recognized that the body itself was an sadly frail vessel. The essential E.C. Tally, contained within the matrix of his computer brain, could function in an acceleration of a thousand gravities, a field which would squash his human form into a shallow pool of mashed bones and liquids. He could handle temperatures of a couple of thousand degrees, enough to leave behind only a few teeth from his surrounding body.

And this was, of course, his *second* body. The second one would never be quite the same. He could not admit it to anyone, but he had felt far more committed to the preservation of his first embodiment. He would treat this one well, of course, and maintain it in working order if he possibly could, but if and when it failed . . .

Which it might well be about to do. The durability of his brain had left him too insensitive to his body's danger. E.C. Tally, in his zeal to help, had entered Paradox at maximum thrust and concentrated his attention on an unsuccessful attempt to locate Hans Rebka. He had not considered the problem of deceleration, until the central disk was increasing rapidly on his display. By that time it was too late to do much. He quickly set his suit thrust for maximum reverse, but the inward force field was working against it, delaying his slowdown.

He reviewed options.

Option 1. He could head for the open center of the disk, brave the swirling dark in the middle, and hope that the force that prevented anything from leaving Paradox would slow him down gradually as soon as he was beyond the central point. He did not have high hopes of that. More likely, the field would stop his motion firmly and finally in a few millimeters. That could be enough to destroy even his hardened brain.

Not promising.

Option 2. He could aim instead for one of the diamond-shaped openings in the wall of the disk. What lay within was anybody's guess, but he judged that Hans Rebka was more likely to have headed there than for the central region.

Option 3. There was no Option Three.

Tally simulated a human sigh, made up his mind, and angled for the nearest opening in the disk. He shot inside, feeling a sharp tug from the membrane at the entrance, and at once became aware of a difference. His suit's thrustor—at last—was working as it was supposed to work. He slowed down rapidly, and smashed into the inner wall with no more than a bruising collision.

His pseudo-pain circuits cut in, but all they offered was a stern warning to take good care of his valuable body. Tally ignored that, and turned to look around for Hans Rebka.

And there he was! No more than twenty meters away in a big, curving chamber more stuffed with furnishings and equipment than any room that Tally had ever seen.

He turned toward Rebka. In fractions of a millisecond, he became aware of several strange facts.

First, Hans Rebka was no longer wearing a suit of any kind. Second, there were three of him, all female. And third, not one of the three was Hans Rebka.

The three women did not seem at all surprised by his arrival.

"Two months," the shortest one growled, as soon as Tally was out of his suit. She was black-haired, big-muscled—a female version of Louis Nenda. Tally guessed that she hailed from a high-gravity planet. "Nearly two damn months since we arrived here."

"And twenty-one days since I came in to rescue them." The second speaker, hawk-nosed and sharp-cheekboned, pulled a face at E.C. "Hell of a rescue, eh?"

"Not your fault," the dark-haired woman said gruffly. "We were all fooled. Thought we'd cracked Paradox, all ready to go out big heroes." She waved her hand at the pair of tiny exploration vessels hovering near the entrance to the chamber. "None of us had any idea that the damn thing was *changing*, so we might not be able to get out. Same for you, I guess."

"Oh, no." Tally had at their urging removed his suit. The chamber was filled with breathable air and felt a little on the chilly side of pleasant. Gravity was low but not uncomfortably so. The women had somehow pulled fixtures from the walls, and were using them as furniture. The result was odd-looking, but formed a comfortable enough living area.

"We knew," he went on. "Hans Rebka and I, we knew Paradox had changed."

The three woman exchanged glances. "A right pair of Ditrons you two must be," said the woman with the prominent cheekbones. "If you *knew* it had changed, why did you come in?"

"We thought it would be safe."

The looks this time were a lot less veiled. "Actually," Tally went on, "I did not enter because I thought it was safe. I knew it was not. I came in to rescue Hans Rebka."

"That's different." The short, dark-haired woman shook her head. "Well, we sure know how that works. What happened to your buddy?"

"I have so far been unable to locate him."

"Maybe we can work together." The third woman, tall, blond, and skinny, waved a hand to Tally, inviting him to sit at a table constructed from two food cabinets laid on their side. "I don't normally think much of men, but this is a case where we need all the help we can get."

"Ah." E.C. Tally sat down carefully at the table, and lifted one forefinger. "In order to avoid a crucial misunderstanding, I should make one point perfectly clear. I am not a man. And now, to begin at the beginning—"

"Not a man?" The blond woman leaned across the table and gave Tally a careful head-to-toe inspection. "Not a *man*. You sure could have fooled me."

"I am not a woman, either."

The woman flopped down on the seat opposite Tally. "And I thought we were in trouble before. All right, we'll do it your way. Begin at the beginning, like you said, and take your time. We've got lots—and it sounds like we'll need all of it."

✦ Chapter Eighteen

Another half day, and still no sign of J'merlia. Darya was worried. Kallik clearly was not. The little Hymenopt was systematically making three-dimensional reconstructions of the other five walls of the hexagonal chamber, using her new computer program on the images that Darya had made earlier.

She did not ask for help. Darya did not offer any. Each had her own obsessions.

Darya kept running the first picture sequence, over and over. All data on stellar velocities was back on board the *Myosotis*, and without that information she lacked an absolute means of measuring time. But the general pattern of the sequence was clear. Somewhere, far in the past and far from the worlds of the Fourth Alliance, an unidentified species had achieved intelligence and space flight. The spreading green points of light showed the stars that the clade had reached. Later, probably thousands of years later, another clade had escaped their home world and set off to explore and colonize. The second clade, judging from the location of the orange points of light, was the Zardalu.

They had spread also, speedily, aggressively. Finally they met and began to swallow up the worlds of the green clade.

So far, so good. Not much was known about the

Zardalu expansion, but there was nothing in the display at variance with recorded history.

But now came a third clade, shown on the display in deep ruby-red. This one, according to its point of origin, represented humanity. It started out from the home world of Sol, and began a tentative spread outward. It never stood a chance. The expanding tide of Zardalu-orange caught and swallowed the first scattering of red points. It swept past Sol and on through the Spiral Arm, swamping everything else. Finally every green and red light was replaced by a point of orange flame.

That was the situation when the supergiant reference stars seemed to be in their present-day positions. Darya halted the progression of images. According to what she was seeing, the Spiral Arm was supposed to be, *today*, what it clearly was not: a region totally under Zardalu domination.

Darya stared and pondered. This was a picture of the Spiral Arm as it would have been had the Great Rising against the Zardalu never occurred. If the Zardalu outward drive had continued unchecked, every habitable planet of the Spiral Arm would have eventually come under the dominion of the land-cephalopods. The worlds of humans were gone, destroyed or confiscated. Humanity was enslaved or exterminated, together with all other species operating in space.

And the future?

There were more frames in the image sequence. Darya ran it onward. The stellar positions began to change again, to an unfamiliar pattern. Time advanced, by many thousands of years. But the pattern of color never altered. Every star remained a steady orange. Zardalu, and Zardalu alone, ruled. At last the orange points of light began to vanish, snuffing out one by one. The Spiral Arm became empty. It remained devoid of intelligent life, all the way to the final frame of the sequence.

Darya turned off the display in her helmet. She did not switch her visor to outside viewing. It was better to stare into blackness, and disappear into a maze of thought.

Here was not one mystery, but two.

First, how had Quintus Bloom been able to show on Sentinel Gate a *realistic* display of the Spiral Arm's colonization—past, present, and future? He did not show the false pattern of Zardalu domination. Darya could not believe that he had *invented* that display. He had found it somewhere within Labyrinth, in this inner chamber, or more likely in some other of the thirty-seven.

Second, what was the significance of this display of Spiral Arm evolution, so clearly contrary to reality? The Builders were an enigma, but Darya could see no possible reason for them portraying on the walls of Labyrinth a *fictitious* history of the Arm.

Now to those mysteries, add a third:

What was the nature of beings for whom the natural way to view a series of two-dimensional images was to stack them on top of another, in three dimensions?

Darya's mind felt clear and clean, her body far away. Her suit was unobtrusive, quietly monitoring her condition and making automatic adjustments for heat, humidity, and air supply. She might have been back in her study in Sentinel Gate, staring at the wall and not seeing it, oblivious to sights and sounds outside the open window. At last a faint voice began whispering its message to her inner ear: *Invert the process. Solve the third mystery, and its solution will answer the other two questions.*

Darya cast her thoughts back over the years, to gather and sieve all the theories she had ever read, heard, or thought, about the Builders.

Old theories . . .

. . . they vanished over three million years ago,

ascending to a higher plane of existence. The Artifacts are mere random debris, the trash left behind by a race of super-beings.

. . . they became old, as any organism must grow old. Knowing that their end was near, and that others would come after them, they left the Artifacts as gifts to their successors.

. . . they left over three million years ago, but one day they intend to return. The Builder Constructs are no more than their caretakers, preserving Artifacts on behalf of their once and future masters.

. . . the Builders are still here, in the Spiral Arm. They control the Artifacts, but they have no desire to interact with other species.

And new theories . . .

. . . according to Quintus Bloom: The Builders are not part of the past. They are from the *future*, and they placed their Artifacts in the Spiral Arm to affect and direct the course of that future. When key events reveal that the future is on the right course, the Artifacts will change. Soon after that, the Artifacts will return to the future from which they came. Those key events have occurred. That time of change is here *now*.

. . . according to Darya Lang: An idea sprang into existence, full-formed in her mind as though it had always been there. The Builders are *not* time travelers from the future. They lived in the past, and perhaps they live in the present. We cannot perceive them, and communication between them and us is difficult, perhaps impossible. But they are aware of us. Perhaps they also have sympathy for us, and for the other clades—because they are able to *see the future*, see it as clearly as humans see a scene with their eyes, or Cecropians with their echo-location.

They lived in the past . . . a race able to see the future . . .

Except that at any moment of time there could be no single, defined future. There were only *potential* futures, possible directions of development. Present actions decided which of those potentials would realize itself as *the* future, one among an infinite number of alternatives. So what did it mean, to say that the Builders were able to see the future? Was it more than a refined ability to perform extrapolation?

Put the question into more familiar terms: What did it tell you about the structure and nature of Darya Lang, that she was able to *see*? What physical properties of her eyes made her able to look close at a nearby flower (as the Builders were able to see tomorrow, in time), and then far off to a distant landscape (as the Builders could see a thousand years hence)?

Darya's trance was complete. She sat at the brink of revelation, its message tantalizingly beyond her grasp. She saw in her mind the blurred, milky wall of the chamber, with its clear (but cryptic) three-dimensional message. Humans and Hymenopts could not grasp that message all at once, in its entirety. They needed to have it broken down into single frames, to see it a thin slice at a time.

But perhaps the Builders had no such need. . . .

Darya sensed the first faint ghost of a different kind of being, one so alien in nature that humans, Cecropians, Hymenopts, and Lo'tfians—even Zardalu—were all close cousins.

If she were right, every one of her questions would be answered. The *logical* pieces were there. All she needed was confirmation—which meant more data.

She turned her visor to external viewing. "Kallik!"

She started, as the Hymenopt popped up right in front of her. Kallik had been waiting, eight legs tucked neatly beneath the round furry body.

"I am here. I did not wish to disturb your thoughts."

"They were disturbing enough by themselves. Did you process the other five walls?"

"Long since. Like the first one, they exist now as sequences of images."

"Can I see them?"

"Assuredly. I have reviewed one of them already. But with respect"—Kallik sounded apologetic—"I fear that it is not what you are hoping to see."

"You mean it's not a set of images of Spiral Arm clade evolution, the way that the first one was?"

"No. I mean that it is just such a set. It shows a representation of the Spiral Arm. However, it suffers the same problem as the one which we previously examined. By which I mean, it does not resemble what Quintus Bloom reported, and it is also quite inconsistent with what we know to be the true history of Arm colonization."

They were deep within Labyrinth, with no idea how, when, or if they would ever escape. Darya decided that she must be crazy. There was no other way to explain the sense of satisfaction—of *delight*—that filled her at Kallik's words. She could not justify her conviction that she was going to achieve her life's ambition. But she felt sure of it. Before she died, however soon that might be, she was going to fathom the nature of the Builders. She was already more than halfway there.

Darya laughed. "Kallik, what you have is *exactly* what I'm hoping to see. As soon as you are ready, I want to take a look at every one of those sequences."

Any male Lo'tfian who has been removed from the home world of Lo'tfi and its breeding warrens is already insane. If a Lo'tfian slave and interpreter is also deprived of his Cecropian dominatrix, he becomes doubly mad. J'merlia, operating far from home and without orders from Atvar H'sial, had been crazy for some time.

Added to that, he now faced an impossible problem: Darya Lang had ordered him to look for a way out of Labyrinth. He had to obey that command. But it forced him to exercise freedom of choice, and to make decisions for himself.

A direct command to leave the others—and one that obliged him, for as long as he was absent, to operate without commands!

J'merlia was a mightily distressed Lo'tfian as he started out from the innermost chamber of Labyrinth. And, before he had gone very far, he was an extremely confused one.

In the short time since they had entered, Labyrinth had changed. The way back from the inner room should have led through a short tunnel into the chamber that teemed with the whirling black vortices. Vortices there certainly were, but only two of them, floating sedately against opposite walls. Neither one moved. Return through the chamber was trivially easy, as J'merlia quickly demonstrated.

The next one ought to have been as bad, with its fierce sleet of orange particles opposing any returning traveler. But when he got there, the storm had almost ended. The handful of little flecks of orange that hit his suit bounced harmlessly off and drifted on their way.

Logically, J'merlia should have been pleased; in fact, he became more worried. Even the walls of the third chamber did not look the same. They had dark windows in them, beyond which other rooms were faintly visible. There was also a translucency to the walls themselves, as though they were preparing to dissolve into grey vapor and blow away.

J'merlia went on. And then, just when he was wondering what unpleasant surprise he might find in the next room, he emerged from the connecting tunnel and saw a very familiar sight. Right ahead was the

Myosotis, floating in the great helical tube, just as they had left it.

The remaining chambers had not *changed*; they had vanished. Six chambers had collapsed into four. A dangerous escape had become a trivially easy one, and J'merlia's task was apparently completed. He was free to turn around, go back, and tell Darya Lang that they could leave Labyrinth any time they felt like it.

Except for a small detail. One form of insanity bears the name, *curiosity*. J'merlia floated up toward the ship to make sure that it was intact, and found that not far ahead was one of those strange dark apertures in the wall of the tube.

He moved closer until he could see through it, into another chamber. There was a suited figure there, moving slowly away from him. J'merlia stared, counted suit appendages, and made his helmet resonate with a hundred-thousand cycle whistle of relief. Eight legs. Thin, pipe-stem body. Narrow head. A suit identical to his. It was J'merlia himself, and what he had taken for an opening in the wall was no more than a mirror.

Except that—curiosity seized him again. He was moving *toward* the opening, and the suited figure was moving *away* from it. He was staring at the *back* of the thin body.

J'merlia kept moving forward, slowly and cautiously, until he was within the opening. The figure he was following moved, too, floating toward a window on the opposite side of the chamber. J'merlia went on through to the second chamber. His double went ahead also, apparently into a third room.

J'merlia paused. So did his quarry. He back-tracked toward the opening into his original chamber. The figure ahead of him reversed and did the same.

The mystery was solved. He was pursuing himself. Somehow this region of Labyrinth must include a mirror, but a *three-dimensional* mirror, one that exhibited an exact copy of the chamber in which he was moving.

Like any sensible being, J'merlia preferred to have someone else doing his thinking for him and making his decisions. All the same, he had plenty of intelligence of his own. Wandering the Arm with Atvar H'sial had also given him much experience of what technology can do. He had never heard of a three-dimensional mirror like this, but there was no great magic to it. He could think of three or four different ways that such a mirror-room might be built.

He was at the aperture, that comforting notion still in his head, when the angular figure in front of him turned its body, stared off to the left, and began to move rapidly in that direction. It was heading toward the central chamber of Labyrinth.

Now *there* was something new. The anomaly brought to J'merlia a new awareness, that he was playing a game in which he did not know the rules. He turned also, to head back to the middle of Labyrinth.

Again he halted in amazement. The bulk of the *Myosotis* should have been hanging right in front of him. There was absolutely no sign of it—no sign of anything in the whole chamber.

J'merlia realized, too late, that he had done something horribly stupid. What made it worse, he had been warned. Quintus Bloom had pointed out that an explorer could "cross over" into another one of the thirty-seven interiors of Labyrinth, but there was a built-in asymmetry. When you went back through the same window, it might be to a new interior region, different from the original point of departure.

Which new interior?

J'merlia remembered the strange cross-connection charts plotted out by Quintus Bloom, and how Darya Lang had puzzled over them. Neither Bloom nor Lang had been able to specify a rule. If they could not do it, what chance for a mere Lo'tfian?

That was a question J'merlia could answer: No chance at all. He was lost and alone in the multiply-connected, strangely changing interior of Labyrinth, without a ship, without a map, without a dominatrix, without companions. Worst of all, he would be forced to disobey a direct order. He had been told to return to Darya Lang and Kallik after just a few hours.

J'merlia had only one hope. If he kept hopping through the connecting windows, no matter how much the interiors might keep changing, nor how many jumps he might have to make, he had an infallible way of knowing when he reached the one he wanted. For although the interior of one chamber might look much like another, only one of them could contain the *Myosotis*.

No more useless thought. Time for action. J'merlia headed for the first window between the chambers. No *Myosotis*. And the next. Still no ship.

He kept track of the number of chambers as he went. The first eight were empty. The ninth was worse than empty. It contained a dozen black husks, dusty sheets of ribbed black leathery material thickened along their center line. J'merlia went close and saw wizened faces, fangs, and sunken cheeks. *Chirops*. A not-quite intelligent species, the favored flying pets of the Scribes. What were they doing here, so far from their own region of the Arm? And where were their masters?

The shriveled faces were mute. The bat-wings were brittle, vacuum dried, their ages impossible to determine.

J'merlia left that room at top speed. The twenty-first chamber had him screeching and whistling a greeting. Two suited figures came drifting toward him. Not until he was close enough to peer into the visors did he realize that they too were victims of Labyrinth. Humans, without a doubt. Empty eye sockets stared out at him, and naked teeth grinned as at some secret joke. They had died hard. J'merlia examined their suits, and found the oxygen had been bled down to the last cubic centimeter. The suit design was primitive, abandoned by humans a thousand years ago. They had floated here—or somewhere—for a long, long time.

But not as long as the contents of the thirtieth chamber. Seven creatures floated within it. Their shapes suggested giant marine forms, with swollen heads bigger than J'merlia's body. The glass of their visors had degraded to become completely opaque. How many millennia did that take? J'merlia carefully cracked open one helmet and peered inside at the contents. He was familiar with the form of every intelligent species in the Spiral Arm. The spiky, five-eyed head before him was unrelated to any of them.

J'merlia pondered the contradiction as he went on: Labyrinth, according to Quintus Bloom and Darya Lang, was a *new* Artifact. It had not been here one year ago, much less a thousand. Yet it contained antique relics of bygone ages.

When the chamber count passed thirty-seven he wondered if he might be missing some other vital piece of information. He kept going, because he had no other real option. At last the rooms began to seem different, the windows between them becoming steadily larger. There was still no sign of the ship.

A male Lo'tfian, according to the Cecropian dominatrices, had no imagination. It did not occur to J'merlia that he too might move from chamber to chamber until he died. After the eighth hour, however, he began to wonder what was happening. He had been through more than three hundred chambers. His procedure in each was the same, developed for maximum speed and efficiency. He made a sideways entry, so that he could glance with one eye down toward the center of Labyrinth, seeking his ship; at the same time he noted the location of the window that would lead him to the next chamber. Dead aliens, of recognizable or unrecognizable form, were no longer enough to halt his progress.

He was so far into a routine procedure that he was almost too late to catch the change when it finally came.

The ship! He could see it. But he was already zooming on toward the window for the next chamber—and if he went through there was no knowing how long it would be before he again found this one.

J'merlia hit maximum suit deceleration, and realized in the same moment that it would not be enough. He would sail right out through the aperture on the far side of the chamber before he could stop.

There was only one thing to do. He switched the direction of the thrust, to propel himself laterally rather than slowing his forward speed. The sideways jump was enough for him to miss the opening and smash straight into the chamber wall.

A Lo'tfian was tough, and so was J'merlia's suit, but the impact tested them both to the limit. He bounced back, two of his thin hindlimbs broken and his torso bruised all along its length. His suit hissed suddenly with lost air, until the smart sensors detected and repaired the small stress rupture at a joint.

J'merlia turned end over end, too breathless to produce a desired whistle of triumph. He had succeeded! He was many hours late, but at last he was back in the same chamber with the *Myosotis*.

He righted himself with some difficulty—one of his attitude controllers was also broken—and found that his thrustors still operated. He drove toward the waiting ship.

That was when he was glad he had produced no triumphant whistle.

It was a ship, certainly. Unfortunately, equally certainly, it was not the *Myosotis*.

✦ Chapter Nineteen

By the end of the second day trapped in the hiatus, three of the four travelers on board the *Gravitas* were not at all happy.

The absence of ship's lights was an inconvenience, but it was the lack of power that would eventually be fatal. Louis Nenda had already done the calculation. The air circulators were not working, but natural thermal currents plus the ship's own steady rotation would provide enough convection to keep a breathable atmosphere in the ship. However, after about six days the lack of air generators and purifiers would become noticeable. Carbon dioxide levels would be perceptibly higher. Five days after that, the humans on board would become lethargic. Four days more, and they would die of asphyxiation. Atvar H'sial would survive maybe a week longer.

Quintus Bloom was not afraid of dying. He had a different set of worries. He was convinced that Darya Lang was far ahead of him, scooping discoveries that should rightfully be his. A dozen times a day, he pestered Nenda to *do* something, to get them moving. Twice he had hinted that Louis had arranged all this on purpose, deliberately slowing their progress as part of a conspiracy to aid Darya Lang. Nenda wondered if somehow Atvar H'sial had managed to communicate her own paranoia about Darya to Quintus Bloom.

The blind Cecropian was in some ways the least affected by their plunge into the hiatus. She could tolerate carbon dioxide levels that would kill a human, and her own seeing, by echo-location, was independent of the interior lights on the *Gravitas*. But the loss of power meant that communication with Glenna Omar through the terminals was no longer possible. Atvar H'sial had again become completely dependent on Louis Nenda and his pheromonal augment for anything that she wished to say to or hear from the others.

The exception in all this was Glenna. Logically she, pampered by a life on Sentinel Gate where every wish and whim could be satisfied, should have been most affected by the drastic change to life aboard the *Gravitas*. But it was a continuing oddity of the Spiral Arm that the inhabitants of the richest worlds played the most at primitivism. So about once a year, the fortunate dwellers on Sentinel Gate would deliberately head out to their forests and prairies, equipped with sleeping bags, primitive fire-lighting equipment, barbaric cooking tools, and raw food. After a few days in the wilds (but never more than three or four), they would return to abundant hot water, robotchef meals, and insect-free lodging. There they assured each other that they could "rough it" as well as anyone, if ever they had to.

Glenna had played that game a dozen times. She was trying a new variation of it now. The luxurious passenger suites of the *Gravitas* were equipped for cozy and candle-lit evenings, where dining tête-à-tête was often a tasteful prelude to romance. Glenna went from suite to suite and took the candles from every one. She used them all to provide subdued lighting for her own suite only, and invited the others to attend the soirée. Atvar H'sial's invitation had to be transmitted through Louis Nenda. The Cecropian received it, and replied with a pungent pheromonal combination that Nenda had never before encountered. It felt like the

Cecropian equivalent of a Bronx cheer. He took it to be a rejection of the offer.

Louis Nenda arrived first, wondering if it was a mistake to show up at all. He did so only from a long-held principle: that he needed to know everything that happened on any ship he was piloting. And if he were absent, who knew what Quintus Bloom and Glenna Omar might plot between them?

Nenda stared gloomily at fifteen candles, arranged strategically around the boudoir. The oxygen used in their burning would shave several hours off their lives, but in the circumstances that didn't seem like a big deal.

Glenna obviously thought this was going to be one swell party. She had her blond hair piled high on her head, to show off to advantage her long, graceful neck. The clinging cotton dress that she was wearing, cut hair-raisingly low at front and back and with a split from ankle to hip, showed a good deal more than that. She pirouetted in front of Louis, revealing what appeared to be several yards of leg.

"How do I look?"

"Astonishing." That at least was the truth. He heard with relief the sound of footsteps behind him. Quintus Bloom appeared, wearing an expression that Louis could interpret exactly. *I'd rather be some place else, but there is nowhere else. And anyway, I can't afford to miss something important.*

Wafting in with Quintus Bloom came something else. A hint of pheromones, too weak to be caught by anyone but Nenda.

"At. I know you're there, waiting outside. I thought you decided not to come."

"I have no desire to attend what I suspect to be designed as a human multiple mating ritual. However, I wish to know what is said about other matters. Like you, I am opposed to any conspiracy of which I am not a part."

"What I thought we would do is this." Glenna, unaware of the exchange of pheromonal messages going on around her, was playing hostess. "Since we're here, in such *primitive* conditions, I thought we ought to tell stories to each other the way our ancestors did, thousands and thousands of years ago, sitting terrified around their camp fires."

Dead silence. Louis didn't know about Quintus Bloom, but he had sat terrified around a camp fire a lot more recently than that.

Oblivious to the lack of response, Glenna went on. "Sit down, both of you." She waited until the two men were in place on the divan, half a yard of space between them. "Now, I'll be the judge, and the one of you who tells the best story will get a *special* prize."

She squeezed into the space between them and placed a warm hand on each man's thigh. "Since we're almost in the dark, we ought to talk about scary or romantic things. Who wants to start?"

Blank silence.

"Did I not warn you?" The message drifted into the room with an overtone of satisfied humor. "If I may offer advice, Louis, I say: Beware the special prize."

Nenda glared at the door. As if things weren't bad enough, Atvar H'sial was laughing at him.

"Oh, come on, Louis!" Glenna squeezed his leg to bring his attention back to her. "Don't play hard to get. I know from what Atvar H'sial told me that the two of you actually met *live* Zardalu, when everybody else thinks they've been extinct for eleven thousand years. That must have been frightening, even for you. What are they like?"

"You don't want to know."

"Oh yes I do!" She slid her hand along the inside of his thigh, and added breathily, "You know, I find this sort of thing just makes me *tingle*."

That, and everything else. Nenda admitted defeat.

Glenna was as single-minded in her own way as Quintus Bloom.

"We said we wouldn't talk about the Zardalu, At, but I'm going to. Maybe a touch of them will slow her down."

Nenda turned to Glenna. "You wouldn't find a Zardalu exciting if you ran into one. You won't, of course, because they live only on Genizee, here inside the Anfract. But they're enough to make anybody jump. For starters, they're huge. Seven meters long when they're at full stretch. The head of a full-grown Zardalu is as wide across as this divan. They are land-cephalopods, so they stand or slither along on half a dozen thick tentacles. Fast, too, faster than a human can run. The tentacles are pale blue, strong enough to snap a steel cable. The head is a deep, deep blue, as blue as midnight on Pelican's Wake. A Zardalu has two big blue eyes, each one as wide across as my outstretched hand. And under that is a big beak."

Glenna's hand had stopped moving on his thigh. Nenda glanced across to see her expression. She was staring at him with wide, avid eyes, mopping it up. So much for his theory that she would be frightened. The surprise came from the other side of her. Quintus Bloom was also staring at Nenda. He looked puzzled. His hand reached out to form a shape in the half-light.

"A beak with a hook on it," he said slowly. "Like this." His hand turned to curve downward. "Hard and blue, and big enough to seize and crack a human skull. And under it a long slit of a mouth, vertical. The head runs straight down to the torso, same width, but separating the two is a thing like a necklace of round openings, each one a bit bigger than your fist and running all around the body."

"Breeding pouches." Nenda stared across at Quintus Bloom, his annoyance with Glenna forgotten. "How the devil do you know all this? Have you been reading reports about the Zardalu that we took to Miranda?"

"Not a word. I'd never in my whole life read or heard any physical description of one."

"You mean you've actually *seen* a live Zardalu?"

"No. A dead one. But I had no idea what it was." Quintus Bloom's eyes were wider than Glenna's. "When I was exploring Labyrinth, I came across an interior chamber with five creatures in it. Each one had started out huge, but when I got to them they were shrunken and wizened. They had been vacuum-dried, and they looked like enormous desiccated plant bulbs. I didn't even realize they were animals, until I came close and saw those eyes. That's when I decided to hydrate one— pump warm water into each cell, until it came back to its original size and shape and color." His gaze moved to Nenda. "Seven meters long, head and torso of midnight blue. Eyes with lids, like human eyes but a hundred times the size. Tentacles pale blue, ending in fine, ropy tips. Right?"

"Exactly right. That's a Zardalu to the life. Or to the death." Nenda caught a quick question from Atvar H'sial, who was following the conversation as best she could from Nenda's scraps of pheromonal translation. He passed it on to Bloom. "What's your interest in the Zardalu?"

"I care nothing for Zardalu—living or dead." Bloom's beaky nose jutted superciliously at Nenda. "My interest is in the Builders, and only the Builders. But you have raised a question that I cannot answer."

"*An unforgivable sin.*" But Louis sent that remark only to Atvar H'sial, along with his translation of Bloom's arrogant comments.

"You assert that the Zardalu live only in one place," Bloom went on. "On Genizee. What makes you think that your statement is true?"

"I don't *think* it, I know it. At the time of the Great Rising, the Zardalu were just about exterminated from the Spiral Arm. Only fourteen specimens were saved, and they were held in stasis until a year ago. They went straight from there to Genizee. I know all that, because I was there when it happened. The only one not on Genizee today is a baby, brought back to Miranda by Darya Lang and her party. Why does that get you so upset?"

Bloom glared back at Nenda. He seemed quite unaware of the flicker of the ship's lighting, or the tentative moan of electrical systems returning to power. "Because, you ignoramus, of the implication of your words. Think, if you are at all capable of such a thing, of these facts. First, every Zardalu except one infant is to be found on Genizee, and only on Genizee. Second, I discovered the dried corpses of *five* Zardalu floating in an interior chamber of Labyrinth. Third, Labyrinth is a *new* Artifact. It did not exist eleven thousand years ago, or a century ago, or even a year ago. Put those items together, and what do you get?"

One thing you got, very clearly, was that Glenna's romantic evening was not going quite according to plan. But that was unlikely to be what Quintus Bloom had in mind for a conclusion. In any case, Nenda's thoughts were moving to other things. He knew what the flicker of light meant: the *Gravitas* was emerging from the hiatus.

"What *do* you get?" His question was automatic. Whatever it was, it was less important than regaining control of the ship.

But now, after all that build-up, Quintus Bloom had apparently decided not to supply an answer. He rose to his feet, brushed off Glenna's hold on his sleeve, and strode out of the boudoir.

"Use your tiny mind, and work it out for yourself," he snapped over his shoulder.

"Quintus!" Glenna wailed, and ran out after him.

"Most interesting." The drift of Cecropian pheromones came in more strongly. "I assume that you made the same deduction as Quintus Bloom?"

Nenda did not move, not even when the pheromonal question was followed a moment later by the stately entry of Atvar H'sial's crouched form. The Cecropian's yellow horns turned to face him, then Atvar H'sial shook her head and just as slowly departed.

There was no need for words. She knew that Louis had made no deductions at all. He couldn't see what there was to be deduced.

He remained brooding on the divan. Live Zardalu only on Genizee. Dead Zardalu discovered on Labyrinth. Labyrinth a new Artifact. So what? All that might say something to Bloom and to Atvar H'sial, but it didn't offer one syllable to Louis. Anyway, with power restored the ship needed his attention. So maybe he had his own question: When there were so many smart-asses around, why was he only one who knew how to fly the *Gravitas*?

He was still asking himself that when Glenna returned. Her chin was up and her manner jaunty as she circled the room blowing out the candles.

It didn't fool Louis for a second. She was upset as hell. He felt unexpected sympathy. "Hey, take it easy. You'll get another shot at him. You know Quintus. He's too wrapped up in his godawful Builders to take notice of anything."

"It's not just that." Glenna sat down next to Nenda. She lifted the hem of her dress and dabbed at her eyes with it. "I was hoping we'd have a really pleasant evening, something to make us feel good. It started so nicely. And then it all fell apart."

"Yeah. It just wasn't your night. But don't let it get to you. I've had nights like that. Lots of 'em." Louis patted her warm shoulder consolingly, and flinched when she leaned back into the crook of his arm.

Glenna snuggled closer. "You know, you were the only one who even *tried* to tell a scary story, the way I wanted." She reached up to put her hand over his. "I think that was really nice of you."

Louis edged away along the divan. "Yeah, well. I dunno. Not that nice. We were stuck in the hiatus, we all had nothing to do. Might as well tell stories to each other. Now we're clear, though, and I have to get busy. Gotta start figurin' out how we make it through the Anfract."

He was pulling his hand free of hers when all the lights went out again. There was a dying groan from the ship's electrical system.

"Damnation!" Louis sat through a long, waiting silence. Finally he heard a giggle from the darkness next to him.

"Back in the hiatus! Oh, dear. Not my night, Louis. And not your night either, it seems." Glenna lowered her voice, changing its sad overtone to a more intimate one. "But you know, this could be *our* night."

It didn't need an augment to pick up the message of *her* pheromones. He heard a rustle of fabric falling to the floor. A warm bare foot rubbed along his calf, and he stood up abruptly.

"You're not *leaving*, are you?" She had felt him jerk to his feet.

Leaving. He certainly was.

Wasn't he?

Nenda made a sudden decision. The hell with it. In the middle of a hiatus, what else should he be doing?

"No, I'm not leaving. Definitely not leaving. I just thought it might be nice to make sure the door was closed. Tight."

Atvar H'sial was an alien without the slightest interest in human sex. All the same, Louis didn't want snide pheromonal comments as an accompaniment to what he was going to do. He didn't have much faith in his skills as a lover in the best of circumstances.

It was a side benefit of staying, he decided, as he groped his way back toward Glenna. She was a very experienced woman. She would be used to sophistication. One night together, and chances were she would never come near him again.

✦ Chapter Twenty

The Builders had made things to last. The exteriors of their free-space structures might bear minor pitting from meteor collisions, and the interiors always collected dust, but the overall Artifact remained as hard and indestructible as the day they were fabricated.

Hans Rebka knew all this. So it was absolutely astonishing to tug open a wall cabinet as he was examining the chamber's food supplies, and feel the cabinet itself move a fraction as he did so.

He braced himself, gripped the sides of the cabinet, and pulled harder. The whole cupboard ripped away from the wall. Hans went rolling away across the chamber, holding on to a cabinet without a back. Not only that—when he returned to look at the wall, he found that part of it contained a big crack.

That started a whole new train of thought. He could not travel *outward*, toward the surface of Paradox, because of the one-way field. He could not travel directly toward the center, because the inner wall of the chamber was smooth and impenetrable. But maybe he could break through a side wall, and so progress around the circumference of the torus. Even if he found no way to escape, at least he could look for E.C. Tally.

Smashing through walls might be possible, but it surely wouldn't be easy. Before he began, Rebka went once more to the opening through which he had originally entered. A brief experiment told him that the one-way field was still in operation. Also, unless his suit's instruments were not working correctly inside Paradox, the outer boundary of the Artifact had moved much closer. For as long as humans had known of its existence, the radius of the Artifact had always been measured as twenty-five kilometers; now the boundary was no more than five kilometers away. Paradox was shrinking. More evidence of profound Artifact changes.

Rebka returned to the inside of the chamber. At the back of his mind he couldn't help wondering how small Paradox might become—and what would happen to the central region and its contents if the outer boundary came all the way in to meet it.

Well, he'd either discover a way to escape, or find out the hard way the consequence of the final shrinkage. Meanwhile . . .

He went across to the wall and wondered about the best way to attack it. His suit tools contained fine needle drills, but nothing intended for major demolition work. One way might be to pull a massive cabinet free, and propel it with his suit thrustors at the weak point of the wall.

Rebka went across to the damaged section from which he had pulled the food cabinet and thumped it experimentally with his gloved fist. He was hoping to gauge its thickness. He was astonished when his fist went right in, the whole surface crumbling away to flakes under the blow.

He moved in close and examined the material. The wall was about four inches thick, but impossibly weak, so soft and friable that he could powder it between his thumb and forefinger. It had not been like this when he first entered the room. Just to be sure, he went back to the exact place where he had hit the side wall earlier. One punch now, and his hand went completely through.

He leaned forward and found that he could see into the next chamber. From a superficial inspection, it was no different from the one he was in. There was no sign of E.C. Tally.

Hans Rebka enlarged the hole until it was big enough for him to pass through it, and headed for the far side of the new room. This time he did not pause to select any special place. He drove feet-first at a space on the wall between two gas supply lines, and was not much surprised when it disintegrated under the impact.

He went through and stared around him. Another empty chamber. At this rate he was going to destroy every room in the torus looking for E.C. Tally. Unless the whole place crumbled to dust by itself, with no help from him. It seemed to be heading that way, weaker by the minute.

One more time. Rebka launched himself forward. Again the wall collapsed beneath his impact. Again he drove on through, and found himself in still another room.

But here, at last, was something different. Radically different. He emerged amid a cloud of powder and wall chips, and ran straight into something solid.

He heard a startled grunt, and felt a sudden grip on his arms. Right in front of his face and staring into his visor was a thin, fair-haired woman. She was not wearing a suit, and her face and hair were covered with chalky dust.

She sneezed violently, then glared at the wall behind him in disbelief. "I've bashed that wall a hundred times in the past week, and never made even a dent in it. Who are you, some kind of superman?"

"No, indeed." A familiar voice spoke from behind Hans. "This is not a superman. Permit me to perform the introductions. This is Captain Hans Rebka, from the planet Teufel, and lately of Sentinel Gate."

The three women were sisters, from the salt world of Darby's Lick. Rebka had never been there, but he knew its reputation and location, in the No-man's-zone of dwarf stars between the Phemus Circle and the Fourth Alliance.

"So you're from Teufel," said Maddy Treel, the oldest, shortest, and darkest of the three. "We've all heard of that. *'What sins must a man commit, in how many past lives, to be born on Teufel?'*"

Those words threw Hans back at once to his childhood. He was on water duty again, a terrified seven-year-old, waiting for the night predators to retreat to their caves; five and a half more minutes, and the *Remouleur*, the dreaded Grinder, would arrive. Margin of error on water duty: seven seconds. If you are caught outside when the *Remouleur* dawn wind hits, you are dead . . .

Maddy Treel went on, jerking Hans back to the present: "But I believe Darby's Lick can give Teufel a run for its money, at least if you're a woman. I guess I don't have to tell you why we came to Paradox. We wanted a better choice than the ones women have, salt-mining or breeding. When they asked for volunteers, we jumped at it."

They were sitting around the makeshift table. Hans Rebka had been persuaded to remove his suit, but only after he had been back to the hole through which he had entered and examined it. He remained mystified. There was an atmosphere on the other side, but it was pure helium. Something was able to keep gases contained within each chamber, even when the wall between them had been partly destroyed. Impossible. But no more impossible than the diamond-shaped entrance to the chamber, which somehow did the same thing. Air within did not escape to the vacuum outside.

"I've done a bit of salt-mining," Rebka replied absently to Maddy. "On Teufel. It wasn't all that bad."

She snorted. "*Uranium* salts? The good news was, after a year of that no one talked about breeding any more."

"I never had to handle uranium. Maybe Teufel's not so bad after all. I couldn't wait to get out, though. Nobody wanted to breed me, but a lot of things wanted to kill me. Anywhere else looked better. But I don't know if I was right." Rebka gestured around him. "The future here doesn't seem too promising. Did you know that Paradox is shrinking?"

"You mean, the whole thing's getting smaller?" Lissie Treel, the tall skinny blonde who had caught Rebka on his arrival, stared at him in disbelief. "How can it? It's always been the same size."

"Sure. And it's always had a Lotus field inside, and it never stopped anything from getting out before." Rebka shrugged. "Paradox is changing—fast. Don't take my word for it. Go have a look for yourself."

Lissie frowned at him, stood up, and headed across to the diamond-shaped entrance. She was back a few seconds later.

"Shrinking, and changing color. No reds any more. What's going on?"

"It is not Paradox alone." E.C. Tally was sitting cozily between Maddy and Katerina Treel. After he had explained to them who and what he was, the three sisters had assured him that they liked him a lot better than if he had been a *real* man. "According to a new theory back on Sentinel Gate, changes should be occurring in all the Artifacts. It is evidence that the purpose of the Builders has at last been accomplished."

"So what *is* the purpose?" Katerina asked.

E.C. Tally stared at her unhappily and blinked his bright blue eyes. It occurred to him that this was one feature of the Quintus Bloom theory which remained less than wholly satisfactory. "I have no idea."

"It may not make much difference to us what the purpose is." Lissie came back to sit across from Hans Rebka. "If Paradox keeps shrinking, we'll get squished out of existence. Since it's down to two kilometers, instead of twenty-five—"

"Two!" It was Rebka's turn to jump up. "It can't be. It was close to five less than an hour ago."

"Don't take my word, to quote you. Go see for yourself."

Everyone rushed for the entrance, with E.C. Tally bringing up the rear.

Maddy Treel got there first. "It sure as hell *looks* closer." She stood there, head tilted to one side. "Hard to judge distance when you can't be sure the fringes haven't changed."

"They have not." This, unlike the purpose of the Builders, was something about which E.C. Tally could be completely confident. "My eyes are unusually sensitive, enough to see reference stars within the rainbow fringes. Refraction has been changing their apparent positions. The outer boundary of Paradox is indeed shrinking. Assuming that the present rate of change is maintained, it will achieve zero radius in"— he paused, not for calculation but for effect. He had remained completely still to make his observations, and in the first millisecond after that he had performed all necessary data reduction —"in twelve minutes and seventeen seconds."

"Achieve zero radius?" asked Katerina.

"That's E.C.'s polite way of describing what Lissie called getting squished out of existence." Rebka was on the point of asking Tally if the embodied robot was sure, until he realized that would be a total waste of what little time they had left. E.C. was always sure of everything. "We've got twelve minutes."

"To do what?" Maddy had adjusted to the facts as rapidly as Hans Rebka.

"Four things. First, we all put suits on again. Second, we board your ships." Rebka scanned the two small exploration vessels. "Just one of them, for preference. Might as well stick together. Which one has the stronger hull?"

"Katerina's our engineering expert. Katie?"

"Not much in it. The *Misanthrope's* a little bigger, and a little faster. My guess is it's also a bit tougher." Katerina turned to Rebka. "What are you planning on doing? Neither hull was built for strength."

"That will be our third action." Rebka was already half into his suit, but he paused and gestured at the inner wall of the chamber. "Once we're aboard we send the ship full tilt at that."

"No way. We'll be flattened!"

"I don't think so. Paradox isn't just *shrinking*—it's falling apart around us."

"But suppose we do break through the inner wall?" Katerina was in her suit, and leading the way to one of the scout ships. "We'll be just as badly off. We'll still be inside Paradox."

"Did you notice what was at the center of this torus of chambers when you came in?"

"You mean that black whirlpool thing?" They were inside the *Misanthrope*, and Lissie was already at the controls. She turned to Rebka. "We saw it all right—and we stayed well clear of it. We may be wild, but we're not crazy. I hope your head's not going the way I think it is."

"Unless one of you has a better idea. I say we have no real choice. If we don't go there under our own power, we'll finish by being squeezed into it. I'd rather enter in this ship, with some say in how we fly."

"He *is* crazy." Katerina turned to Maddy for support. "Just like a man. All they want to do is order us around."

"I am not a man," E.C. Tally said quietly. "Yet I am obliged to concur with Captain Rebka. I also saw the center of Paradox as I entered, and I suspect that he and I have information unavailable to you. That vortex strongly resembles the entry point for a Builder transportation system."

Lissie abandoned the controls and spun around in the pilot's chair. The other two sisters moved alongside her.

"Go on," Maddy said softly. "You can't stop there. How would you know what a Builder transportation system looks like? So far as I know, there isn't any such thing."

"You pretend you know what you're doing," added Katerina, "but you did no better than us at steering clear of Paradox. Worse, because you told us you *knew* things were changing here."

"We maybe weren't too smart." Rebka glanced at his suit's clock, then toward the chamber entrance. "Four more minutes. The outer boundary of Paradox is squeezing in. Look, you've either got to believe us, or it will be too late to do anything. E.C. and I know what a Builder transport system looks like because we've been through a few of them."

Lissie and Katerina turned to look at Maddy. She glanced at the shattered wall of the room, where Rebka had broken in. "What does a Builder transport system do to you? And where does it take you?"

"You survive, if you're lucky, but you don't enjoy it. As for where it takes you, I don't know how to answer that." Rebka shrugged. "Wherever it wants to."

"No comfort there. I should have known better." Maddy Treel tapped Lissie on the shoulder. "Make room, sis. Soon as we're ready to fly, hand over to him."

"You mean, let that *man* fly our ship!"

"I know how you feel. Have to do it, we're up Drool Creek without a paddle." Maddy glared at Rebka. "With who-knows-what for a guide. I hope you're as good at getting out of trouble as you are at getting into it."

"Strap in, everybody." Rebka didn't respond to Maddy, but he moved to the copilot's chair next to Lissie. "It may not make a damn bit of difference, but I'll feel better if we're all secured. Ready?"

Lissie nodded. "Any time. Just don't ruin my ship!"

"Not a chance." Rebka threw the local drive to maximum and aimed directly for the chamber's inner boundary.

With forty meters in which to accelerate, the *Misanthrope* took over a second to reach the wall. Plenty of time to visualize a ship with its drive set to maximum hitting an impenetrable barrier. The drive thrust would continue until everything ahead of the engines was a centimeter-thin compressed layer.

Rebka saw the final meters of approach as a blur on the forward screen. He felt a shock, but it was no more than a moderate jolt that threw him forward against his restraining belt. Then the screen was a chaos of flying fragments.

He cut the power in the same instant. The ship could not reverse its thrust, there was not time for that. They were flying on, with the same velocity as at impact. How fast? Forty meters, accelerating at five standard gravities. E.C. Tally would know, but there was no time to ask.

Too fast, at any rate. Much too fast for finesse. Rebka could see again; the cloud created by the disintegrating wall was dispersing. The ink-black swirl of the vortex was almost dead ahead. He had time for a lateral thrust, enough to aim them a little more squarely at the center. That was his last act before the vortex took control.

The sensation was familiar. It would never be pleasant. Hans felt the vortex close in on him, a tightening spiral that shrank until it felt no wider than his body. The torsion began, forces that racked his body in sections, twisting from head to neck to chest to hips to legs to feet. It increased steadily, shearing him until the pain was unbearable. Rebka had no breath left to scream. He squeezed his eyes shut. It was no comfort to imagine what Maddy, Katerina, and Lissie must be thinking about him at this moment.

It was impossible to say how long the pain lasted, but it ended abruptly. Rebka opened his eyes and stared around him, relieved to see that the ship and its contents were unaffected by the crippling forces that he had felt. Maddy and her sisters were bulging-eyed and gasping, but that was just psychological after-effects. The Builder transport systems, if they delivered you at all, did so leaving you physically intact and unharmed.

But delivered you *where*? It could be in the Anfract, or inside some other distant Builder Artifact, or even in Serenity, thirty thousand lightyears outside the plane of the galaxy.

Rebka peered at the screen in front of him. There was not much information to be gained from that. He was seeing a pattern of near-parallel lines like an optical illusion, a streaming glow of white on a dense black background.

"Tally?" The embodied computer was the best bet, with every major feature of the Spiral Arm stored away in his head. "Do you know where we are?"

"Unfortunately, I do not." E.C. Tally sounded very cheerful. Rebka recalled, with some envy, that pain in Tally's case offered warning signals without discomfort. "However, it is almost certain that we are no longer within Paradox."

"I can tell that much. What about the other Artifacts? Do any of them look like that, on the inside?" Rebka gestured at the screen.

"Not remotely like that. The pattern we are observing would be considered striking enough to have been reported, even if images of it were unobtainable. Might

I suggest that you record it on the imaging equipment of this ship?"

"Never mind the scenery." Maddy Treel had her breath back. "You can study that any time. What about the whosit out there? I want to know if it's dangerous."

Rebka and E.C. Tally turned. Maddy was staring at a different screen, one that showed a view to the rear of the *Misanthrope*. The pattern of lines was there too, no longer parallel but curving away and apparently slightly converging. But in front of those, much closer to the ship and rapidly approaching it, was something else. A black, spindly figure, its body twisted a little to one side.

Rebka stared in disbelief. He opened his mouth to speak, but E.C. Tally was well ahead of him. The embodied computer had done a rapid comparison of every feature of the dark figure, from number of legs to suit design to antennas and probable frequencies.

"If you will permit." He turned, reached across Lissie—still stunned to silence by the transition through the Builder vortex—and flipped four switches. "Our general communication channel is now open. This is E. Crimson Tally. Do you wish to come aboard?"

The speaker system of the *Misanthrope* clicked and whistled. "With respect, I would like that very much. I recently suffered a most unpleasant impact, and I wish to perform certain repairs."

"You can't let that thing onto our ship!" Maddy Treel grabbed E.C. Tally's right arm as he reached forward to activate the airlock. "You're crazy! That's an alien out there. I don't care if it is hurt—it could kill us all if it got inside."

"Oh, no." E.C. Tally leaned forward, and with his left hand pressed the lock control. "You do not have to worry. He is an alien, true enough, but he would never hurt anybody. You see, it is only J'merlia."

✦ Chapter Twenty-One

Experience makes everything easier. Darya had struggled hard to interpret the first series of images that she and Kallik had obtained from the wall of the hexagonal chamber. Now, as she examined the second series, she wondered what she had found so difficult.

Blue supergiant stars served as references, fixing the scale and overall geometry of the Spiral Arm. Their movement in space also made them into celestial clocks, measuring how far before or after the present a particular image was set. Without knowing stellar velocities, the time scale was relative rather than absolute, but it was enough to judge the progress in Spiral Arm colonization.

The second image set proved similar to the first, except that this time the orange markers of Zardalu control spread across the Arm, engulfed the worlds of the earlier green clade, and then suddenly vanished.

That matched Darya's understanding of history. Instead of going on to dominate the Spiral Arm, the Zardalu had themselves been annihilated in the Great Rising.

After a dozen images with no colonized worlds at all, a dull red spark appeared at Sol's location. The red markers spread, and were joined by the yellow of another clade. Darya noted the location. Cecropians. The two clades grew until their boundaries met. After that the boundary line remained steady, while both clades grew rapidly in other directions.

Darya nodded to herself. This was the past shown by Quintus Bloom. And presumably the future, also.

Darya waited. Suddenly yellow points of light began to surround the region of red ones. Finally, when englobement was complete, the yellow markers spread inward. Red points of light flickered out one by one, and yellow took their place. Finally yellow lights alone were visible through the Spiral Arm. Cecropians ruled the Spiral Arm. And then, far enough in the future that the supergiant reference stars had moved to noticeably different positions, there was a final change. The yellow lights began to blink out, one by one, until almost all were gone. For a long period the Spiral Arm showed just one yellow point, close to the original clade world of the Cecropians. Then it too winked out. The Arm had lost all evidence of intelligent life.

This was *not* the future displayed by Quintus Bloom—far from it. In this series of images, as in the last set that Kallik had displayed, the final sequence showed an end point for the Spiral Arm with no inhabited worlds.

Darya puzzled over the display for a long time, running and re-running the image sequences. They were false pasts and futures for the Spiral Arm. Could she be seeing an *entertainment*, a fictional presentation? The Builders were so remote, so enigmatic, it was difficult to accept them as having recreations of any kind. But maybe all thinking beings needed a break now and again.

Finally she nodded to Kallik to move to an image sequence drawn from a different wall.

The now-familiar first scenes came into view. Blue supergiant marker stars, no colonized worlds. The orange sparks of the Zardalu came, and at last went. Humans appeared in a lurid red, Cecropians in yellow.

They existed side by side, spreading outward for a long, long time, until a clade of glittering cyan appeared from close to the inner edge of the Spiral Arm.

Darya stared at the location, and could think of no species at all in that part of the Spiral Arm. Human exploration vessels had been there, but had found nothing. She glanced at the supergiant markers. The scene was far in the future.

The cyan clade worlds grew until they met humans. Cyan then at once began to disappear. Humans were taking over the worlds of the new clade, as glowing red swallowed up cyan. That went on until the new color had vanished completely. And then, as though a process had been started that could not be stopped, red began to consume yellow. The Cecropian worlds dwindled in number, not steadily but in sudden spasms of contraction. The clade shrank back toward the original home world of the Cecropians. A final spark of yellow gleamed there, until it was replaced at last by a gleam of red.

Humans, and humans alone, ruled the Spiral Arm. The millennia rolled on, the supergiant marker stars crept like tiny blue snails across the face of the galaxy. Finally, red points began to flicker out of existence. Not in a systematic pattern this time, but randomly, one by one. A handful, widely scattered across the Spiral Arm, hung on as dots of ruddy light. At last they began to vanish. Darya was finally staring at a Spiral Arm where again only the marker stars could be seen.

"Excuse me if I interrupt your thoughts, but do you wish to see the next sequence?" Kallik was standing by her side. Darya had no idea how long she had been waiting there.

She shook her head. Since her findings made no sense, additional data were more likely to confuse than to clarify.

Darya realized how tired she was. How long since

she had slept? How long since they had entered Labyrinth, how long since they arrived in this chamber? She couldn't even guess.

Still there was no sign of J'merlia. She and Kallik should have gone searching long since. The fascination of the polyglyphs had held her.

The worst of it was, she wouldn't be able to sleep now no matter how she tried. And it was not because of worry over J'merlia. Darya knew her own weaknesses. She might close her eyes, but the image sequences were going to keep running, running, running, visible to an inner eye that could not be closed. They would remain until something in her brain over which she had no control permitted them to vanish. Then she would rest.

"Kallik, do you mind if I talk to you?" Hymenopts, unlike mere humans, never seemed to become weary. "I'd like to share some thoughts, think out loud at you."

"I would be honored."

"Did you watch all three sequences with me?"

"Yes, indeed."

"But you didn't see Quintus Bloom's presentation, when he was on Sentinel Gate?"

"That was not my good fortune."

"Pity. Did you, by any chance, examine the recording of the presentation in Bloom's data files on the *Myosotis*?"

It occurred to Darya that for someone who had asked to share her thoughts, she was doing rather poorly. So far everything had been a question. But Kallik did not object.

"I examined the records on the *Myosotis*, and I found them fascinating."

"Good. So you saw what Bloom says he found in Labyrinth, and we've both seen what we found here."

"*Some* of what we found here. With respect, three image sequences remain to be displayed."

"That's all right. We'll get to them. We need to think,

frame a hypothesis, then use the other image sequences to test it."

"That is a procedure fully consistent with the scientific method."

"Let's try to keep it that way. First, Bloom's image sequence. It was consistent with our past, and what we know of the past of the other clades. It showed a future with all clades present, and it showed a Spiral Arm full of colonized worlds. Now for a question: Was that the *only* image sequence that Bloom found?"

"We lack the data to provide an answer." Kallik stared all around her with her rings of eyes. "However, we do know that Quintus Bloom came to a hexagonal chamber like this one, even if it was in a different interior."

"Which is very probable. But you mean, he must have wondered what was on the other five walls, wherever he was? I agree. He seems a thorough research worker. He must have examined all six walls. But now let's talk about what *we* found. Three different histories of Spiral Arm colonization. The past in two of them was plausible, but in every case the far future was different. Agreed?"

"Certainly. Different from each other, and also different from what Quintus Bloom reported."

"Good. Now I've got my own ideas, so I don't want to lead you on this. What do you see as the single biggest difference between what Bloom reported, and what we have been finding?"

Kallik's exoskeleton did not permit her to frown, but her perplexity showed in the delay before she responded. "With respect, I see two major differences."

That remark was not one that Darya had been expecting. "*Two* differences?"

"Yes indeed. First, we find that the Spiral Arm in the far future is *empty*. There are no populated and colonized worlds. Quintus Bloom found the opposite, an Arm where some clade occupied every world."

"That's the difference that hit me. So what's the other one?"

"The image sequence displayed by Quintus Bloom showed Builder Artifacts. The sequences that we have seen so far offer no evidence of such Artifacts. In fact, they show no sign whatsoever of the existence of the Builders, now or in the past. But this"—Kallik waved a jointed forelimb around her—"is certainly a Builder Artifact. It is proof that the Builders, whether or not they exist today, certainly existed at one time." Kallik stared unhappily at Darya. "With respect, Professor Lang. It appears to me that our very presence here, in an Artifact, *proves* that Quintus Bloom's claim must be correct. Only a Spiral Arm containing Artifacts can be the *real* Spiral Arm."

During her scientific career, Darya had developed immense respect for experimental data. One little fact was enough to destroy any theory ever constructed, no matter how beautiful and appealing it might seem.

Now she was facing one ugly and very big fact: Builder Artifacts appeared in Bloom's images, as Kallik had pointed out, but not in the ones that they had seen. There was no way of arguing around that, no way of dismissing it as irrelevant or unimportant.

The smart action at this point was also the simple one: accept that Quintus Bloom's images represented reality, while the new ones, whatever they might be, did not. With that full acceptance, Darya would at last be able to relax and get some sleep.

She might have to do that—but not quite yet. One of her ancestors must have passed along to her a good slug of stubbornness. She was almost ready to quit, but first she had to see the other three image sequences.

Kallik, at her direction, patiently prepared to run them. During the set-up period, Darya's tired brain took off on a new line of thought.

Labyrinth was a new Artifact. On that, she and Quintus Bloom agreed one hundred percent. Not only did it look new, with none of the long-deserted appearance of every other Artifact that Darya had ever encountered, it was also too close to the populated planet of Jerome's World to have escaped detection through thousands of years of exploration and observation.

There was more. Not only was Labyrinth new, it was not in any way hidden. Whoever built it, *intended* it to be found. Darya felt sure of that, although her thinking was now far indeed from the testable, provable world of hard evidence.

Don't stop yet. If Labyrinth were found, it would also be explored. The designers of Labyrinth expected that at some time, an intelligent being—human or alien—would reach this very chamber. Someone would stand here, as Darya was standing, and stare at the milky, streaky walls. They would puzzle over their meaning and significance. Once you accepted that such discovery and exploration were inevitable, then the idea that the sequences Darya and Kallik had seen so far were no more than Builder fantasies became ridiculous. The three sets of images—the Spiral Arm past, present, and future—were solid, important data, as real and meaningful as what Bloom had discovered. Whoever found the inner chamber of Labyrinth was supposed to deduce what it all meant.

And then do what?

That was the point where Darya's thinking stuck. She was supposed to stand just where she was, and conclude—what? It was like some sort of super-intelligence test, but one that she was failing.

She sighed, and came back to reality. Kallik had been ready long ago, patiently waiting.

"All right." Darya nodded. "Let's see what we've got in the other three."

At first it seemed nothing but more mystery and disappointment. The fourth sequence showed a very simple progression. The green clade, the one that Darya had never managed to identify, arose far away in the Spiral Arm. The green tide spread, sun after sun, until the Arm was ablaze with green. No other clade ever appeared. At a time not long after the present, the green points of light began to pop out of existence. Finally all were gone, and the Spiral Arm remained empty to the end of the display. No Zardalu, no humans, no Cecropians. And never a sign of the bright magenta that had marked the Builder Artifacts in Bloom's display.

Darya hardly had the heart to ask Kallik to continue. It felt like someone else who nodded, and said. "Let's try the next one."

The sequence began. And Darya moved suddenly, totally, into mental high gear. The display in her suit visor seemed to become twice as bright. *Artifacts!* Points of vivid magenta were scattered in among the supergiant reference stars.

And now the green clade was appearing, soon followed by the orange of the Zardalu. At last, here came the red of the human clade. Clades grew, met, intermingled, traded off regions among them. Finally the Spiral Arm was filled. It continued to be filled, thousand after endless thousands of stars. This was Quintus Bloom's display. The only difference was that during his presentation he had focused the attention of the audience on the spread of the human clade. The earlier spread and collapse of the Zardalu, and its subsequent re-appearance, had been deliberately ignored.

Why would Bloom have done such a thing?

Darya could answer that: he had ignored *what he could not explain*. At the time of his presentation he had no idea that the Zardalu were once more in the Spiral Arm, re-populating on their original clade-world of Genizee. Bloom wanted all his evidence to support his conclusions.

The sixth sequence started, but it no longer contained surprises. It was another "false history" of the Spiral Arm, where the Zardalu came and went; Cecropians and humans fought for star systems with the green clade, and finally conquered. Yellow then battled ruby-red, and finally won. The Spiral Arm filled with Cecropians; and, after a short period, began to empty. The yellow points of light blinked out. At last the Arm again showed no sign of intelligent occupation. At no time was there any evidence of Builder Artifacts.

Darya was sure that Bloom had reconstructed image sequences for all six walls. She had great respect for his intelligence and his thoroughness as an investigator. But having examined all of them, he had selected just one.

And who could blame him? Only one contained Builder Artifacts, which certainly in the real world were scattered through the Spiral Arm. It was reasonable to reject the other five, as nothing more than a strange invention for an unknown purpose.

Reasonable, but Darya could not do it. Her inner voice told her that the other five histories of the Spiral Arm were all equally relevant. Their existence, and the way in which the two-dimensional images had been stored in three dimensions, provided a message for any visitor to Labyrinth. Understand the histories and the images, and you would understand a lot about the Builders. Or—invert the process, as before—if you fathomed the nature of the Builders, then the existence of multiple histories and the reason that the scenes were stored in such odd fashion would be explained.

It was a crucial moment, one that needed all her

concentration. Instead, to her huge annoyance Darya found her thoughts drifting off. She could not rid her mind of Quintus Bloom's face, with its half-disguised red sores, and his confident and persuasive voice as he said to his audience, "If you answer that the Builders had that magical power to predict the far future, then you assign to them talents that strain my belief past bearing."

But it was not magical power. Not at all. It was a different physical nature, one which changed the definition of prediction. The idea came into her head again. A species able to *see* the future. Not *predict*, she thought dreamily, as Bloom would have it, but *see*.

The fact that she was falling asleep no longer upset her. She knew the way her mind worked. When it had a problem, sleep was impossible. She could not rest until the problem was solved.

So now . . .

Her thoughts as she faded into sleep carried a perverse comfort. She could stay awake no longer, therefore something deep inside her subconscious said that all necessary data were now in place. The problems of the Builders and of Labyrinth were solved.

Everything clarified to a pleasant simplicity. When she awoke, she would persuade her subconscious to behave honorably, and reveal to her its solution. Then they would find J'merlia, and return to the ship.

And then, at last, they could go home.

✦ Chapter Twenty-Two

Two days in the hiatus were disturbing, but not really dangerous. In a well-equipped ship all you had to do was sit tight, endure darkness and silence, and wait to emerge. Sometime. Somewhere.

The rest of the Anfract offered no such assurance. The difference between a hiatus and the Anfract main body was something that Louis Nenda did not define in words, but had he done so, "passive danger" and "active danger" would have served well enough to separate the two of them.

Active danger, unfortunately, was on the menu for today.

Two hours after they emerged from the final night-long hiatus, Louis was sitting pale, red-eyed, and exhausted at the controls of the *Gravitas*. He would much rather have been sleeping, but sleep had to wait. They were in more trouble. Entry into the Torvil Anfract was always a risky business, but the Anfract had once possessed at least a few constant features that an explorer could rely on.

Not any more. In the past there had been a consistent thirty-seven lobes. Now that number had decreased to eleven. The internal geometry of the place used to be fixed. It had recently changed—and was still changing. Boundaries between the lobes slid one way and another, shifting, merging, vanishing. The regions of macroscopic Planck scale had become unpredictable.

All of which told Nenda that his old flight plan could be thrown out of the airlock. He would have to fly the Anfract using a combination of experience and good luck. Judging from the past year, he was long on the first but rather short on the second.

He concentrated his attention on the feature directly ahead of the *Gravitas.* In a region of spacetime not noted for its welcome to approaching ships, the Maw was nobody's favorite. Explorers with a taste for metaphor described it as a hungry, merciless mouth, waiting deep within the Anfract to crush and swallow any ship that mistimed the passage through. Nenda, after his last night's experience, favored a rather different description, but he had no illusions about the danger they were in. The Maw showed ahead as a grim, black cavity in space. There was no point in getting Quintus Bloom or Glenna Omar agitated, but that total blackness meant something to Louis: every light cone pointed inward. The ship was already past the point of no return. They were moving at maximum subluminal speed, and they would go rushing into the Maw no matter what they did.

If they passed through successfully, on the other side they ought to find a dwarf star that burned with an odd, marigold light. Around that star orbited Genizee, the home world of the Zardalu. And around Genizee . . . Darya?

Louis wondered. It had all sounded supremely logical back on Sentinel Gate. Darya Lang had insisted that the Torvil Anfract was an Artifact, but no one had believed her. Her reputation was at stake. She would have come here, seeking proof. Bloom was sure of that, and Louis had been persuaded.

Now, he had his doubts. Darya, like Louis, knew only one way into the Anfract. The *Gravitas* was a lot faster than Darya's ship, the *Myosotis*. So why had the ship trackers on the *Gravitas* seen no sign of Darya and her ship? It was possible that she was still ahead of them, on the other side of the Maw. But it was just as possible that the Maw had swallowed her—as in a couple of minutes it might eat the *Gravitas*. The Maw filled half the sky ahead, wide and gaping and infinitely menacing.

Louis felt a gentle touch on his shoulder and jumped a foot.

"Jeets!" He turned his head. "I wish you wouldn't creep around like that. You might at least have told me you were coming."

"*My apologies.*" Atvar H'sial's pheromonal response lacked any shred of sincerity. No Cecropian ever felt apologetic about anything. "I did not wish to disturb you at what appeared to be a crucial moment."

"Disturb away. It won't make any difference what I do for the next two minutes. We're going through that Maw, like it or not. I can't stop us."

"Then this is a good time for discussion." Atvar H'sial settled down next to Louis. "With Genizee ahead, it is time to make our detailed plans. How do we take one adult Zardalu, and avoid taking a hundred—or being taken by them? I should point out that we would have had more privacy for this meeting earlier, within the hiatus. But you were unavailable."

"You might say that. And speakin' about what went on in the hiatus . . ." Louis had his eye on the circular perimeter of the Maw. A pale violet ring had formed there. It was growing *inward*, a closing iris, so that the black center of the Maw was steadily shrinking. They had to pass through that central tunnel. The violet region would disintegrate ship and crew. "I'll talk plans, but first I got a question for you. I know you've been chatting with Glenna Omar through that terminal hook-up you made. What did you tell her about Darya Lang?"

There was a pause in the flow of pheromones—too long, in Louis's opinion.

"About me and Darya Lang," he added.

"It is possible that I suggested your interest in Professor Lang might be excessive. What makes you ask?"

"Something Glenna said when we were in the hiatus."

"To you?"

"More to herself. She laughed, and she said, 'I'd like to see Darya Lang do that.'"

"But what was she doing at the time?"

"Oh, nothing special. Nothing you'd be interested in." Louis cursed himself for starting this topic of conversation. "Hold tight, At. We're almost there, but this is going to be a close thing."

The Maw filled the sky. The outer annulus had spread rapidly inward. It was more like an eye ahead of the ship now, a violet iris with at its center a tiny contracted pinpoint of black pupil. The *Gravitas* had to pass into—and through—that narrow central tunnel before the opening closed completely.

Nenda tried to judge dimensions. They ought to clear the opening all right. But how long was the tunnel? If it narrowed and tightened while you were inside it . . .

Louis ignored the symbolism—he was feeling sensitive this morning—and kept his eyes on the displays.

The *Gravitas* was inside, racing along a narrow cylinder of glowing violet. He was staring at the forward screen, where a pinprick of black still showed. The end of the tunnel. Approaching fast—and closing even faster.

The sky ahead turned black. They were almost through. There was a squeal and a dull *crump*, shivering through the whole ship. At the same moment, half the alarms on the bridge went off simultaneously. The lights failed, as though they had entered some new hiatus. After a split second the emergency power cut in, and Nenda could again see the control board.

He swore.

"Are we through?" Atvar H'sial had heard the curse, since her echo-location picked up all sounds. But she was not able to interpret it.

"Through—with half our ship." Nenda scanned the monitors, assessing the degree of damage. "No, a bit more than half. I guess we count as lucky. But the Maw trimmed off quite a piece of the stern." He began the inventory. "Lost all the aft navigation and communication antenna. Lost the fine-guidance motors. Lost the auxiliary air supply and water supply units. And the worst news: the Bose generators are gone. No more Bose transitions. From this point on, the *Gravitas* has to travel at crawlspeed."

"I see." There was no hint of alarm in the Cecropian's response, but she understood the implications. "Assuming that we are able to emerge successfully from the Anfract, how far is it to the nearest inhabited planet?"

"Couple of lightyears. Mebbe ten years travel time going subluminal."

"An unacceptable option."

"Not an option, though, 'less you got some ideas."

"Problems with the ship are not my province. They are yours. However, I perceive that this is perhaps not the best time to discuss the strategy of Zardalu capture." Atvar H'sial rose and made a stately departure from the bridge.

Nenda did not protest. Anyone who took a Cecropian as a business partner had to accept that race's contemptuous view of all other species. Louis admired outrageous gall in any creature, human or alien. In any case, he suddenly had a thousand things to do. Top priority was an inventory, first of everything that remained on the *Gravitas*, and then everything that had been lost to the Maw. This ship, like all but the smallest unit construction vessels, had been built with fail-soft design philosophy. Chop it in half, and each piece would still have some residual capability. It would be able to support life, and perhaps to fly. But the details of what was left were going to be crucial.

Mid-ship auxiliary engines would let them move. The *Gravitas* could make a sluggish planetary landing on anything that had less than a standard surface gravity, and achieve an even more lumbering take-off. Nenda could not advise anyone that they were coming, but he hadn't intended that anyway. The aft bulkheads would have locked automatically when the ship lost its stern. Nenda could not determine without direct inspection what might remain beyond them, but their doors were big enough to serve as an entry for a mature Zardalu.

So what had definitely been lost? Nenda studied the plan of the *Gravitas*.

The suits, for a start. Unless some happened to be stowed temporarily in the bows, he would be making no space-walks. Superluminal communication equipment was gone—no chance of sending a fast message of distress. Two of the three exit locks were on the lost section. One lock was left, unless you counted the hatches in the stern of the ship as possible improvised access points. What else? Much of the ship's computer equipment. And every cubic meter of cargo space.

Whatever they might find in the Anfract or on Genizee, not much of it could go back to Sentinel Gate aboard the *Gravitas*. A Zardalu, if they managed to snag one, would have to travel in the general passenger quarters along with the rest of them.

Nenda grinned to himself as he imagined Quintus Bloom's reaction to that. Bloom and Glenna Omar were safe enough, because they were in passenger quarters, up close to the bows of the ship. But the first sight of a live Zardalu ought to wipe that sneer off Bloom's face.

Louis was no less exhausted than ten minutes ago, but he was suddenly on top of the world. They were alive! They had come through the Maw in a closer scrape than anyone in recorded history. They still had a functioning ship. The problem of working them out of the Anfract and all the way back home was the sort of challenge—Atvar H'sial had been quite right—that Louis absolutely thrived on. And just ahead, no more than a few hours travel even at subluminal speeds, the forward screen showed a bright marigold disc.

They were heading for Genizee's sun. For Zardalu. And—just maybe—for Darya Lang.

The thought processes of a Cecropian can never be mapped precisely on to those of a human. Atvar H'sial, if pressed, would have explained that thought was conditioned by language. Human language was coarse, crude, one-dimensional, and incapable of subtle overtones compared with pheromonal speech. How could a poor human possibly be expected to express or to understand the nuances and shades of implication which were so natural to even an infant Cecropian?

The problem was nowhere more acute than in conversations with Glenna Omar.

The raw facts were not in dispute. During the hiatus Louis Nenda and Glenna Omar had spent many hours together, locked away in a single chamber. They had surely occupied themselves in the bizarre human mating ritual.

But had the ritual been *successful*?

Atvar H'sial struggled with the primitive human tongue, and tried to ask her that question. *Success* in this case had nothing to do with *procreation*, the production of another generation of humans. It was rather an outcome-defined success, wherein two results had to be achieved simultaneously. First, the obsession of Louis Nenda with the human female Darya Lang had to be broken. That was unlikely to occur in a single other mating. Second, therefore, as a prerequisite of the first the willingness of Glenna Omar to continue a close interaction with Louis Nenda had to be established. The interaction must continue until that first outcome was absolutely guaranteed.

Atvar H'sial could have expressed all that, including the subtle interaction between the first and second desired outcomes, in a single, short burst of pheromones. Instead she was obliged to structure her thoughts in cumbersome human sentences—and then, no less a problem, to interpret Glenna Omar's response. Once again, Atvar H'sial mourned the loss of her slave, J'merlia.

It did not help that much of the ship's computer storage, including the on-line dictionaries and thesaurus for human speech so painstakingly developed by Atvar H'sial, had been chewed up in the Maw. What was left as back-up was a mangled remnant, and she was not sure how to make use of it. To make matters worse, Glenna herself was languid, yawning, and apparently half asleep. When Atvar H'sial, laden with translation equipment, entered the boudoir, Glenna was consuming a great lump of sticky sweet confectionery. She was smiling to herself, a far-off dreamy smile of satisfaction. The passage through the Maw and the subsequent fate of the ship apparently worried her not at all.

Atvar H'sial unfurled her antennae in frustration as she sought to frame the first question.

YOU SPENT MANY HOURS IN YOUR QUARTERS WITH LOUIS NENDA, WHILE THE SHIP WAS TRAPPED IN THE HIATUS. CAN YOU DESCRIBE TO ME YOUR EXPERIENCE DURING THAT TIME?

Glenna had talked with the Cecropian a dozen times since the *Gravitas* left the region of Sentinel Gate. Repeated experience had not made Glenna feel fully comfortable. You had to face facts. Chatting about your sex life with what was, when you got right down to it, no more than a smart monster bug was never going to equate to drawing-room conversation.

"I'll talk about my *feelings*, if you like, so long as you don't want physical details. A lady has a right to privacy. You want me to describe what sort of time I had?" Glenna thought for a moment. "It was a total blast."

Not a promising beginning. *Blast* = explosion, discharge, detonation, fulmination.

WAS THERE AN EXPLOSION WHILE YOU WERE WITH LOUIS NENDA?

"*An* explosion! There were half a dozen of them—on both sides. I know that off-worlders are supposed to be something special, compared with the men on Sentinel Gate. But nobody ever told me to expect anyone like Louis." Glenna smiled, arched her back, and stretched tired arm and leg muscles. Her worries about privacy were disappearing. After all, the Cecropian was Louis's partner. She must already know what the man was like. A maniac. "It was awesome."

Awesome. The word was not even given; was it the same as *awful* = dreadful, terrifying, appalling?

"He was amazing," Glenna went on. "An absolute *animal*."

Animal = wild beast, brute, less than human, lower life form.

LOUIS NENDA WAS LIKE A WILD BEAST WITH YOU?

"He certainly was. Over and over. Want to see the tooth marks? I'd think we were all done, but then something would get him going again."

Going = leaving, departing, exiting.

And tooth marks. That needed no dictionary. Louis Nenda had attacked Glenna Omar, and departed.

As Atvar H'sial ought to depart. But it was not the Cecropian way to give up unless there was no other alternative. She needed Glenna Omar, to immunize Nenda from the Lang female. She dug in, ready for a long effort at persuasion.

YOUR EFFORTS ON MY BEHALF, NO MATTER HOW
FRUITLESS, ARE TO BE COMMENDED . . .

Louis Nenda, monitoring everything on the damaged
ship, was listening to Glenna and Atvar H'sial with six
different kinds of satisfaction. He could have given the
Cecropian the use of a decent dictionary, but why spoil
the fun? It would make no difference to the final result.
Atvar H'sial was persistent. She and Glenna would sort
out their misunderstanding eventually, provided they
kept talking.

As for Glenna's comments . . .

It was no surprise that Louis had had the time of
his life. It had left him drained and half-dead, of course,
but that was the way a fantasy ought to leave you. A
native Karelian like Louis Nenda might, in his dreams,
meet and take to bed a woman from one of the richest worlds of the Fourth Alliance, a beautiful woman
with long, supple limbs and skin so soft and creamy
that you felt it would bruise at a touch. In your dream
world the lady might even fake pleasure. But for her
ecstasy to be *genuine*, for her to say afterwards to a
third party that it had been wonderful—that went
beyond fantasy. It was so improbable, it must really
have happened.

Quintus Bloom's intrusion, coming when it did, made
Louis want to turn around and strangle him.

"I have been monitoring the damage reports." The
beaked nose came pushing over Nenda's left shoulder.
Bloom was staring at the status flags. "Are we in a
position to continue my mission?"

Nenda turned his head. No sign of fear or concern
was visible on Bloom's face. He was plenty tough, in
his own way. *My* mission, eh? They would see about
that.

"We can continue." Louis nodded to the screen. "See
that star? We'll soon be in orbit around Genizee."

"Excellent. Any sign of Darya Lang?"

Bloom was not so much tough, Louis decided, as protected from all outside worries by the strength of his own obsession.

"Not a hint. We beat her to it, or more likely she went someplace else."

"Either is satisfactory." Bloom considered for a moment. "The records I made during our entry to the Anfract remain intact, but I would prefer more tangible evidence to take back with us to Sentinel Gate. As one who knows this region well, do you have suggestions?"

No doubt in Bloom's mind that they would get back. Nature—and now Louis Nenda—looked after drunks, idiots, babies, and Quintus Bloom.

"Certainly." It was time to improvise. Louis had his own agenda. "The planet Genizee contained structures that could only have come from the Builders."A perfectly true statement, even if those structures had been fast disappearing when Nenda and Atvar H'sial made their hasty departure. "So a landing on Genizee might serve a double purpose. First, it will allow you to obtain the evidence you need. And second, I can take a good look at the external damage to the ship."

"Very well. Proceed." Bloom was already leaving.

"One other thing." Nenda's call halted him at the door. "Genizee is the home of the Zardalu."

"I have no interest in Zardalu."

"Maybe not." Louis throttled back his irritation. "But they'll have plenty of interest in you—and in tearing you to bits. When we land, let me deal with 'em. I can talk to them."

"Such was already my intention. I consider it part of your duties."

That, and everything else that comes to your mind. Louis turned to monitor once more the conversation between Glenna Omar and Atvar H'sial. He cursed. Too late. The Cecropian had gone, and Glenna was relaxed on the divan, her face as unlined and innocent as a small child's.

Louis stared at the scene, and felt dizziness and a surge of intense desire. His blood sugar must be very low. He would give anything right now for one of those sticky, sugary confections sitting on the low table next to Glenna.

Nenda had left Genizee, swearing never to make another landing there. Here was the landing he would never make. The *Gravitas* came wobbling down toward the familiar sandy shore. Zardalu were emerging from the sea and the tall, sandstone towers at the water's edge, long before the ship made its touch-down.

Aware of the poor condition of the ship's equipment, Nenda worried that they would plummet the final fifty meters and squash a batch of the welcoming committee. It wouldn't help the subsequent conversation. Or maybe, knowing the Zardalu, it might help a great deal.

The *Gravitas* flopped in sideways, dropping like a wounded duck at the very edge of the beach. Zardalu slid out of the way at the last moment, and returned at once to form a crouching ring around the ship on land and in the water.

There was no point in putting off the critical moment. Nenda, with Atvar H'sial right behind him, opened the one working hatch on the side of the ship and stepped out onto the sand. He was aware of Glenna Omar and Quintus Bloom, curious and unafraid, standing behind him at the hatch. He was strangely calm himself. Maybe constant exposure to horrors was making him blasé. Unfortunately that was one very easy way to get yourself killed.

Louis beckoned to the biggest Zardalu. It lifted its monstrous body and slipped noiselessly forward like a gigantic blue ghost. Right in front of Nenda it subsided in a sprawl of thick tentacles.

"Just as we promised, we have returned." The clicks and whistles Louis used were in the master form of the old Zardalu slave language, but that hardly mattered. What counted was going to be the reply. How had things been going here, in the months since he and Atvar H'sial left?

"We have dreamed of your return."

In slave talk! Nenda waited, until the broad head bowed and a long tongue of royal purple stretched four feet along the beach. He placed his boot firmly on it for five seconds, easily long enough to satisfy the ritual requirement, and then stepped back. He resisted the urge to scuff the slime from his boot. What Bloom and Glenna Omar thought of all this nonsense was anyone's guess. They certainly didn't realize the possible danger.

"It is time for our other pledge to be fulfilled. We have proved that we are able to come and go from Genizee as we choose. Now it is time for us to prove that we are able to take you with us."

The head of midnight-blue rose and turned, to scan the waiting circle. "We are ready. We await only your permission."

Now for the tricky bit. "Not all can go at once. We will begin by taking with us a single individual, as a demonstration. After that we will organize for the departure of larger groups."

There was a long, long silence, while all Nenda's worries about growing too blasé slipped silently away.

"That will be satisfactory. If the Masters will wait for a few moments and permit a turning of the back."

"It is permitted."

The big Zardalu swiveled its body around without moving its tentacles. It made a short speech in a language that Nenda did not understand at all.

A *very* short speech. Surely those few clicks were not enough to explain what Nenda had said. But all the other Zardalu were backing away. Thirty meters. Fifty meters.

The Zardalu in front of Louis turned back to face him. "It is done. I am the chosen Zardalu, and I am ready to go at once. It will be desirable to move with speed, once we begin."

"No point in waiting." Louis turned, and was gesturing Atvar H'sial back into the hatch when the noise began. It came from everywhere in the ring of waiting Zardalu, a high-pitched buzz that rose rapidly in volume.

He took one look, and knew exactly what had happened. Zardalu never changed. The big one hadn't *explained* anything at all to the rest. It had decided who was going, and just commanded the others to stand back—giving Louis, for a bet, as the source of the order.

The thought wasn't complete before he was at the hatch. Atvar H'sial, even quicker on the uptake, was already through and had swept Quintus Bloom and Glenna Omar along in front of her. Louis took a swift look behind. The self-appointed Zardalu representative was at his heels, while a hundred furious others were gliding in hot pursuit.

Nothing ever went the way you planned! Louis threw himself through the hatch. It was anybody's guess whether the big Zardalu would be able to squeeze in after him, but if that one could, so could others.

Louis didn't wait to find out. He bee-lined for the controls and slapped in the lift-off sequence. The *Gravitas* started its rise, tilting far to the left. Nenda knew why. The big Zardalu was wedged halfway through the hatch on the side of the ship and was struggling to wriggle in farther. A dozen others had grabbed the tentacles that were still dangling outside. The ship was lifting with twenty tons of excess and unbalanced mass. But it was lifting. And the Zardalu in the hatch was flailing with one free tentacle at the hangers-on.

Louis watched, with no regret at all, as the first of the hanging Zardalu lost its grip, dropped a couple of hundred feet, and splattered on a line of jutting rocks that bordered the beach.

After that it was just a matter of time. The ship was still rising. The Zardalu outside were shaken off, one by one. It no longer mattered whether they fell on land or water. At this height both were equally fatal. The last one to go had managed to attach its suckers to the underside of the *Gravitas*. It clung on until the ship was almost at the edge of Genizee's atmosphere. But even a Zardalu had to breathe. Nenda watched it drop at last, a near-unconscious ball of defiantly thrashing tentacles. He even felt faint sympathy as it vanished from sight. You had to admire anything, human or alien, that just didn't know when to quit. The big Zardalu, after enormous effort, had squeezed its bulk all the way on board. Not before time, either, because the ship was losing air through the hatch. Nenda slammed it closed, nipping off the ends of a couple of tentacles that were slow to pull out of the way.

The Zardalu did not seem to mind. It lay on the deck for a few seconds, breathing hard, then lifted its head and stared around. Glenna took one look at the vicious beak and ran to stand behind Louis. She put her arms around him and clung to him, hard enough to make his rib cage creak.

Nenda ignored that. He stepped closer to the Zardalu and waited until the great cerulean eyes turned in his direction.

"I hope you have not caused me a problem." He used the crudest form of master-slave talk.

"Problem?" The Zardalu sounded terrified. "Master, why are you unhappy?"

"I'm not unhappy. But others may be. What about the ones who just got killed? What about all the ones who were left behind?"

"The dead do not feel happy or unhappy." Now the Zardalu sounded more puzzled than afraid. "As for the rest, why would they have reason to complain? I acted as any one of them would have acted. What other behavior is possible?"

Which was probably, to a Zardalu, a wholly reasonable position.

Louis gave up any attempt to understand aliens.

Or humans. Quintus Bloom had narrowly escaped death. He was standing within six feet of a creature who at Nenda's command would tear him into small pieces and swallow the fragments. And he was scowling at Louis.

"I did not authorize lift-off from Genizee. What about my evidence of Builder activities there? Return me to the surface at once."

The temptation was very great. Pop the hatch open for a second, and say the right word to the Zardalu. Then Nenda would have revenge for all Bloom's put-downs and insults. Bloom would have his own put-down, one that went a long, long way. He would be returned to the surface all right—just as he had ordered.

It was Glenna Omar who saved Bloom. But not by siding with him. She released her hold on Nenda and turned angrily.

"How dare you talk to Louis like that! I'm sure he did what was best for us. He took off because he had to. Didn't you see them? Hundreds of things like— like *that* thing—" she waved at the Zardalu, but averted her eyes from it "—waiting down there for us."

Louis was beyond confusion. In his experience—and he had plenty—no one had *ever* jumped forward to defend him, as Glenna was defending him. And Quintus Bloom seemed equally amazed. Glenna Omar had been allowed on the expedition specifically to admire and report back in glowing terms everything that Bloom did. But now she was *criticizing* him—and approving the unauthorized actions of some squat, swarthy barbarian from the middle of nowhere.

It was at this tense, intense, and incomprehensible moment that the alarm system of the *Gravitas* sounded. The ship's remaining sensors were warning of a major emergency.

Too many crises, all different, and one right after another. Louis was fairly sure that he was in the middle of a long sequence of alternating dreams and nightmares. He had reached another piece of the dark side. Close your eyes, relax. Unfortunately he dared not take the risk.

The first information came from the viewing screens that showed what lay ahead of the ship. They once more displayed the pattern of singularities that had prevented escape from Genizee during Nenda and Atvar H'sial's last visit. Now, however, the singularities looked a good deal more ominous, dark bands with sudden lightning flashes across them mixed in with the pale wash of a gently wavering aurora. There were other differences, too. No saffron beam of light was stabbing out from the artificial hollow moon of Genizee, ready to return the ship to the planet's surface.

Good news. Except that a beam of vivid purple from the same source had locked on to the *Gravitas*. It was pulling them directly toward the hollow moon, at a steadily accelerating pace.

Nenda inventoried the ship's interior. The big Zardalu was lying quietly on the floor, inspecting the ends of its two clipped tentacles.

Fair enough. Louis couldn't think of one useful thing to tell it to do in an emergency. No allowance had been made in the *Gravitas*'s design for strapping in a body that size. If it didn't move, that was a blessing.

Atvar H'sial, who couldn't see the screens, presumably had no idea what was happening unless she could smell it from Louis's natural pheromones—he had found no time to send a message to her, but he must stink of fear. Anyway, no help there.

Quintus Bloom was turning accusingly toward Louis, but his mouth was still only half-open when the lights went out. All the screens turned dark. A moment later, Glenna's arms went round Nenda from behind and ran like starved animals down his body. "Louis!" Her whisper was right in his ear. "It's another hiatus!"

It wasn't, though. It was more serious than that, and Louis knew it even if no one else did. He jerked forward, away from Glenna's embrace. As he did so the lights came back on and the screens flickered again to life.

He reached for the controls, guessing that anything he did would make little difference. In the couple of seconds that the lights had been off, the hollow satellite of Genizee had vanished. In its place stood a spinning ball of darkness.

Louis swore aloud. He knew exactly what that was, and he wanted nothing to do with it. The *Gravitas* was being drawn, willy-nilly, into the black tornado of a Builder transportation vortex. He had enough time to wonder where and if he was likely to emerge. But in the middle of that thought the vortex seemed to reach out, grip him, and mold its fierce embrace like a great animal constrictor around his whole long-suffering body.

Louis probably screamed. He was not sure. A scream was certainly justified.

Glenna all last night, then the Maw, and now the vortex. Hadn't he been assigned more than his fair share of out-of-this-world squeezing?

✦ Chapter Twenty-Three

Two more days, and still no sign of J'merlia. With or without him, Darya had to decide how she and Kallik proposed to escape from the interior of Labyrinth.

It went beyond concern over suit supplies of air and food. Darya felt the breath of change, like an invisible wind all around her within the Artifact. Hour after hour, the chamber *moved*. A haze in the air came and went. The walls themselves drifted and tilted to meet at slightly different inclinations. The effect was most noticeable at the wedge-shaped end. When Darya had first examined it the angle between the walls had been acute, no more than a few degrees. Now she could place her gloved hand down into the broad gap, far enough to touch the end with her fingertips.

The final decision, like all major turning points in Darya's life, seemed to make itself. One moment she was crouched near the end of the chamber, wondering what could have happened to J'merlia. The next, she was heading for the dark funnel of the entrance.

"Come on, Kallik, we've learned all we're going to learn in this place. Time to get out."

Don't stop to wonder about the condition of the outer chambers, or of the ship that she had left behind there. Logic was good, but too much logical analysis inhibited action. Darya had heard it seriously suggested

that the original human cladeworld, Earth, had degen-
erated to an ineffectual backwater of a planet because
computer trade-off analysis had increasingly been used
as the basis for decision making. On purely logical
grounds, no one would ever explore, invent, rejoice,
sing, strive, fall in love, or take physical and psychological risks of any kind. Better to stay in bed in the
morning; it was much safer.

If you were lucky enough to have a bed. Did the
Builders sleep, eat, laugh, and cry? Did they feel hope
and despair? Darya paused at the narrow exit from
the innermost chamber. *Follow the streaky white lines.*
The *Myosotis*, complete with beds and bunks and all
the other niceties that she had not seen for days, lay
in that direction.

"With respect." Kallik had come up close behind and
was edging ahead of Darya. "My reactions are faster
than yours. It is logical that I lead."

Logic again. But Darya found this point difficult to
argue. With Hymenopt reaction times, Kallik could be
fifty meters away while Darya was still wondering if
there might be a danger.

"Be careful. Things in here are *changing.*"

As if Kallik needed to be told. Her senses were more
acute than Darya's, her reasoning powers in no way
inferior. She was already away, shooting along the tunnel
to the next chamber. Darya followed, expecting when
she arrived to see Kallik far ahead and fighting her
way through the moving maze of vortex singularities
that they had faced on the way in. To Darya's surprise
she found that the Hymenopt had not progressed
beyond the end of the tunnel. Kallik was floating with
folded limbs, obviously waiting.

"Too dangerous?" Darya approached the end of the
tunnel. She expected to see the energetic vortices,
zipping back and forth past the tunnel entrance. What
she saw instead was one great pool of swirling black,

as though a single vortex had taken up station at the chamber entrance and waited for them there.

That impression faded as she moved to Kallik's side. The usual circulation pattern was visible, sure enough, and it came from a bloated monster of a vortex. However, it did not fill the whole chamber. There was room for a human—or a Hymenopt—to squeeze past on either side. It might be safe enough, provided that the dark whirlpool did not increase again in size.

"What's the problem?"

Kallik did not reply in words. Instead she pointed to the black heart of the pool. At first Darya saw nothing, a darkness so complete that instead of delivering illumination the vortex center seemed to draw light away from the eye. After a few moments a faint ghost of an image rippled into that darkness, then just as quickly vanished. Darya was left with the subliminal impression of a distorted cylinder, a long ellipsoid with each end sheared off and replaced by flat planes.

Before she could speak the spectral image came again, and again slipped away.

Again. And again, lingering a moment longer.

"Next time, I think." But even before Kallik's quiet comment, Darya knew what she was seeing. It was a Builder transportation system, in the very act of giving birth. Something or someone was being squeezed and corkscrewed through a narrow spacetime canal— Darya would never forget the feeling—and any moment now would be delivered into the chamber ahead.

The vortex trembled. Smooth blackness became in an instant a dazzling flash of blue and white. Darya's suit visor cut out with photon overload. When the visor again admitted light, Darya saw that the chamber in front of her contained something more than the whirling singularity. A dull grey ship of unfamiliar design floated beside the dark whirlpool. And the vortex itself was changing. With delivery over it was dwindling, tightening, shrinking back to normal size. After a few seconds it faded to grey. At last it became an insubstantial fog, a wraith through which the chamber beyond was visible. And then it was gone.

Darya started forward. She halted when the ship in front of her began to change. Hull plates slid aside, and the smooth grey surface was broken by open dark circles. Darya froze. Even someone from the peaceful worlds of the Fourth Alliance knew enough to recognize weapons ports.

"Ristu 'knu'ik. Utu'is's gur'uiki." A blare of warning came from the ship ahead, accompanied by supersonics that raised the skin on Darya's arms to goose pimples. Something within the ship had recognized what Darya herself had forgotten—that the chamber was filled with air. Breathable or unbreathable, the gases would carry sound signals.

"Can you understand that gobbledygook?" Darya spoke on the private suit channel.

"No. But I think I recognize it." Kallik was moving slowly to one side, studying the swollen cylinder ahead from different angles. "It is a language peculiar to the worlds of the Cecropian Fringe, where the Federation meets the Communion. I have heard it spoken, but regrettably I have had no prior opportunity for study. J'merlia would surely understand it."

Perfect. Come in, J'merlia, wherever you are. "Keep still, Kallik. Those are weapons ports."

"I know." Kallik had stopped the sideways crabbing, but now she was moving forward. "Permit me to ask something. What is the nearest Artifact to the Cecropian Fringe?"

It was an odd time for such a question, but this particular one didn't call for any thought. Information on all the Builder Artifacts was so ingrained in Darya that the answer came as second nature. "It's the Kruskal Extension—what most people call Enigma."

"Thank you. Are there inhabited worlds close to Enigma?"

"Three of them. Humans call them Rosen, Lao, and Nordstrom, after the original human explorers of Enigma. But as I recall, there are no humans on any of the three. High mass, all of them, and I don't think we could breathe the air on Lao."

"Which is one way of avoiding territorial conflict. But with thanks to you, we perhaps have what we need." Kallik was still drifting forward, tracked by blunt nozzles protruding from the weapons ports. She switched to external suit broadcast and produced a piercing series of audible but near-supersonic howls. To Darya's ears it was a painful scream of buzz-saws, nothing like the knotted speech pattern that had greeted them from the ship.

There was a long silence, during which Darya waited to be dispersed to atoms. At last an answering set of screeches came from the ship.

"Excellent. That is Tenthredic, or a variant of it in which I have at least rudimentary speech capability." Kallik gestured to Darya to move forward with her. "The inhabitants of Lao are Tenthredans. They qualify, at least biologically, as remote cousins of mine."

"Cousins! But they're all set to shoot at us." The threatening nozzles had not moved from their targets, and Darya could see glowing cross-hairs within them. Another awful howl, to her ears like a final warning, came from the ship.

"With respect, I think not. They are merely expressing their own sorrow, alarm, and confusion. I told them who we are, and where they are. That news is distressing to them. Less than half an hour ago, they and a sister ship were entering Enigma to explore it—six hundred lightyears from here." Kallik was heading directly for a hatch on the ship's side. "A certain apprehension on their part is not perhaps too surprising."

❖   ❖   ❖

The stages of Kallik's logic, as soon as she explained them to Darya, seemed absurdly simple:

One: The original message was in a language used in the Cecropian Fringe.

Two: Since the ship had emerged from a Builder transportation system, it must also have entered one.

Three: Transportation system entry points are associated with Builder Artifacts.

Four: The Fringe itself does not contain any Artifacts, but Enigma lies close to it.

Therefore, the newcomers probably originated on a world close to the Fringe, and also close to Enigma.

Which made the puzzle of Labyrinth, and the arrival of the ship, no less perplexing. In all recorded history there had been no evidence of Builder transit vortices—until one year ago. Now vortices were popping up everywhere, and making nonsense of all human rules for superluminal transportation.

Added to that, Labyrinth itself was changing *again*, more and more obviously. Darya and Kallik, on board the Tenthredan ship, were supposed to guide them all back to open space. As far as Darya was concerned, the Tenthredans were more likely to escape by flying their ship straight at the walls than by listening to her. *Nothing* in Labyrinth was as it had been when they entered. And the changes continued.

She nodded at the solid-bodied, blunt-headed creature poised over the control panel. The family resemblance to Hymenopts was obvious, but with their red eyes, hooked jaws, prominent stings, and banded abdomens of bright black and maroon stripes, the Tenthredans seemed far more obviously menacing than Kallik. There were five of them, and they were all watching her suspiciously with one ring of crimson eyes, while staring at Kallik with the other. The Hymenopt, gesturing to the far end of the chamber, seemed to be explaining some subtle point to the pilot. The Ten-thredan was gesturing in turn, and apparently disagreeing violently.

"What's the problem?" Darya had to change her own role from that of useless supernumerary. "We know that's the only way out. We have to go through the tunnel, even if it means blasting a way through with the weapons system. Tell her that."

"Him. At this stage of the life cycle a Tenthredan is male. I am doing my best, but we are communicating with great difficulty because of my inadequate language skills."

Kallik did not seem to be aware of the irony in her apologetic comment. Darya did. When she and Kallik first met, the Hymenopt had spoken no word of any human tongue. Now, less than one year later, Kallik was completely fluent in several human languages—and Darya neither understood nor could utter a single syllable of Hymenopt.

"He agrees that the ship will not pass through the tunnel easily," Kallik went on. "However, he remains reluctant to employ extreme force."

"Tell him we don't care any more how much he damages Labyrinth. We do whatever we have to, to get out."

Darya marveled at her own response—no one back on Sentinel Gate would ever believe that it came from the mouth of the compiler of the *Lang Universal Artifact Catalog*. She had always argued, vociferously, for the preservation of every element of every Artifact. Even Kallik was shaking her head.

"Don't you see, Kallik? We must damage Labyrinth if we want to escape."

"Indeed, yes. But with respect, Professor Lang, that is not the point at issue. The pilot is reluctant to use weapons at this stage because of what his sensors suggest is in the next chamber."

Darya peered at the black void of the tunnel as it showed on the screen. "He can't possibly see anything."

"Not with visible signals. He is receiving a return sonic profile, indicating that the chamber beyond holds a ship. He argues, with reason, that no weapon should be used until more information is available. Suppose that in the chamber beyond lies the Tenthredan sister ship, transported like them, but to a slightly different location?"

Something—at last!—to do, more meaningful than attempts to become an instant speaker and understander of Tenthredic howls and screams. Darya was on her way to the hatch almost before Kallik had finished speaking.

"Tell him I'll have a message back to you in just a few minutes. And would you also tell him that I'd feel a lot more relaxed if he'd point those weapons in a different direction while I'm out in front of the ship? I get the feeling this whole group is a bit trigger-happy."

"That may unfortunately be true, Professor Lang." Kallik called after her when Darya was already in the lock. "With respect, I suggest that you proceed with extreme caution. The Tenthredan reputation is not for steady nerves. It is undesirable to excite them."

Just what Darya needed to hear. She went into the tunnel, very aware of the array of vaporizing weapons pointing at her back. Midway along the narrow corridor she paused. Suppose that what she found in the chamber ahead was dangerous, so much an immediate threat to Kallik and the Tenthredans that it had to be destroyed at once? What would she do? She was no cool hero like Hans Rebka, willing to direct fire onto his own position if it was required to save a larger group.

But she could not remain in the middle of the tunnel forever. Even if she did nothing, the nervous Tenthredans might decide it was time to shoot. Darya sighed, and started forward.

Whatever was in the chamber beyond, it was unlikely to be another ship—unless it was *her* ship. Quintus Bloom had discovered Labyrinth and talked of it on Sentinel Gate, but so far as Darya knew the Artifact was otherwise unknown except on the backwater planet of Jerome's World. No one there had shown interest in exploring it—or anything else, for that matter. Darya's expedition to Labyrinth was presumably the second visit in its whole history. So if there *was* a ship in the next chamber . . .

She came to the entrance and halted again. When a person was so consistently wrong, it was time to give up having opinions.

The elongated bubble of the vault ahead contained no sign of the hail of orange particles that had threatened them on entry. What it held instead was a single hump-backed object at its far end. Small, and of an unfamiliar design, but certainly a ship.

"Kallik, can you hear me?"

"Certainly."

"Then tell your buddy that he was quite right. There is a ship through here." Darya hesitated. This one carried no sign of weapons. Nothing moved on its surface. Was it possible that she was facing a dead vessel, a derelict that had floated in Labyrinth for eons?

"Kallik, you can tell the Tenthredans that this is not their sister ship. It's much smaller, and a completely different design. I'm going to take a closer look. If there is anyone inside I will try to make contact with them."

There. That was one way to force yourself to take a dangerous action. Announce an intention, and then be too embarrassed to admit that you were afraid to go through with it. Darya wondered how a professional would approach a situation like this. There seemed to be few options. The ship itself did nothing to suggest any interest in her presence.

She examined the hull in front of her, then headed for the single lock. It was a standard design, used everywhere from the inner worlds of the Fourth Alliance to the farthest reaches of the Zardalu Communion. She knew just how it worked. No excuse for backing off and returning to the unpleasant company of the Tenthredans.

Darya reached for the manual control on the outside of the lock. It turned easily in her grip. She rotated the control all the way and swung the airtight hatch inward on its beveled hinge.

As she entered the airlock she swore a silent oath: If she emerged from this alive, she would never again poke fun at Professor Merada and his quiet, cloistered life on Sentinel Gate.

✦ Chapter Twenty-Four

Hans Rebka stood in front of the Treel sisters, sharply aware of their glowering disbelief. He couldn't blame them. The old term for the problem was "credibility gap."

Maddy, Lissie, and Katerina had been stranded in the interior of Paradox. They were facing eventual starvation, but that was a form of death they understood.

Along came E.C. Tally: a human male, a man, which counted as a major strike against him, but at least a man who might offer possible salvation. Then Tally had explained that he had not come to save them. He was trapped himself, and he knew of no way out; and anyway he was not a man. After a lot of explanation, they were beginning to believe him.

Enter Hans Rebka. Definitely a man, and a friend of E.C. Tally, who brought with him the bad news that the prison of Paradox was no longer as safe as it seemed. He had led them out of their chamber—but not to safety. No. He had taken them and the *Misanthrope* into a diabolical ink-swirl that he called a vortex, and it had wrung them out like wet dishcloths until they had wanted to die.

They had survived. And were they safe when they finally emerged? That was a matter of opinion. Certainly they were no longer anywhere within Paradox, or any other place that Rebka or Tally had ever been or heard of. They had arrived inside some strange new prison. Rebka had made it clear that so far as he knew the vortex had flung them into unknown territory. He could tell them nothing about the place. It might be no more than a different choice of tomb.

Enter J'merlia. An alien who had certainly *not* been with Rebka and Tally on Paradox, a life-form very far from human, but a life-form *known to Hans Rebka and E.C. Tally*. And vice versa. When J'merlia had entered the *Misanthrope* he had greeted the others joyfully, as long-absent friends.

Was Hans expected to explain all this to the Treel sisters?

He couldn't explain *any* of it, even to himself. Instead, he was asking his own questions.

"Let's get this straight." He had persuaded J'merlia to shed his suit, then closed the hatch on the *Misanthrope* and locked it. "You say that you and Kallik and Darya went to *Sentinel*? Why there?"

"We know the Sentinel Artifact," Maddy Treel said gruffly. "But who the devil are Kallik, and Darya?"

"They are both females. That should please you." Rebka found himself glaring at the senior Treel sister. It was tempting to start playing battle-of-the-sexes. But that would solve nothing. "I'm sorry. Darya Lang is a researcher on Sentinel Gate. She compiled the Lang Artifact Catalog. And Kallik is a Hymenopt with whom we've all worked before. J'merlia, are you suggesting that *this* is Sentinel, where we are now? It's nothing like any description of Sentinel that I've ever seen."

"Oh, no." J'merlia was as confused as anyone, but he was obviously delighted to be with Rebka and Tally. Finally, he had someone to make his decisions for him. "We left Sentinel because it had changed and was not at all as we expected. We went on to a different Artifact: Labyrinth."

"No such Artifact!" Lissie glared at Hans Rebka. "What are you trying to pull? We know the Lang Catalog as well as anyone. There's nothing in there called Labyrinth."

"It's a new Artifact." He didn't expect that comment to be well-received. It wasn't.

"Bullshit! All the Artifacts are millions of years old." Lissie turned to E.C. Tally for support. "You say you don't have circuits that allow you to lie. So tell me: How old are the Builder Artifacts?"

"All are at least three million years old—except for Labyrinth, which does appear to be quite new." E.C. Tally had hoped for facts, and was getting arguments instead. "If you would just permit J'merlia to complete his explanations . . ."

"He's right." Unexpected support came from Katerina Treel. She had taken a strand of her long, dark hair and was thoughtfully chewing on it. Socially acceptable behavior on Darby's Lick. It almost made Hans Rebka nostalgic for home, back in the crudities of the Phemus Circle.

"I don't care how *old* things are," Katerina went on. "I'll settle for just three things. Number one, I want to know where we are *now*. Number two, I want to know how to get out of here, and back to open space. And number three, I want no more damned *surprises*." She turned to J'merlia. "Now, get on with it."

"But that's what I was trying to tell you." J'merlia had wondered when he would be allowed to speak again. "We went to a planet called Jerome's World, and then on to Labyrinth. We found a way in, and we followed a path that led all the way to a central chamber. But we had been forced to leave our ship, the *Myosotis*, in the outer part of Labyrinth. So while the others examined the middle chamber, I went back to make sure that the ship was all right. I located the *Myosotis*, in the same condition as when I left it. But then I made a mistake. You see, Labyrinth has thirty-seven separate sections, or it did when we entered. I think it has a lot less now, it keeps changing—"

"Like everywhere else," Maddy said grumpily.

"—but I accidentally went through into another part of the interior, and I couldn't get back to where I started. I was still trying to return to the *Myosotis* when I saw your ship."

"Hold it there." Maddy held up her hand. "Let's make sure we understand what you're telling us. First, we're sitting right now inside an Artifact called Labyrinth?"

"Correct."

"And Labyrinth is *new*—that's why it's not in the Lang Catalog?"

J'merlia hesitated, and Maddy caught that hesitation. "Is it new, or isn't it?"

"I was assured that it is new, by Darya Lang and everyone else. But I am not sure." J'merlia told of what he had seen in his long wanderings through Labyrinth, of desiccated black bat-like figures, of human skeletons in ancient suits, and of long-dead five-eyed marine giants like nothing in the whole Spiral Arm. Worst of all, to his eyes, had been the silent forms of a dozen Cecropians, so untouched by death that only a breath seemed needed to bring the Lo'tfian dominatrices back to life.

His listeners sat in silence when he was finished. Maddy Treel finally cleared her throat. "All right. Labyrinth is supposed to be new, but it has old things in it. Maybe they got here the same way we did. But we won't solve anything by sitting here. The main thing is, do you know the way out?"

"I do. It is very simple. All you have to do is head along the direction of the spiral tube that increases in size. You should come to one of the exit points."

"Fine. So that takes care of the second of Katerina's want list. We can get out of here. And I say let's do it, right now. We'd like more explanations, but they can wait."

"But what about Darya Lang and Kallik?"

"You told us yourself that they should have no trouble reaching your ship, and it's intact. You couldn't find your way back there, but that was your own fault. Anyway, this is *our* ship, and we use it as we choose. Katerina, you heard what we have to do. We follow the direction of the expanding spiral, and it takes us back to open space. Let's go, before something else happens. I agree with you, we don't want any more surprises."

Maddy Treel had been leaning against the cabin wall. She suddenly sat upright and cocked her head. Rebka, Tally, J'merlia, and her two sisters were all sitting in front of her. But the faint sound she could hear was coming from *behind* her. It was the air-lock of the *Misanthrope*, opening and closing on its molecular hinges.

Maddy sighed, and swore under her breath. Katerina's third want was going to remain unsatisfied.

The explanations started all over again with a new level of tension, helped slightly by the fact that Darya Lang was indisputably a woman. She had given Hans Rebka a single look of anger and disdain, then ignored him. The Treel sisters liked that. After presenting a united front for a while they had now changed to what Rebka suspected was their natural condition. They were beginning to squabble among themselves, Lissie and Katerina kicking back against Maddy's age and presumption of seniority.

They finally agreed to listen to Darya's story, but patience and polite behavior didn't last very long. Darya began well, disposing of one source of J'merlia's perplexity in two sentences. "Labyrinth *is* new, but it contains old things that had been locked inside other

Artifacts for ages and then were *brought here*. Just as you were brought here."

"So I was right," Maddy said.

"I'm not an old thing," E.C. Tally objected. "I'm almost new."

"And I don't give a damn whether Labyrinth is full of something old," Katerina interrupted. "Or something new, or even something borrowed and something blue."

"Orange," said E.C. Tally. "The Builders prefer orange."

Katerina glared at him. "Are you sure you're not a man? As I was trying to point out, we were brought here, and that's enough for me. Who cares if Labyrinth is crammed to the rafters with Tenthredans, or Hymenopts, or Lo'tfians, or purple-spotted blue-bummed green-balled Fambezuxian male sexist hooter-honkers. And *you*—" she had seen Tally ready with a puzzled look and a question "—can shut up and learn about those later, from somebody else. I want *out*, and I want out *now*."

Maddy ignored her sister's outburst. "But *why* were we brought here?" she asked thoughtfully. "And what happens next?"

Darya clenched her teeth. So much for the rest of them sitting and listening to any description of Labyrinth. They had no interest at all in hearing what she had to say. "I have no idea why you were brought here. Or what will happen next." She stood up and firmly closed her suit's helmet. "But I'm not going to sit here and listen to you argue with each other. If you want out, then go. I told Kallik that I would return and reveal to her exactly what I found, and I am going to do just that. I have promises to keep."

It made a fine exit line. Darya gave Hans Rebka one last cold look, that said, *I won't deal with you now, you worm, but just you wait*; then she left.

She did not like what she found beyond the airlock.

She was in the same chamber, but there had been major changes. The space had somehow increased in size. Its walls had become translucent, and she could see the faint outline of other rooms beyond. Worse than that, the way back, which had been open and easy, was blocked. At the entrance to the tunnel stood the familiar but unwelcome sight of another transportation vortex.

It was still swelling and building. Darya waited. This time she knew what to expect. The pattern was developing in the same way as before: darkness, growing on itself and with a center of swirling, absolute black. Then a ghost image, flickering for the briefest moment across the dark bloated heart.

It took longer this time, because the final size of the vortex was so big that it filled almost the whole expanded chamber. Darya retreated to the illusory shelter of the *Misanthrope* at the far end. She noted that in spite of Lissie's ultimatum the ship had not changed its position. She thought she could see it shaking a little. The fighting among the sisters inside was something better imagined than experienced.

The spectral image became stronger, flashing twice into near-visibility. It was a ship, and a big one, with a slightly peculiar profile. She saw why when it finally popped into full existence and she could examine it for more than a split-second at a time. The new vessel had begun life as a sleek ship with an advanced Fourth Alliance design, but somehow a large part of the aft section had been sheared away. Before she could evaluate the extent of that damage, a hatch on the side was swinging inward. Three human figures jetted out, followed a few moments later by a gigantic fourth shape.

A *familiar* gigantic shape. A Cecropian. Darya's eyes were ready to pop out through her visor. She was beyond surprise when the leading human came zipping over to her.

"What, may I ask, are *you* doing here?" The nasal, arrogant voice had not changed a bit. "Access to this Artifact is supposed to be tightly controlled."

"She must have been dumped here, like we were," another voice said, just as familiar. "Hey, Professor, how's it goin'?"

Darya shook her head hopelessly and gestured to the *Misanthrope*, still motionless beside her. "Let's go in there and talk. It can't get any messier inside, and I don't want to be out here when the next shipment arrives."

Darya was wrong. It got much messier within the *Misanthrope* before five minutes had passed, because in less than that interval the next shipment did arrive. Kallik, finding the road between the chambers open, appeared with two of the Tenthredans.

The Treel's exploration ship had been designed for a crew of three, with emergency space for a couple of extra passengers. Packed inside it at the moment were the three Treel sisters, Hans Rebka, E.C. Tally, J'merlia, Louis Nenda, Glenna Omar, Quintus Bloom, Atvar H'sial, Kallik, and the two still-anonymous Tenthredans. Plus, of course, Darya herself.

It would have made more sense to reconvene on the *Gravitas*, but the Treel sisters refused to board any vessel that lacked superluminal capability. As Katerina pointed out, anyone who left Labyrinth on a subluminal ship faced a long crawl home. The presence on the *Gravitas* of a live, adult Zardalu was of less consequence. Maddy and her sisters just didn't believe Louis Nenda, and his comment that passage through a Builder vortex had changed the Zardalu's attitude toward space travel and subdued it considerably was taken as embroidery on an implausible fabrication.

Not everyone was talking at once. It merely felt that

way. The only happy being of any species seemed to be Quintus Bloom. He was grinning, and he had started to lecture everyone who would listen as soon as his suit was open.

"Exactly as I expected." The prominent nose was raised high in satisfaction. "Events are occurring *precisely* as my theory predicted."

That wasn't the way Darya remembered things. She looked at Bloom, and then carefully scanned everyone else crowded into the cabin. The expressions on the faces of the nonhumans and of E.C. Tally were largely unreadable, but the rest were a study in contrasts. Maddy and Katerina Treel were edgy and impatient, eager to leave Labyrinth as soon as possible. It was only a matter of time before they threw everyone off their ship and fled. Maybe they were the smart ones. Their blond sister, Lissie, had been caught instantly by the Bloom charisma. Her deep suspicion of men had been charmed away, and she was standing right in front of him and hanging open-mouthed on to his every word.

Next to Lissie and Bloom, Hans Rebka stood in his usual crisis mode, monitoring everything and everyone, self-contained and serious. He noticed Darya staring at him and his expression turned to one of acute discomfort.

He ignored everybody else and came across to stand by her side. "Darya, we have to talk."

"Indeed?" She stared at him coldly. "I don't know that I have anything to say to you. And it's the worst possible time for talking."

"It may be the worst time, but it could be the only chance we'll ever have. No matter what happens to us, I want to set something straight."

"I suppose you're going to tell me that Glenna Omar was in your bedroom by accident. That nothing happened between the two of you."

"No. That wouldn't be true. I know I hurt you. But

Glenna really doesn't mean anything to me, and she never did. I never meant anything to her, either. I was just another man to add to her collection, another trophy for her bedroom wall."

"Why should I believe that?"

"Darya, just *look* at her. Look at Louis Nenda. Can't you see it? What do you think they've been doing?"

Nenda stood four or five steps away. He seemed exhausted, his swarthy face paler than usual and his eyes marked beneath by dark bruised smudges. Glenna Omar was standing very close to him, her shoulder rubbing against his. Glenna—Darya decided that the world must really be coming to an end—was wearing no make-up, and her long hair was pulled back and tied casually away from her face. She too seemed tired. But her whole body spoke of languid contentment.

The sight induced in Darya a strong feeling of irritation, not all directed toward Hans Rebka.

"We can't talk now," she said. "Maybe later."

"If there is a later." Hans took her hand in both of his. "If not, I want to tell you that I'm sorry."

"There won't be a later, unless we stop talking and do something." But Darya did not pull her hand away. Instead she focused her attention on Quintus Bloom, who alone in the cabin seemed to be on a real energy high.

"You claim you predicted all this?" She interrupted Bloom's stream of words to Lissie Treel. "I don't remember that."

"Then you were not paying attention." The beaked nose turned aggressively in her direction. "And despite my explanation on Sentinel Gate, I suspect that you still do not accept the nature of the Builders. Why, otherwise, would you have come to Labyrinth uninvited?"

Uninvited. As though Bloom personally owned the Artifact. But he was sweeping on.

"Recent events provide ample confirmation of what is happening. Consider the evidence. Fact: Paradox shrinks and vanishes, and Rebka and the rest of them are shipped to Labyrinth through a Builder vortex. Fact: The Torvil Anfract changes beyond recognition, and while that change is still occurring my party is sent here through another vortex."

Darya studied Bloom's gleaming smile and unnaturally bright eyes, and realized a great truth about herself. She and Quintus Bloom were both ambitious, both smart, both hard-working, and both dedicated. To most observers, they must appear very similar. But there was one difference, and it was the crucial one. Darya was on the right side of the line between great enthusiasm and total obsession. She would always have doubts about herself and the correctness of her ideas. Bloom, somewhere on the way from his childhood on Jerome's World to his appearance on Sentinel Gate, had crossed the line. He was crazy. Nothing in his life was as important as being right. The idea that he might be *wrong* was impossible for him to accept psychologically.

The child is father to the man. Orval Freemont, Bloom's first teacher long ago on Jerome's World, had read the young John Jones/Quintus Bloom exactly.

Darya compared his expression again with all the others. They were in trouble, with danger and perhaps death awaiting them in the next few hours. Some people might say that Quintus was uniquely brave, because he was so cheerful and self-confident. The truth was quite different. Bloom felt no fear, because he had no sense of danger; he could not, because danger was irrelevant to him. All that mattered was the confirmation of his theories about the Builders.

Which, in Darya's opinion, had one fatal problem: the theories were *wrong*. She might never persuade Bloom of that, but her own self-esteem insisted that he must at least be told that there were other ideas in the world. It was still the worst time and place for an argument. On the other hand, as Hans had pointed out, there might never be another chance.

Darya stepped closer, edging Lissie Treel out of her position right in front of Quintus Bloom. "The Artifacts are changing, no one disputes that. I even agree that they seem to be disappearing. But those are *observations*. They do not provide an explanation of *why* things are happening."

"My dear *Professor* Lang." Bloom made the title into an insult. Incredibly, despite the chaos around them, he was deep into his condescending lecturer's mode. "*I* can provide that explanation, even if no one else can. Everything forms part of one simple, logical sequence of events. As I told you once before, the Builder Artifacts were all planted in the Spiral Arm *from the future*, by our own descendants. When their purpose has been served, the Artifacts will vanish—as they are now vanishing. And what, you may ask, of Labyrinth itself? It is a *new Artifact*. Why then was it created, and why have we been brought here? I will tell you. Our descendants have their own curiosity. They are not content to learn of our times as part of history. They wish to see things for themselves. Labyrinth is the final Artifact, a transit terminus to which the interesting contents of all other, older Artifacts are being transferred. I knew this, as soon as I saw my first live Zardalu. The only living Zardalu are on the planet Genizee, but I had seen *mummified* forms before—on Labyrinth. Those corpses must have originated in some other Artifact, where they arrived at least eleven thousand years ago, before the Great Rising. The same process is at work in all the Artifacts. And once the transfer process is complete—which will be very soon now—Labyrinth will return to the far future. Whoever and whatever is here on Labyrinth at that time will go with it. *I* intend to go with it. I will meet the Builders—our own distant descendants! Is that not the most thrilling prospect in the whole Universe?"

It *was* thrilling. Darya could feel her own positive response. Standing next to her, Lissie Treel was nodding enthusiastically. Quintus Bloom was one hell of a salesman. He was dreadfully plausible.

He was also *dead wrong*.

Darya would never be as persuasive a speaker as Quintus Bloom, but her stay in Labyrinth had provided plenty of time to organize her thoughts.

"What you say sounds good, but it leaves too many questions."

"Indeed? I challenge you to name even one of any relevance." Bloom was still smiling, eyebrows arched and prominent white teeth flashing to show his overlong, pink tongue. But his attention was now all on Darya. In a cabin crowded with noisy people and aliens, the interaction had become an intensely personal one.

"Right." Darya took a deep breath. "I'll do just that. First question: Everyone admits that the Builder Artifacts have been around for at least three million years. Some of them are much older than that. Humans and the other clade species have been in space for only a few *thousand* years. If the Builders are our descendants, what was the point of planting their Artifacts *so long ago*? They had no relevance to humans for almost all of their lifetime."

"There is no doubt—"

"It's still my turn. Second question—and this is the big one. You found your way into the central chambers of Labyrinth, and you discovered how to read the polyglyphs. I give you all the credit in the world for that—it was a staggering accomplishment. I don't know if Kallik and I would ever have figured out that we were seeing potential messages, without your lead. But knowing it could be done, we deciphered the walls ourselves. I didn't say *wall*, you will notice, but *walls*. Every one of them portrayed a different series of images of the Spiral Arm, past, present, and future. Now, I suspect that you were not in the same central chamber as we were. But you still had a hexagonal room, and six walls. My bet is that five of them revealed a history different from the history that we know. So here's my question, and it's actually two of them: Why didn't you show the alternate histories, along with the real one, in your presentations? And second, what is the *point* of those other histories? And while I'm at it, let me throw in a third question: Why did the Builders choose such a strange way to display information, building the image sequences into the walls in three dimensions?"

Darya paused for breath. Once the questions started it was difficult to cut them off. She noticed, with shameful satisfaction, that the smile had vanished from Quintus Bloom's bony face. He was finally frowning.

"Additional research will of course be needed to answer those questions. Or, if we remain here, we will soon be in a position to ask questions directly—of the people who created Artifacts, Labyrinth, *and* polyglyphs."

Bloom gestured to the ship's display screens, which Darya had for the past few minutes been ignoring. The interior structure of Labyrinth had broken down further. Walls were vanishing, windows between chambers enlarging. Darya could see through into half a dozen other chambers, as they collapsed into each other like a connected series of soap bubbles. Within each one was a confusing blur of activity. She saw three new swelling vortices, dozens of small dots that could be figures in suits, and a trio of ships of unfamiliar design.

"Do you doubt," Bloom continued, "that Labyrinth itself is still changing? That it is preparing to return to the future?"

"It's changing, yes. But Labyrinth is *not* from the future, or going there." Now came the critical moment. "I can answer *every one* of my questions that you insist will need 'additional research.' And I can do it now. *Because I understand the nature of the Builders.*"

Suddenly, the intense personal dialogue had changed. Hans Rebka was listening hard, and so were Louis Nenda and Glenna Omar. Kallik and J'merlia had ended their conversation with Atvar H'sial, and were looking Darya's way. J'merlia, crouched beneath the Cecropian's carapace, was sure to be offering a pheromonal translation of everything. Darya became aware of her own doubts, as surely as she had felt Bloom's overwhelming certainty. But it was not the time to back off.

"Let's begin with the easy one. You *did* discover alternate histories of the Spiral Arm on the other walls of the inner chamber. You chose *not to present them* in your seminars, because they conflicted with the theory that you were offering. Do you want to deny that?"

Quintus Bloom's stony stare was enough of an answer.

"So I'm sure *you* know the main point displayed in all those alternate histories," Darya went on, "even though no one else does. I have half a dozen of the image sequences with me, if we ever get out of all this and anyone wants to see them. But I can summarize. In every alternate history, a clade or group of clades arises to colonize and populate the Spiral Arm. Sometimes the clade is one that we know well, sometimes one we have never encountered. Sometimes the development happened far in the past, long before humans came on the scene. But in every case, as we go on into the future, some single clade achieves dominance. And after that, no matter which clade rules, the colonization at last collapses. The Spiral Arm is left empty, with no populated and civilized worlds.

"Now, my first thought was the simplest one. We

were examining not alternative histories that were rooted in reality, but some kind of fiction. It seemed unlikely, but who knows? Perhaps the Builders had their own idea of entertainment. Fiction seemed more probable than the alternative: that what Kallik and I were looking at was in some sense *real.*"

"Which it clearly was not." The supercilious sneer was back. "I examined the other image sequences, of course I did. However, I saw no point in burdening my audience or my argument with palpable fantasies. Alternative contrived histories, or fictitious imagined futures, have no relevance or interest to serious researchers."

"If the image sequences contained nothing else, I would probably agree with you." Darya could feel her own competitive juices bubbling. "But there was something else, something that you either did not notice or did not want to mention. One past and future of the Spiral Arm portrayed *our* past, and perhaps our present and future. That one, alone of all pasts and futures, shows the growth and continued presence of *multiple clades.* Many species, not just one, share the future of the Arm. And unlike all other cases, that sequence does not end in the collapse of civilization. It shows a far future in which the Arm is populated, healthy, and stable. And there is one other point, the most important of all: Our version of history, and our version alone, *contains Builder Artifacts.* There is no sign of Artifacts in any other alternative history."

"Stop right there." Bloom held up his hand, palm facing Darya. "Do you realize that you have just destroyed whatever minimal credibility your argument might have had? You accept a scenario that shows the future of the Spiral Arm. There is no way to know such a future, *unless it is shown to us by beings who themselves are from that future.*"

"*Wrong.* That's what stopped me, for the longest time. I asked myself: *how could any being, no matter what it was like, know the future*? It might make predictions; we do that all the time. But this would have to go far beyond prediction. I wondered. Could a being exist who *saw* the future, as we see things around us? If such an entity did exist, what would be its essential properties?

"I didn't have an answer—until I saw the polyglyphs on the walls of Labyrinth. Normally a picture is a two-dimensional idea. These were *three-dimensional* pictures, and the third dimension represented *time*. I asked myself, What kind of being would find it natural to treat time as a dimension no different from any other? And I found an answer: A being with *finite extension in time*."

"Gibberish!" Bloom glanced around, seeking support from the others in the cabin. "What she is saying is physically ridiculous and implausible."

"To us, maybe. But to the Builders, *we* are implausible. We are totally *flat*, living within an infinitely thin slice of time. No wonder the Builders find us difficult to communicate with. We perceive space as three dimensions, but we move through time always trapped in the moment of the immediate present. We have no direct experience of anything else, past or future. A being with finite size in time as well as space will move forward through time, just as we do, but it will also have *direct experience* of what we perceive as the immediate past and the immediate future. To *see* in any dimension, it is necessary to have a finite size in that dimension. They see the future, as we see things in space. And, like our vision, their time-vision can see detail close up, but only the broad outlines farther off."

Darya could sense a change in the atmosphere within the cabin, people moving and turning away from her and Bloom. But she was too absorbed to stop, and in any case he was the one who had to be convinced. She spoke faster.

"I could accept this idea conceptually, but I still had a major problem: We talk about 'the future' as though it is a well-defined thing. But it isn't. The future is a *potential*, it can take many different forms. Depending on what we do—and what the Builders did—many different futures might be possible for the Spiral Arm. And at last I understood. The Builders *see*—and illustrated, for our benefit—*potential* futures. That's what the polyglyphs showed. Different walls, different possible futures. And of all those possibles, only one permits stable growth and continued civilization. It is the one where the Arm is populated and dominated by *multiple clades*. And the Builders, with the use of Artifacts planted long ago, have created the possibility of that future."

Darya, struggling to make her points as clearly as she could, hardly saw her surroundings. Her mind was filled with the vision of the Builders, performing actions in the past and present, then peering out far ahead to watch the shifts and changes of a misty set of futures. They could not *guarantee* a future, they could only increase its chances. How did those options look, to the strange Builder senses? Did alternatives fade or sharpen, as different actions were taken or considered that would vary the future? How much *detail* were they able to see? The rise and fall of a clade, yes. But what about the smaller options, of economic power and influence?

Someone was tugging impatiently at her arm. She glared, expecting it to be Quintus Bloom. Instead it was Hans Rebka. Bloom himself was pushing his way into a crush of other people, all milling around the cabin.

Darya turned her annoyance onto Rebka. "What a nerve. I was talking to him!"

"No." He began to pull on her arm, dragging her after the others. "You just thought you were. For the past thirty seconds you haven't been talking to anybody. You're as bad as he is, you know, when you get going. Come on. We have to find a way out of here. Everything is falling apart. You can tell us all about the Builders some other time—if we're that lucky."

✦ Chapter Twenty-Five

It was like being engaged in a public debate—at the moment when the stage falls out from under you. Darya had been pumped up for a verbal duel-to-the-death with Quintus Bloom. She had no illusions; the fight was far from over. But now, without warning, both Bloom and audience had departed.

Darya, glancing at the screens for the first time in many minutes, could see why. Labyrinth was becoming unrecognizable. The walls were dissolving. Darya could see right through them. She could observe, as through a fine gauze curtain, the whole of the helical structure right down to the tightest innermost chamber.

And Labyrinth was *simplifying*. One spiral now, not thirty-seven. One great coiled tube, filled with novelties.

The bulging vortices had vanished, leaving in their place a horde of new arrivals. The Spiral Arm, revealing its diversity . . .

. . . ships, from the newest design of the Fourth Alliance to the ponderous and ancient bulk of the legendary Tantalus orbital fort. The corrugated surface of the fort crawled with a thousand identical vessels like twelve-legged metallic spiders. Nothing in today's Spiral Arm remotely resembled them. Beyond the fort was a transport vessel for Hymenopt slaves, with next to it the disk and slim spike of an original McAndrew balanced drive. Most of the ships in the whole mismatched flotilla were drifting in one direction, toward an exterior wall of Labyrinth.

. . . writhing free-space Medusae, Torvil Anfracts in miniature, rainbow lobes shimmering like sunlit oil on water.

. . . alien creatures, familiar and strange, suited or naked to space, dead or alive, fresh or mummified. Some of the beings without suits were leaping easily through space from ship to ship. Some of the others were legless, eyeless forms. Far from their homes in deep oceans or on gasgiant planets, they twisted helpless in the gulf. The interior of Labyrinth could support life unassisted, although it was strange that everything could breathe the same air. But how had those giants ever been carried to the interior of an Artifact?

Moving through the whole mass, guiding and shepherding, were thousands of miniature Phages, small twelve-faced solids no bigger than Darya's hand. They showed every sign of intelligent behavior.

Darya recalled the common wisdom of the Fourth Alliance: Intelligence was not possible in an organic structure below a minimum mass. That mass far exceeded the size of these mini-Phages.

Did that mean these were remotely controlled, or were they built of inorganic components? Or could a finite size in *time* more than make up for a reduced size in *space*? What Darya was able to see might be not a whole Builder, but a mere flat projection of it, the tiny slice apprehensible to the senses in what humans described as "the present." Perhaps *total* spacetime volume was the important parameter for intelligence. From a Builder point of view, humans and their alien colleagues must occupy an infinitesimal region of spacetime, with body size in space multiplied by the width of a vanishingly small section of time. Such a small spacetime volume, the Builders might argue, did not permit the development of intelligence.

The mini-Phages darted energetically to-and-fro. But that was not what had caused the excitement on the *Misanthrope.* Darya turned and saw, for the first time, the dark shape hanging beyond the translucent outer walls of Labyrinth.

Another vortex. And not just *a* vortex. The whole of the space on one side of Labyrinth was occupied by the Grand Panjandrum of all vortices, bigger than the Artifact itself. It was slowly swelling. Either it was truly growing in size, or Labyrinth was creeping steadily closer to it. Whichever was true, the end point would be the same. Labyrinth would be engulfed.

Rebka was still gripping Darya's arm, steering her closer to the hatch. She resisted.

"Why not stay here with them? They're getting ready to leave Labyrinth." She pointed to Katerina Treel, suit closed and in place at the ship's controls. Her two sisters were trying to push people out of the lock. There was too much noise to hear what they were shouting.

"Who?" Rebka had to shout, too, leaning close to Darya's helmet. A deep, booming noise like the tolling of a gigantic bell filled the cabin with a regular tone. It was coming from somewhere *outside* the *Misanthrope.* "Who could stay here? You, me, Tally? What about Nenda, or Atvar H'sial and the other aliens? What about Glenna or Quintus Bloom? There isn't room in this ship for everyone."

"My ship!" Darya found herself screaming. "We can use my ship—the *Myosotis.*"

"You want to bet on finding it, with that lot out there?" Rebka's gesture took in the swarming chaos beyond the lock. "There isn't much room on the *Myosotis,* even if you were sure you could get us there. And Nenda's ship can't fly superluminal."

"So what are you thinking?"

"The same as everyone else." They had finally reached the lock and struggled through it, Rebka still firmly attached to the arm of Darya's suit. He pointed to the periphery of Labyrinth, on the side away from the monster vortex. The ships from the interior now hung there in space, a strange mixed fleet that had somehow passed right through Labyrinth's external wall. "All the ships with no crews seem to have been steered out there. We pick a type that we know how to fly—one with a Bose Drive on it."

"Those ships weren't there when we came to Labyrinth!"

"Nor were a lot of other things. They are now."

"Hans." She stopped dead, shaking her arm free. "Don't you see, it proves I'm right. The Builders are here, *now*—and they are helping. They want anything alive and intelligent to be able to escape before Labyrinth vanishes completely. *That's* why they are taking the ships outside, ready for use."

"Someone is moving the ships, but that doesn't prove you are right. Maybe the Builders are just making sure that anyone who wants off can get off. Maybe *he* is right, and we are heading for the future—along with anyone else who stays in Labyrinth."

Rebka was pointing to the tall figure of Quintus Bloom, floating at the center of a knot of people and aliens. The two Tenthredans had disappeared, but most of the others from the *Misanthrope* were circling around Bloom as though bound to him by some odd form of gravity. Darya looked for Louis Nenda, and at first could not locate him. Then she saw a dark-suited figure floating toward them from the *Gravitas*, which had begun its drift toward Labyrinth's outer wall. A Cecropian was at Nenda's side. They were towing behind them, trussed tightly in a clumsy, improvised suit, a gigantic tentacled creature. A *Zardalu*! Nenda and Atvar H'sial had risked the trip back into the other ship, while all of Labyrinth disintegrated around them, to rescue a *Zardalu*? Darya couldn't believe it, but there was no time to stay and ponder.

She left Rebka to himself and pushed her way through to the center of the cluster. "We have to get out of here fast, on one of those." She waved at the jumble of ships. Already some of the new arrivals were heading for them, with the urging of the mini-Phages. The steady, booming, bell-like tone filled the whole of Labyrinth. It came from the region of the ships, drawing attention to them. "Look at that vortex. We don't have more than another ten minutes."

"Great!" Bloom laughed like a lunatic, audible even without his suit's transmitter. There was still plenty of air in Labyrinth. "Ten minutes more, and we will enjoy the experience of a lifetime. We will advance to the far future, and meet our own descendants. Who would want to miss that?"

"The Builders don't come from the future. *Those* are the Builders, or the servants of the Builders." Darya pointed to the mini-Phages. "That vortex won't take you to the future. It will kill you! Look at the way everything is being steered away from it and toward the ships."

"Steering is for sheep and cattle. The future doesn't want followers—it wants *leaders*." Bloom scanned the group around them. "I'm staying on Labyrinth. Who's with me? Don't bother to say anything, Professor Lang. I know your answer."

"You're insane! The Builders live on some other plane of existence, a place where humans probably can't survive for a second." Darya gestured to the junkyard of ships. Some of them were already edging away from the outer wall of Labyrinth, their hulls and locks swarming with the diminutive figures of humans and aliens. "We have to go and grab a ship for ourselves, while we have time."

If we have time. She could see the looming vortex

on the other side, a swirling mouth holding the whole Artifact within its jaws.

No one moved. Darya was in agony. What was wrong with them? Was it the force of Bloom's personality—fascination at the idea of traveling to the future—simple reluctance to be thought afraid?

As though reading her mind, Hans Rebka moved to Darya's side. "Sorry, Bloom. I don't know if you're right, or if Darya is right. And I don't really care. I've seen hard times, but I like life well enough to want to go on with it. I vote for the ships. I'll save my trip to the future for another day."

He moved away from the center of the group and began to study the ships more closely. They were all different, and it wouldn't do to select one that he did not know how to fly.

"Don't try to justify cowardice," Bloom called after him. "It never works." He turned his back deliberately on Rebka. "Miss Omar? I know that you at least are not afraid. Will you come with me?"

Glenna hesitated. "I'd like to come. If it would please you . . . Only . . ." She turned to where Nenda was fighting to control his trussed Zardalu. Despite his previous assurances of its change in attitude, it was far from docile. He had just punched it between its glaring eyes, and it was struggling to free a tentacle big enough to squash him to bloody mush. "Louis, will you be going?"

"Goin' where? Into *that* thing?" Nenda jerked his head toward the hovering vortex. "You outa your tiny mind? The one we come through to get here squeezed me flatter than a Sproatley smart oyster. That one's a thousand times the size. If I never go near one of them again in my life, it'll be too soon."

"That settles it, then. I'm not going, either." Glenna turned to Bloom. "Quintus, I'm not going."

"I heard you the first time. I am not deaf. Since

when does the advice of a barbarian space anthropoid dictate your actions?" Bloom glared right through Glenna, as though she had ceased to exist. "What about the rest of you? Tally? Here surely is a challenge worthy of an embodied computer's powers. Atvar H'sial—Kallik—J'merlia? Do you not wish your own species to be represented in the future? Which of you is ready to embark with me on the greatest adventure in history?"

But Glenna's decision had somehow turned the whole group. They had been clustered around Bloom as their center of gravity. Now, without a word, they began to drift toward Hans Rebka. He pointed to one of the ships, twice the size of any of the others.

"That's my choice. I think I've even seen pictures of it before. That's the *Salvation*, the ship Chinadoll Pas-farda used to roll over the darkside edge of the Coal Sack. People have wondered where she and her ship went for two centuries. Now we have to make it earn its name. But we'll have to be quick."

The vortex beside Labyrinth was beginning its work. The Artifact was rotating faster as Rebka led his odd convoy toward the chosen ship. Behind him were Louis Nenda and Atvar H'sial, carefully towing the captive Zardalu. Kallik, J'merlia, and Glenna Omar followed them, as close as the wriggling Zardalu permitted. Darya brought up the rear with E.C. Tally. She found herself threading her way through a menagerie of creatures and objects, flotsam and jetsam delivered to Labyrinth from a thousand other Artifacts. A group of a dozen Ditrons, abandoned by their owners, hooted like foghorns and giggled as Darya passed by. The high-domed skulls suggested plenty of intelligence, but that was an illusion. The Ditron's head was a resonance cavity, designed to produce as much sound as possible in mating calls. The brain itself was a mere couple of hundred grams tucked away at the back.

Darya kept well clear of them. She skirted a huge creature like a spiral galaxy in miniature, thorny swirls of body with one enormous pale-blue eye the size of a child's paddling pool set at its center. The eye tracked her as she passed by. The urge to stop and examine that alien was almost overwhelming, until she saw out of the tail of her own eye a nine-foot squirming streak of green. It was a Chism Polypheme, hurtling its corkscrew body toward one of the ships.

Dulcimer? Could that really be Dulcimer, the leering Polypheme pilot who had first taken them into the Torvil Anfract? Well, if so he would have to look after himself. He should be able to do it—anyone who was fifteen thousand years old had to be a survivor.

But what was Dulcimer doing *here*? Did it mean that *every* other Artifact had already vanished from the Spiral Arm, its contents transferred to Labyrinth? The thought left her numb. She had devoted her whole career to the study of the Builders and their creations. If they vanished and left no evidence that the Artifacts had ever existed, what would she do with the rest of her life? Future generations would probably not even believe that the Builders had existed. They would become part of the myths and legends of the Spiral Arm, no more accepted than fairies and trolls and the Tristan free-space Manticore, no more real than the lost worlds of Shamble, Midas, Grisel, Merryman's Woe, and Rainbow Reef. The images that she was carrying of the Labyrinth polyglyphs would be regarded as no more than clever fakes, produced by eccentrics as hoaxes to fool gullible people.

Maybe Quintus Bloom was doing the right thing. No one could ever accuse him of not living up to his beliefs. If the Artifacts went, and you had devoted your life to them, perhaps you should go with them.

Darya turned to look back. Bloom had not moved. He was staring after them. When he saw Darya looking he raised his arm to her in an ironic salute. She felt a strange sense of loss. The great debate would never continue. She would have no chance now to persuade Bloom that he was wrong, that the Builders were of the past and present, not of the future. She would never again hear that confident voice, with its hypnotically persuasive style of presentation, discoursing so knowledgeably on the Artifacts. Despite all his faults, she and Quintus Bloom shared one thing that set them apart from most of the rest of humanity: they were fascinated by every aspect of the Builders.

Bloom turned and began to move toward the vortex. It dwarfed him to insignificance. Darya could not take her eyes away as the tiny figure headed for the dark swirl of its center. He seemed to hover for one moment, right at the edge of the maelstrom. One arm waved a farewell; she was sure it was to her. In her mind she saw the driven little boy again, determined to be Number One. And then, without warning, the vortex took him.

Where was Quintus Bloom now? Somewhere far in the future, a million years up the stream of time, looking back on today as an event so distant that it merged into human history with cave dwellings or the first flight into space. Or dispersed to component atoms by the shearing forces of a vortex meant to remove from the Spiral Arm every evidence of the Artifact. Or, as Darya preferred to believe, removed to another plane of existence entirely, where the Builders could examine at their leisure whatever their collecting jar of Labyrinth had brought from the final hours of Artifact operation.

There would be a time to ponder those questions. But it was not now. E.C. Tally was pulling urgently at her arm. The remaining contents of Labyrinth were streaming toward the vortex, moving under the influence of that invisible tide. The outer wall was just ahead. The others had already passed through and were heading for the *Salvation*.

Darya felt no more than a slight ripple through her body as she met the wall. It was all that remained of the structure that had once seemed so indestructible and impenetrable. Would the ships themselves keep a permanent form, long enough to be useful? She hurried after E.C. Tally. The hatches of *Salvation* were open; the others were already on board. Louis Nenda reached out as she approached, swung Darya effortlessly inside, and slammed the hatch closed with one sweep of a brawny arm. Hans Rebka was in the pilot's seat, reviewing the unfamiliar controls. He turned to glance over his shoulder at the lock, and saw that Darya had at last arrived. The worried expression left his face and he returned his attention to the power sequence. Five more seconds, and the ship's engines came to life.

Not before time. Labyrinth itself was going. *Salvation*'s screens showed it changing shape, elongating, stretching toward the mouth of the vortex. The walls had begun to glow with internal light, reacting to the stresses on them. The structure was rotating madly, faster and faster.

"Hold on." Rebka was engaging the drive. "This could get rough."

The force from the vortex was reaching out to the ship. As it engulfed Labyrinth it was still growing. Darya felt a painful new force on her body, adding to the thrust of *Salvation*'s own drive.

Combined accelerations increased. A moment stretched on and on. Labyrinth was rolling—twisting—writhing. It distorted until it was a long, thin spiral, pulling out like a strand of melted glass. Beyond it, the vortex pulsed with energy. Bloated and quivering, it was snatching at the ship at the same time as it consumed Labyrinth. The shear forces on Darya's body strengthened, shifted, changed direction.

And then, in an instant, the pain vanished. *Salvation* went bounding forward, free, into open space. Behind it the vortex began to dwindle and die. Stars were visible, shining dimly through it. Shining brighter. Shining bright. Shining clear. Suddenly there was nothing but space between the stars and the racing ship.

"Now comes the real test." Rebka had opened his helmet and was taking deep breaths of ship's air. He knew how nervous he had been, even if no one else did. "But what the devil is *this*?"

He was querying the ship's data base for instructions to take it superluminal, and an unrequested message had appeared on the display.

Whoever you are, you can have this one to keep. Me and Chinadoll have decided to try something different. She tells me that her name, Pas-farda, means the day-after-tomorrow in the old Earth Persian language, and that's where we're going. We hope. May the Great Galactic Trade Wind be always at your back.
     —Captain Alonzo Wilberforce Sloane (Retired)

"Two old mysteries explained—after a fashion." Hans was racing through the superluminal protocol. "You might want to pray on this one, Darya. I'm going to take us superluminal and hope I can hit a Bose point. If it works, we'll be on the way home."

Darya leaned back and closed her eyes. *And if it doesn't? Suppose the Bose Network has gone, too?*

It *had* to work. It would be just too ironic to go through all this, only to discover that you were restricted to subluminal travel and were going to spend the rest of your life in open space, or on Jerome's World.

If they did make it home safely, though, Darya swore to return to Jerome's World. She would personally make sure that a statue was erected there, in honor of the planet's most famous scientist. Quintus Bloom had certainly earned it—even if future generations might not quite know for what.

But they *would* know for what. It was Darya's responsibility to make sure that they did. She must write the whole history of the Builders, from the discovery of the first Artifact, Cocoon, to the vanishing of the last one, Labyrinth, along with its enigmatic displays and their implied warning. She would present every theory that had ever been proposed concerning the nature of the Builders—including her own ideas, and certainly Quintus Bloom's. She would document what the Builders, wherever they might be now, had left behind as their heritage to the rest of the Universe.

And if, a thousand years or five thousand years in the future, people thought of that heritage as no more than a work of epic fiction, that would be acceptable. Myths and legends endure when bare facts are forgotten. Think of Homer, his works remembered when no one today knew the names of any king or queen of the times. King Canute tried to hold back the tide, but who recalled who ruled before him, or after him?

The legend of the Builders.

Darya smiled to herself, as the cabin air glowed blue. *Salvation* was going superluminal.

✦ Chapter Twenty-Six

The atmosphere on board the *Salvation* was somewhere between numbed satisfaction and manic glee. Hans Rebka, sitting in the pilot's chair, knew the cause. Nothing in life produces a more powerful joy than a near miss by the Angel of Death. Their lives had been threatened in the days before Labyrinth vanished, to the point where Rebka would have taken no odds on survival. Yet here they were, alive and on the way home (except for Quintus Bloom, whose present location was anyone's guess but no one's worry).

Hans felt that he was the odd man out, the single exception to the general cheer. He ought to be enjoying the moment, even if in his case it would be no more than a brief interval of peace before the next task. That task would be the most difficult one of his life, if he was any judge, but he could not avoid it—because this time he was assigning it to himself.

The final minutes on Labyrinth had taught him something of profound importance. He had not just *endured* their troubles, he had *enjoyed* wrestling with and beating them. He was a professional trouble-shooter. That was a fancy name for an idiot. Trouble was always dangerous. But it was addictive and stimulating, thrilling and energizing, the ultimate roller-coaster, more exciting than anything else in life. And he was the best damned trouble-shooter he had ever met.

That formed the root of his current problem. He could do this job. Maybe no one else could. But how was he going to break the news to Darya? He could produce plausible but bogus reasons: that he would never be able to stand her sedentary lifestyle; that she could never bear to live in the Phemus Circle. But the two of them had been too close for too long to permit lies and half-truths. So he was going to make her miserable.

Hans realized that, unusual for him, he was procrastinating. At the moment Darya certainly didn't sound miserable. She was standing behind him, humming tunelessly to herself and massaging his neck and shoulders. She probed stiff-fingered into his trapezius muscles, hard enough to hurt. It felt great.

"Relax, Hans," she said. "You're too tense. What has you so knotted up?"

"I was thinking that we fit really well together."

"Mm." The grip on his shoulders tightened. "The men from Phemus Circle. One-track minds. I don't believe you, you know."

"You don't think we fit well?"

"Sure we do. But I don't believe that's what you were thinking about when I asked you."

Which only proved that he had been right. He couldn't fob Darya off with false reasons. It had to be the bald truth.

"I'm going back to the Phemus Circle, Darya. I have to."

Her fingers froze on his back. "You've received orders?"

"No. Worse." He turned to face her. "I made the decision for myself."

Her hand came up again to touch his cheek. "Can you tell me why?"

He could hear her uncertainty. "I want to explain, Darya, but I don't know if you'll understand. Maybe no one can understand who isn't from the Phemus Circle."

"Try me."

"You think you know the Phemus Circle, because you've visited it. But you don't *really* know the Circle at all. Maybe you have to be born there. When I was stuck inside Paradox, I started thinking about my childhood on Teufel in a different way. Half my friends died before they were ten years old, from predators and drought and malnutrition, or while we were on water and food duty. It seemed inevitable at the time. I've finally realized it's anything but. It doesn't *have* to be that way—on Teufel, or anywhere else. Since I became an adult I've been sent to one world after another, wherever and whenever a bad problem appeared. I study the situation, and I solve the problem—every time. The infant deaths on Styx, the encephalo-parasite on Subito, the runaway biosphere on Pelican's Wake, infertility on Scaldworld, the crop die-off on Besthome, the universal sleep on Mirawand, the black wave on Nemesis—there isn't one that has beaten me. It's a great feeling, shipping home and thinking: *that's another one in the bag.*

"I had to leave the Phemus Circle completely before I could recognize a different truth. I haven't been *solving* problems, you see, not in any final sense. I've been plastering over them. The real difficulty lies higher, in the government that runs the Phemus Circle. There are excellent ways of modifying planetary biospheres, small changes that don't cost a fortune and don't harm native stock, but translate into enormous lifestyle improvements for human colonists. Hell, I've *done* terraforming, myself, on loan in Alliance territory. We've known the techniques for thousands of years. But I've never once applied those methods in the Phemus Circle. Teufel remains as it was the day I left it. So do all the other god-forsaken Circle worlds."

"*Why?*"

"That's the big question. That's what I have to find out. It's as though the people who control the central government of the Phemus Circle *want* people to live short, stunted lives. They have more control that way. But I'm going to change things."

"How?"

"You keep asking questions I wish I could answer. I have no idea *how*. But I'll do it, or I'll die trying. I'm sorry, Darya. Will you forgive me?"

"Forgive you? For what? For being responsible, and brave? There's nothing to forgive. I'm *proud* of you, Hans."

"But it means that we won't—"

She silenced him by leaning forward and kissing him gently on the lips. "There. We're going to see a lot of each other whenever we have a chance, but we are going to have separate jobs and separate lives. Right?"

"That's one reason I feel so bad. To talk to you this way, just when your work has been destroyed."

"Destroyed?" Her laugh was not at all the laugh of a broken-hearted woman. "Hans, I've got the best and fattest job ahead of me that a research worker could ever have. Before all this started, I was happy to study beings whom I thought had left the Spiral Arm at least three million years ago. Now I have all that old knowledge, plus more new information than I ever hoped for. And with Quintus Bloom gone I'm the *only* person, the only one in the whole Arm, with all the information. Don't you see it's my *duty* to produce a final, definitive study of the Builders? I'll even include Bloom's theory, though I know it can't be right."

"How can you be sure of that?"

"You'll be sure, too, if you think about it. Because you know Quintus. If he is in the future, and they have time travel, he would make one action his top priority. What would it be?"

Hans frowned. "He'd send a message back. To prove to everybody that his theories are right."

"Exactly. And he would do it in a way we couldn't possibly overlook. No cryptic polyglyphs for *him*, no hiding in the middle of an Artifact. So he *can't* be right. But he'll be in my reports anyway, along with every other speculation about the Builders. Can you see what a huge job I have ahead of me? It will take years and years of labor, and I'm going to need all the library support and computer power and research facilities that Sentinel Gate can produce. This is work I can't do on the road. But I'll still have to travel—the Phemus Circle had Artifacts, and it's at the intersection of two of the other major clades. I'll visit you, sure I will, wherever you happen to be. And you can visit me whenever you get the chance, and stay as long as you like."

"I will. No shared home, though. My job will be dangerous. The powers-that-be in the Phemus Circle won't like what I'm planning to do."

"They can't touch me here on Sentinel Gate."

"Darya, they might. If I'm successful, we don't know how desperate they may get."

"I'll take that chance. I'm not afraid of risks, not any more. One day, when I've finished my work, I'll come to the Phemus Circle. We'll share the dangers."

"But no children."

"Hey! I didn't agree to that. They won't live in the Phemus Circle, of course, they'll grow up on Sentinel Gate."

"And be spoiled rotten."

"Are you suggesting that I was spoiled? Don't bother to tell me." She leaned past him to stare at the status displays. "We'll be through the final Bose transition in five minutes. Come to the forward observation port after that. We'll do some practical planning." She stroked the short hair at the back of his neck, sending tingles through him, and was gone.

Hans stared at the controls as another message appeared over the superluminal communications network. Was that *it*, the confrontation that he had so been dreading? Darya was an exceptional woman. And a super-smart one. Because there it was, another Artifact vanishing exactly as she had predicted. Every last one of them was going, according to the bulletins.

The *Salvation* was about to clear its final Bose Transition. Only when that last jump had been taken would he feel free to join Darya. The Bose Network was not a Builder creation, as he had once feared, but its nodes were certainly affected by the presence or absence of nearby Builder Artifacts. He would be far easier in his mind as soon as he was sure that the ship could fly the rest of the way subluminal.

One minute more to the Bose Transition. Hans's expression changed to a scowl as he checked the screen displays for the rear section of the ship. *That damned Zardalu!* He'd feel easier when the jump was over, and easier still when that midnight-blue nightmare was gone from the *Salvation*. Louis Nenda claimed that the beast was safe, but it had managed to work a tentacle loose while the ship was first going superluminal. If it had quietly used that tentacle to free itself, instead of flailing at every fixture within reach, it might now control the whole ship.

Maybe the Fourth Alliance did need a mature Zardalu for study, Hans thought, as the Bose indicator blinked in with a transition accurate to the microsecond. Maybe they would pay a huge reward for it, as Nenda and Atvar H'sial claimed. But did the two of them have to choose the biggest and meanest Zardalu that Rebka had ever seen?

They were feeding the brute now, with great chunks of synthetic meat. Were they trying to grow it even bigger? Well, good luck to them. Hans checked the control settings one more time and stood up. He had more productive—and pleasant—ways to pass the remaining days of subluminal flight.

Nenda and Atvar H'sial were feeding the Zardalu. They were also talking to it. And it was just as well that no one else on board could follow the conversation.

"Don't give me that." Nenda was using the extreme form of the master-slave language. "I saw what you did with just one tentacle free. You smashed bits of the ship all to hell, so me and At got blamed for bringing you aboard. We should have let you rot in Labyrinth. Taking over control of the *Salvation* is one thing, but unstrapping you so you can help do it is another."

"Master." The land-cephalopod, floating in front of Nenda, could scarcely move in its double-strapped harness. But the long purple tongue reached out, inviting him to step on it with his boot.

"You can put that thing away. It's disgusting."

"Yes, Master." Four feet of tongue slid back into the narrow vertical mouth. "Master, I can help you to conquer this ship. I lost control of myself earlier. That is why I broke things. I thought that I was about to die."

"Maybe you are—or worse. The people on Miranda say they want to examine an adult Zardalu. That's you. But when they say 'examine,' they really mean 'dissect.' See, it all depends what I tell 'em. If I say you belong to me, and I need you back, that's one thing. You stay in one piece, no cutting. But if I say you don't belong to me, an' I don't care what happens to you . . ."

"I do belong to you. Completely. I will be your willing slave. Master, do not leave me in the hands of strange humans. My brood-mates and I learned our lesson on Serenity and on Genizee. We know that compared with your Master Race, all other species of the Spiral Arm are weak, pitiful, sentimental imbeciles. Humans are the most resourceful, intelligent, terrifying, and *cruel* beings in the whole Spiral Arm." The saucer-sized cerulean eyes saw a scowl appear on Nenda's face. "And also, of course, the most *merciful*."

"Better believe it. *All* of it. Hold on a minute, though. Gotta talk to my partner." Louis turned to Atvar H'sial. The Cecropian had been monitoring the exchange through Nenda's pheromonal translation. She had been given a censored version of the Zardalu's final comments. Delivery of the "weak, pitiful, sentimental imbeciles" comment had been postponed. Nenda would like to see Cecropian and Zardalu go fifteen rounds with the gloves off, but this was not the day for it.

"At, we got to make a few decisions real soon. We're gonna drop Jelly-bones here off on Miranda, but what next? Do we try to steal this ship? Do we go to Sentinel Gate with the others? And do we make a pickup at Miranda later, when they're all done with Zardie?"

"No, we do not steal this ship. No, we do not go to Sentinel Gate." The emphatic pheromones became charged with suspicion. "Will the Lang female be there? I feel sure of it. We will not go there. But yes, we do collect the Zardalu after it has been examined. That all fits the grand design."

"It does?"

"Certainly. Why steal this ship, which is of indifferent performance? We will have plenty of money when the Zardalu has been delivered to Miranda."

"But no ship."

"Miranda Spaceport offers the largest selection of vessels in the whole Spiral Arm. We will acquire one. We will then claim our Zardalu. If you like, we will visit the Mandel system and determine if your own ship, the Have-It-All, has reappeared there. And then—we return to Genizee."

"Genizee! At, no offense, but you're out of your mind. I spent months tryin' to get out of that place."

"In very different circumstances. First, the Anfract is no longer to be feared. Any dangerous aspects were a consequence of its being a Builder Artifact. The same is true of any problem we had in escaping from Genizee itself. Finally, let me remind you of Quintus Bloom and Darya Lang's assertion: the Zardalu will play an important part, along with the other clades, in the future of the Spiral Arm. And we, Atvar H'sial and Louis Nenda, will control the Zardalu! Already, they think of themselves as our slaves. Let me ask you a question: Do you know of any other planet in the Spiral Arm that we can make completely ours?"

"No place that I'd want to go. We could probably buy Mucus for next-to-nothin', but you can have my share. All right, I'll go for the deal as you've pitched it. But I don't know why you keep goin' on about me and Darya Lang, that's old history." Nenda turned back to the waiting Zardalu. "My partner has pleaded with me on your behalf. We will make sure you don't get damaged too much on Miranda."

"Thank you, Master." The purple tongue came slithering out.

"Put that away. I don't ever want to see it again."

"Yes, Master."

"And after we get you back from the people on Miranda, we're going to take you home. To Genizee. Then you'll help us make plans for all the Zardalu to come back to space. *Under our control.* You understand?"

"Yes, Master. I will serve you faithfully. If necessary, I personally will kill any Zardalu who seeks to do otherwise, or who disobeys you in any way."

"Attagirl. That's what I like to hear. If you're really good till we get to Miranda, I'll let you glide down the gangway on your own tentacles and wow the locals.

That's a promise." Louis turned to Atvar H'sial. "Okay. Done deal. Only thing left is to collect the money."

"That, and one thing more." The Cecropian followed Nenda as he started out of the cargo hold. The phero- mones were oddly hesitant. Nenda wondered. Atvar H'sial was not noted for diffidence.

"What's up, At?"

"I wish to request a great favor of you. These past weeks have been most frustrating for me. I have lacked communication ability with anyone but you. And yet the future of the Spiral Arm, we hear, must involve increased inter-clade activity. Therefore, I have reached a decision. I must perfect an ability to interface directly with humans."

"No problem. We'll get a ship with plenty of com- puter capacity."

"That will not teach me the human outlook, as it is reflected in your curious speech. I will need a com- puter as the interface, true. But I must also converse with a human."

"What the hell do you think I am? A peanut?"

"A patient human. One willing to devote substantial time to the effort."

"Forget it."

"Precisely. Which brings me to my request. Would you consider asking Glenna Omar on my behalf to travel with us, to assist me in perfecting my human speech skills? She already taught me to employ beat frequencies within my echo-location system, and so offer the longer wavelength sounds accessible to humans. Thus, a greet- ing." Atvar H'sial produced a grating low-pitched groan. With a lot of imagination Nenda decided that it could be interpreted as "Hello."

"Why don't you ask her?"

"Improbable as it seems, I think she admires you more than me. The request would be received better from you. Also, you are able to frame it with more precision in human terms."

Nenda swung round and stared up at the Cecropian's blind head. "Let's get this straight. You want me to try an' talk Glenna Omar into signing on with us? Long term."

"Precisely. If you are successful, I will acknowledge a major debt to you."

"Damn right you will. It sounds impossible."

"But you will make the attempt?"

"I don't know. When?"

"As soon as possible."

"Hell."

"I hope not. You will do it?"

"All right. I'll talk to her." Louis glared up at his towering partner. "But I don't want you watching. You'll mess up my style."

"I will not move from this spot until you return."

"Might take a while no matter what she says."

"I will wait. And I will steel myself for the possibility that you will return with bad news."

"You do that. I'd better get it over with."

The passenger quarters were in the bow, far from the cargo hold. Louis started the trek forward, wondering how he was going to handle this. There wasn't a chance in a million that Glenna would agree, but he had to make Atvar H'sial believe that he had done his best.

In the mid-section of the ship he came across Kallik and J'merlia sitting cross-legged on the floor. He stopped as he came up to them, struck by another thought.

"What are you two planning to do, now the trouble's all over?"

Lemon-yellow eyes on their short eye-stalks and doublet rings of black eyes gazed back at him in shared amazement. "Why," said Kallik, "we are coming with you."

"And with my dominatrix, Atvar H'sial," J'merlia added. "What else?"

Which made the presence of Glenna Omar unnecessary. J'merlia was the perfect interpreter. It would be no good telling that to At, though. Louis knew from experience, the Cecropian was nothing if not stubborn. If she insisted that she wanted to learn human speech from a human . . .

"Atvar H'sial is back there." Nenda nodded aft. "Go tell her that the two of you will be staying with us, and say that's fine with me. Tell her I'm on my way to talk to Glenna Omar."

Which just about wrapped it up. A quick and indignant refusal from Glenna, and Louis could break the bad news to the Cecropian. He started out again along the corridor.

Glenna was alone in her bedroom, staring into the mirror. Even now, with the emergency long past, she was not wearing make-up. Her blond hair was piled high, showing the long and graceful neck, and her skin was as clear and smooth as a young girl's. She was wearing a scanty pink slip with a plunging neckline, long gold ear-rings, and nothing else. Her reflection beamed at Louis as he came in.

"Just the man I wanted to see." She did not turn around.

"Yeah?" A bad start.

"You know that after Miranda, the *Salvation* is heading for Sentinel Gate?"

"I hear that's the plan. Darya Lang and E.C. Tally want to go there."

"But Hans Rebka says you won't be going on. You'll stay for a while on Miranda, then take off for some other place."

"Sounds more than likely. Miranda's not the place for me and At, any more than Sentinel Gate."

"Or for me." Glenna spun around in her chair to face him. She stood up and grabbed his hands. "Louis—take me with you. Wherever you're going, I want to go."

"What!" Nenda's defenses came up automatically. "Sorry. Can't do that."

"You like me, I know you do. Why don't you want me with you?"

"I do like you." Nenda hadn't intended to say that. He was baffled by his own surge of feelings. "I like you, sure I do. But it's—well, it's—I dunno. It's not that simple. I have to say no."

"Is it that you are ashamed that you come from a crude, barbaric part of the Spiral Arm, and you know that educated people from any decent place will look down on you?"

"No, it's not that."

"Is it because you have a funny accent, so that civilized persons laugh when they hear you?"

"Never occurred to me. I think I sound fine."

"Is it because you know you're little and dark and ugly, and I'm tall and blond and beautiful?"

"Naw. But don't stop. You're doin' wonders for my self-esteem."

"Because, you see, if it's any of those things I don't care about them at all."

"It's none of them."

"So what is it?" Glenna struck a pose, hand set on rounded hip. "Don't you find me attractive?"

"I think you're the sexiest thing on two legs. Or four." Louis saw her eyes widen, and added hastily, "Not that I've tried that, of course. But you don't know what *I'm* like, Glenna."

"So tell me."

"I've led a hard life."

"And you haven't let it break your spirit. I admire you for that."

"Not an honest life."

"Who is honest? We all tell lies."

"Mebbe. But Glenna, I'm a *crook*, for God's sake."

"And I'm a tramp. Ask anyone on Sentinel Gate,

male or female, they'll tell you. We make a fine pair, Louis."

"No. You still don't get it. Glenna, I've *killed* men."

"And I've done my best to—the hard way. You know that, if anyone does." She moved closer. Her eyes glowed, and she looked ready to eat him. Her hands reached out to touch his chest. "But there's more to it than you think. Louis, you don't understand something, and you may find it hard to believe me when I say it. But cross my heart, it's true. I can't bear the idea of leaving you and going back to Sentinel Gate. My life was easy and safe there, but it wasn't *exciting*. It was deadly dull. I'm no great brain, like Professor Lang. I sometimes hate her for being so good at what she does, but I admire her, too. My job had a nice title, Senior Information Specialist. You know what I did? I moved information I didn't care about from one data storage unit I didn't care about to another like it. You know the biggest thrill I had, all the years I worked there?"

"Meeting Quintus Bloom."

"No. Well, yes and no. My big thrill was meeting some man from off-planet, like you or Bloom, and doing my best to hustle him into bed before he left Sentinel Gate. I didn't care what he looked like, or whether he seemed nice or not, provided he was an off-worlder. I didn't have to get off on it myself, or even enjoy it. The whole challenge was to bed him. I would sleep with *anyone*. I would have slept with Quintus Bloom, though I bet that under his clothes he was wall-to-wall scabs. There. Now I've upset you."

"Let's say you don't make me feel too singled out for special privileges."

"But you *are*. That's what I'm trying to say. Even if you make me go back to Sentinel Gate, I can't be the way I was before. You've changed me, Louis. You are an absolutely wonderful lover, but that's only a little bit of what attracts me to you. You live an exciting life. Being with you is *fun*. You're brave, you're wild, you take risks, you grab enjoyment wherever you find it. You never complain about anything. People on Sentinel Gate make more fuss over a paper cut than you would if you lost an arm." She moved her body against his. "Louis, take me with you. Please."

"You'd get tired of me in a week."

"There's only one way to find out. I'm betting it's not true."

"But what will you do? Can you cook, or make clothes, or clean house?"

"Let's not get ridiculous. I have my talents. You know some of them already. But Louis, you're not being honest with me. I can see it in your eyes. There's something else. *Why* won't you let me be your woman, and go with you wherever you go? Is it some*body* else—that other woman?"

"There's no other woman. And it's not because I don't want you. It's Atvar H'sial. She'll be sure to say no."

"I'll talk to her."

"No! Don't even think of that. Better let me do it."

"You would do that? For me?" Glenna gave him a hug and a kiss that scrambled his cerebral cortex worse than a trip through a Builder vortex.

"I'll try."

"Wonderful!"

"But I know Atvar H'sial. She'll ask a price. She may even want you to go on working with her on human speech."

"I don't mind that. It's *fun*, not work."

Glenna's hands slid down his body. She was all set to steal second base, but Louis pushed her away. "Let me get this over with first. I'll go and talk to Atvar H'sial." He swallowed and stared at Glenna's peek-a-boo pink slip. "Then I'll come right back."

"I'll not move from this spot until you return."

Where had he heard that before? From Atvar H'sial, no less. Louis's pulse was racing as he escaped from Glenna's bedroom and headed aft. His mind was as furiously active as his hormones.

Atvar H'sial was going to owe him, big-time. That was great, especially when he didn't deserve the debt. *Revenge is a dish best eaten cold.* It was a long time since Atvar H'sial had snoozed and made Louis do all the work, when they had first escaped Genizee and were lost in the Anfract; but the memory was still strong.

And they had their Zardalu, worth a guaranteed fortune on Miranda. Plus Kallik, his very own favorite Hymenopt, back once more in Louis's possession. For the first time in years no one in the Spiral Arm was after his blood, or trying to arrest him. The most exciting woman he had ever met in his whole life wanted him and liked him as much as he wanted and liked her.

Louis halted, leaned against a bulkhead, and concentrated his thoughts. It was too much, too good to be true. He needed to discover the hidden snare, the cruel trap that would turn all the wonders to horrors. It was sure to be there, it always was, but where was it? He felt baffled. Maybe he was being dim or naive, but he could not see a single cloud on the horizon.

Finally he sighed and gave up.

Happy endings were for children's stories and fools. *You live in misery, and then you die.* Life, by definition, was not designed to end happily.

Louis continued aft. No happy ending, then. That was a fact, certain as death itself. He was living at the moment in a dream, an imagined world where everything went right.

But—*dreams are real while they last. Could you say more of life?*

A dream sequence was no more than a happy interlude, but maybe a happy interlude could last for an awful long time.

Louis approached the waiting Atvar H'sial. He was going to stretch this one for as long as he could.